MANHUNTER

Manhunter

This is a work of fiction.
All characters and events portrayed in this book are fictional,
and any resemblance to real people is purely coincidental.

For information contact: Shalako Press
P.O. Box 371, Oakdale, CA 95361-0371
http://www.shalakopress.com

ISBN: 978-0-9830608-4-0

Cover design: Karen Borrelli
Photo of Seth Riley taken by author
Editor: Judy Mitchell

PRINTED IN THE UNITED STATES OF AMERICA

Acknowledgments

Every book is the combined effort of many people. The list of people who I depend on seems to grow with each new book.

Thanks to Jamie Hood for her input and ideas.

Thanks to Josie Costa, Pat Decker, Kelly Flynn, Lauren O'Brian and a host of others for helping correct my mistakes.

And most of all hugs and kisses to my wife, Judy, whose expert editing always turns my hieroglyphics into something readable. This book was originally intended to be her Christmas gift. It has instead taken several years to finish, and become a lot of work for her. Thanks Kid, for being patient. I love you.

Dedication

This book is dedicated to my wife Judy, who has been my biggest fan, partner, support and love. Thanks Kid, for believing in me.

MANHUNTER

A Novel by

Major Mitchell

Shalako Press
Oakdale, CA

Prologue

The Indian sat astride his pony viewing the scene below. It had been ten years since he had seen the little cabin with its barn and corrals. The corral fences were now rotting and lay broken, and the roof of the barn was in dire need of repair. But these things were of no interest to Manhunter. His attention was drawn to the fenced-in area beneath the oak tree, beside the pond where he used to water his horses. He dismounted, tying the reins of his brown and white pinto to a bush. Removing his hat, he shook his head and spoke softly to the animal.

"Of all the places between heaven and hell, why did he have to find this one to hide in?" He could not follow the fugitive down to the cabin --- it was sacred ground. The fence enclosed the graves of his wife and son.

Taking the heavy Sharps rifle from its sheath, he loaded it. Squatting, he took careful aim and pulled the trigger. The horse that was tied in front of the house fell. Manhunter injected another cartridge into the magazine as the man ran outside cursing. He fired again, sending the bullet a few inches in front of the bandit's feet. The man ducked back inside.

The chase that had taken him two weeks and hundreds of miles was over. He would wait, and patience was never lacking in Manhunter. The folded poster in his coat pocket said the man inside the cabin was wanted for bank robbery and worth $250.00. Eventually, due to lack of food and water, the bandit would have to leave, and being on foot, he would be easy to capture. The man poked his head through the door and fired his pistol. He answered with a round from the Sharps that caused the door casing to splinter.

Manhunter took the makings out of his shirt pocket and began to roll a cigarette. He had lived with white people long enough to pick up many of their habits. There were times when he wondered if he wasn't more white than Comanche.

The man inside the cabin was now calling curses down on his head.

The nearest town happened to be ten miles south. He paused and smiled before striking the match, wondering if Cotton was still their sheriff. He hoped so. Handing this prisoner to him would force his old friend to do something besides play checkers. Alice might even cook him up some fried chicken and mashed potatoes like she used to.

The man inside appeared just long enough to give him an obscene gesture. Another round sent a chunk of wood spinning through the air.When he got hungry enough, or thirsty, he would give himself up. If he chose to fight, Manhunter would kill him. Either way, the fugitive would go to town and Manhunter would have his reward. The sun sank and darkness came as the Indian sat cross-legged and motionless on the hillside with his rifle in his lap.

Chapter 1

Nothing exciting ever happened in Leon, Kansas, and that was why Cotton liked it. His chair groaned as he leaned back and propped his feet on his desk, scanning that morning's edition of *The Leon Vindicator*. After twenty years of Army life, three of which were spent dodging Yankee lead, he had spent an additional two by patrolling the streets of Atlanta when it was under marshal law. Cotton was looking forward to spending his golden years in relative peace. A relaxing cup of coffee with a newspaper every morning at his desk was exactly what he wanted.

"My God! What'd you put in this?" Cotton glanced up as his young deputy made a face at his coffee mug.

"If you don't like it, make it yourself next time."

"I think I will," he said, and tossed the contents of his mug through the open door and into the dusty street.

Cotton grunted and took another sip from his own mug as the deputy began filling the pot with fresh water. He'd hired Dave Price several years ago against the wishes of the city council, who considered him too young to be a lawman. *Actually*, he thought, *he was*. Dave was only sixteen at the time, but he'd seen something in the boy that caused him to want him. He agreed with the council that Dave was young and rash at times, but he was also honest and eager to learn. It was Mayor Parker who had finally taken his side, and reminded the council how popular Cotton was with the citizens. He also reasoned that it was hard enough to hire a good sheriff in Leon, let alone with his reputation. So in the end, he got his deputy.

Not that there was much need for one. The last killing had taken place some ten years earlier, long before he had become sheriff. Cotton had made the decision to join the Yankee Army and move west in an effort to get away from the horrors of the post-war south, but fighting Indians and chasing whisky peddlers across the Kansas plains wasn't much better. They had been visiting a friend near Leon, when they discovered that the sleepy town bordering the Little Walnut River was looking for a sheriff. It didn't take much convincing from Alice, his wife of twenty-two years, for him to accept their offer. The pay wasn't much…only forty dollars a month, but it left him with plenty of time to work a small farm at the edge of town, and he didn't have to worry about getting shot in the back, or scalped.

His eyes locked onto his favorite column in the newspaper. *Law And Order, by Sheriff Harvey Blankenship.* He ran his fingers through his thinning white hair as he read his own account of the past week.

One of Berta Johnson's chickens had come up missing. He had shot the fox when he came back for seconds, before filing a report and closing the case. Then he had locked Hugh Avery in a cell overnight so he could sober up enough to find his way home. Normally, he would have taken a drunk home and handed him over to an angry wife, but Avery lived some five miles south of town. Besides, Kansas was a dry state, and moonshine was supposed to be illegal, so, he fined Hugh seventy-five cents to cover the cost of breakfast and stabling his horse, then sent him on his way. He filed a report on that one also before closing the case. And that was it, outside of breaking up a fight between two teenage boys who were rolling around in the middle of the street, both of whom claimed ownership of one of the town's dark-eyed beauties. He promptly gave them a kick in the britches and sent them

4

home. He didn't file a report or mention that one in his article. The girl was pretty, and he couldn't blame either one of them.

"What the hell's going on out there?" he said, at the sound of a racing buckboard and wild shouts from the street.

"Looks like Jim Larkin," Dave said, poking his head through the door. "His wife and boy are with him. Something's wrong." He set the coffeepot aside and stepped outside as the wagon came to a halt. A cloud of dust drifted through the door as Cotton reached for his hat. Dave was staring into the back of the wagon by the time it cleared enough for him to see.

"He killed them, Cotton! Killed 'em both!" Jim Larkin yelled. The big man was beside himself, and his wife's tear-streaked face was white as a sheet. Their boy, John, sat stone-like, staring into the distance.

"What are you talking about, Jim? Who killed who?" Cotton gripped the sideboard and reached for the bloody tarp. He let go as Jim climbed over the seat and into the back of the wagon.

"Slim...my stable hand! Dirty bastard killed them!"

"Quiet!" he yelled and motioned toward the noisy crowd that had begun to gather. "Quiet down. Now, who did he kill?"

"Karen, my little girl," Larkin yelled as he jerked the bloody tarp from the mutilated bodies in the back of the wagon.

"Oh, Jesus!" Dave jerked around to heave his breakfast into the street. Several others covered their mouths as Freda Wilson fainted.

Cotton stared at the bodies long enough to understand they once belonged to Karen Larkin and Carl Jenkins, two of the most popular young people in Butler County. Their families were some of the more successful and wealthy families in the county, perhaps the state, if you could believe such rumors. It was also rumored the two had been sweet on each other, and everyone was expecting the families to announce a huge wedding sometime this fall. Not now. *Hell of a way to go*, he thought as he pulled the tarp back over the half-nude bodies. Whoever it was had taken the time to carve up their faces, as well as gutting them like a couple of hogs.

"He killed 'em, Cotton, and stole Lighting! I want that bastard caught and hung! You understand me?"

"Yes, I understand, but first things first. Get down, and come into the office," he said and motioned toward the door.

"I don't wanna go into no office. I want you to catch him!"

"I understand, Jim. But you've got to think of your wife right now. Come on inside. Come on." He added and motioned toward the office with his head. "I'll catch him. I promise." He waited until Jim Larkin had entered the office before turning to Dave.

"Think you're okay to drive this wagon over to Doc Stevenson's?"

The deputy nodded.

"Tell him what happened best you can. Tell him I need to know everything he can find about what killed them."

"Hell, I can tell you just by looking at them," Dave said with a shudder.

"Yes, but I'd like Doc's opinion. Just do it, okay?"

Dave nodded and climbed into the driver's seat. Cotton took one more glance at the tarp before giving a shudder.

"Have him take care of Mrs. Larkin and Joe first. Then get back here as soon as you can, so we can get started."

He closed the door on the angry, milling crowd and pulled a notepad and pencil from the desk drawer. He paused before retrieving a bottle marked *cough medicine* from the bottom drawer and handed it to the shaken man seated across from him.

"Here take a pull on this. I don't know if you've got a cough or not, but it'll settle your nerves." He took a deep breath and picked up the pencil. The sheriff in Atlanta believed you couldn't have too much information, because information was the key to any good investigation. Cotton had built his entire career around that single phrase, but this report was going to be different from anything he had filed before. He began to write, wishing for the first time that he was back

6

in Atlanta.

September 12, 1882. Butler County, Kansas.

Chapter 2

Otis Felts, better known as Slim, sat under an oak tree and rested the prized horse he had ridden on his flight from the Larkin ranch. In his estimation, he was a little more than fifty miles from Leon. He knew the horse was capable of covering twice that, but Otis did not know the country, and had not been thinking too clearly since following Karen to the creek. Instead, he had kept the beast at a gentle pace, while he tried to untangle his jumbled thoughts and cursed himself for what had happened.

"It's that damn curse." Every time he got close to someone or something, the curse he believed he was living under destroyed any possibility of happiness. Being an orphan, Otis had never known his parents or grandparents. His earliest memories were of the home where he had to stay because he was different from other people. Periodically he had fits that racked his body. He tried to control them, but they still came, causing him both fear and pain. One day a kind old lady named Paula Thornson had visited the institution and took Otis home with her. She used to say there was nothing wrong with him that a little love couldn't cure. He began calling her Grandma Paula, and loved her with all his heart.

Then, one night as he tried to light the lamp on the kitchen table, it tipped over, spilling the kerosene. The flames spread quickly through their small wood frame house. He knew he could have saved her, but he had bolted outside, where he stood frozen stiff. Some nights he could still hear her screaming for help. Others had reminded him he was only nine years old at the time and wasn't responsible, but he knew he was. They wanted to put him back into the home, but he refused, and ran away every time they tried to take him there. Finally, Otis ended up on the streets, doing odd jobs and begging for food.

Then there was Dog, a starved mongrel that was orphaned like he was. Dog was the only name he had ever given him, because it fit. They became best of friends and went everywhere together. One day the Jackson boys, two bullies from the other side of town, kicked Dog in the head until he died. Otis tried stopping them, but they were bigger and stronger than he was. They laughed as he cried over Dog's limp body.

"But I got back at 'em, Dog. Yeah, I really got even," he said bitterly. That's when Otis had discovered that his speed and dexterity at handling a knife made him superior to most men. Two days before his eleventh birthday, Otis set out for new territory while Dave and Billy Jackson lay dead behind Turner's Livery Stable.

Otis was always heading for new territory. He couldn't remember if it had been five times or six. And now, it had happened again. It was that damned Carl Jenkins' fault this time. If it hadn't been for him, he might have stood a chance with Karen. But Carl kept coming around courting her, just like Otis didn't matter, or even exist.

Karen was the main reason he had gone to the Larkin ranch asking for a job. He'd wandered into Leon simply hoping to get a handout, and maybe enough work to fill his poke with grub. Then he saw her leaving Walker's General Store with her mother. He fell in love with her right there in the middle of the street. He followed them to the ranch, and feigned himself to be a down-on-his-luck cowboy. He was good enough with horses and cattle, and had little trouble convincing her father to hire him, especially when he lied about having trained race horses in Tennessee. Otis had a feeling Jim Larkin might've loved his prize horse, Lightning, more than his wife or daughter, as he spent every breath bragging about the animal.

Otis began sparking Karen that first day. She giggled at his habit of rocking from one foot to the other when he felt pressed to say something important. But then she smiled and said, "That's sweet of you, Slim. I'll be sure to ask when I need your help with any of my chores."

And she sure enough did. That very next day, she had him hauling water for laundry, chopping wood and even feeding chickens. Otis was happy to do those things on top of the work her father had given him, because they were for the pretty dark-eyed Karen. This continued for several months, with him asking only that she sit with him on the porch in the evening for a few minutes of conversation. Then Carl Jenkins began frequenting the ranch. It had taken several of these visits before Otis realized the young man was coming to court Karen. There was no way he could compete with Carl Jenkins, and he knew it. Carl had good looks, fancy clothes, and his family had plenty of money. All Otis had was stringy hair, buck teeth, and pock-marks on his thin face. His clothes were old and trail-worn, and he only had ten dollars in wages in his pocket. He had stared at himself in the little piece of mirror by the washbasin outside the tack room and knew he'd have to make his move, or it'd be too late.

He cleaned up the best he could and waited until she had seated herself alone in the porch swing the way she'd done every evening he could remember. Then he scampered from the barn with a fresh-picked bouquet of wild flowers and told her he loved her and wanted to marry her. She stared at him opened-mouthed before laughing hysterically.

"You what?" she said, trying to compose herself.

"I...I...said I...uh, want to m...m...marry you, Miss Karen." Otis rocked from one foot to the other as he knotted his hat in his hands. The rocking and hat-twisting became more pronounced with her laughter.

"What's going on out here?" Jim Larkin poked his head

though the door.

"Your stable-hand just proposed to me," Karen said, and held Otis' bouquet for her father to see.

"He what?" The big man laughed as he came to the edge of the porch and stared down at him. "You crazy, boy? You think I'd let my little girl marry the likes of you, even if she said she loved you?"

Otis stumbled backward before turning to bolt inside the barn. He could hear them laughing as he crouched inside Lightning's stall. The huge roan may have belonged to Karen's father, but Otis considered it his horse. He was the one who fed, groomed and exercised it. While Jim Larkin petted and bragged about the animal, he'd not actually ridden the horse once that Otis could remember. He hugged the roan's neck as it nuzzled him tenderly.

"Yeah, you know, don't you, o'l boy? Ain't right or decent to laugh in a feller's face when he's trying to tell how he feels inside. Folks like that have got to understand. Things like that make a feller do things he shouldn't ought to."

He avoided Karen for the next two days by throwing a saddle on Lightning and exercising him in one of the remote pastures. He would return to groom and feed the animal around sunset, then climb into the hay loft and watch her through a crack in the barn siding as she rocked and giggled beside Carl Jenkins in the porch swing. The humiliation he'd felt had begun to fester in the pit of his stomach until he thought he'd burst. Then the fit came on the third day, just after he'd put Lightning back into his stall. He'd only had two of them during the past three months. He had been lucky enough to feel them coming, and had hidden until they passed, but this one had taken him by surprise, and left him thrashing on the ground outside the barn door. Otis could never remember anything that happened during the fits, and had to rely on what others told him, but he did remember hearing their voices from inside a deep tunnel as the fit left him.

"What's the matter with you, boy? Get up from there! You gone completely crazy?" Jim Larkin was yelling.

"Keep away from him, Daddy! He has rabies or

something!" Karen said.

"Oh, go away, both of you! The boy's sick. Go on! All of you!" Mrs. Larkin said.

"Get away from him, Mama. He's foaming at the mouth. He might have gotten bit by a rabid dog!"

"Jim, take your daughter to the house like I said, and leave this boy alone. I'll take care of him."

Otis could hear the laughter of the ranch hands who'd gathered, as they left toward the house with Karen and her father. He waved Mrs. Larkin's offer of help away as his senses began to return, and crawled inside one of the stalls to lie on the soft hay. *Rabies,* was what she'd said. He'd heard that word hundreds of times before. It had become a nickname of sorts. That's what Dave and Billy Jackson used to call him.

"Hey, Rabies. Where're ya goin'?"

"Don't get too close to ol' Rabies, he might bite you."

"Yeah, you might catch whatever he's got."

He'd tried so hard to hide his fits, and now everyone knew. He rolled over clutching his stomach. The pain from her knowing hurt worse than the pain caused by the fit. She'd never want him now, not even to sit and talk to on the front porch. *Keep away from ol' Rabies, you might catch whatever he's got.*

It was about midnight when he heard quick steps crunch the gravel as they crossed the yard and hurried past the barn. He poked his head from the loft opening to see Karen turn the corner of the corral and head toward the creek. He could see her shapely limbs though her white nightgown in the moonlight. Otis decided to follow. He needed to explain that there was no possible way for her to catch what he had. They could still be friends and sit in the porch swing and talk. That's all he wanted. After all, he still loved her.

He'd lost sight of her by the time he scurried down the ladder and out the door. It took him most of ten minutes to stumble onto her and Carl lying in the soft grass, doing things only married people should do. He couldn't rightly remember what happened next, only that seeing Carl Jenkins kissing, touching and doing those things to the girl he loved had somehow caused the festering inside to explode. He came to himself later, sitting beside Karen and holding his boot-knife. Except Karen was dead. He remembered seeing Carl Jenkins some ten yards closer to the creek. He was also dead. He tried waking Karen, and even drug her to her feet, but nothing seemed to work. Then he remembered crying as he washed away the blood in the icy water. The only thing he could do was leave. He saddled Lightning and took Jim Larkin's guns from where he hung them inside the kitchen, along with some food. He was well down the road by the time the sun broke over the treetops. What was troubling Otis right now was, he didn't know where the hell the road led.

He was pulled from his thoughts by the sound of sheep and barking dogs. There were approximately a hundred or more of the smelly creatures headed his way. He had been riding on a small trail, unsure where it led, and at this point not caring.

"Roan, old boy," he paused while tightening the saddle cinches, "I hope you don't mind me calling you *Roan*. I always thought *Lighting* was a stupid name for the likes of you. Anyway, as I was saying, I never really liked sheep much, but this bunch is gonna save us a lot of trouble. If we ride down that trail ahead of 'em, no one, not even God himself, could ever find our tracks."

Otis clucked his tongue as he started the horse ahead of the sheep and on the trail toward Geuda Springs.

Chapter 3

"May God help us." Cotton leaned in the open doorway as he packed his favorite pipe.

"He'll have to, if we're ever going to find Slim with this sad lot," Dave said, pouring two cups of freshly brewed coffee. "Hot-damn!" He dropped the pot back onto the stove with a bang.

"Watch yourself. That handle gets hot."

"Yeah, so I noticed." He handed one of the mugs to Cotton and stared at the milling crowd in the street. There were approximately thirty men, ranging from seventy-year-old Lloyd Hawkins to twelve-year-old Gary Baker.

Cotton grinned as William Beadles, the town's founding father, stopped his buggy in front of the office. The man was dressed in black, and carried a ten-gauge shotgun propped against the seat next to him.

"Hope you don't plan on going along with this three-ring circus, and using that Long-Tom. There wouldn't be enough of anyone you nailed to tote back and hang."

"Not hardly." Beadles scratched his chin as he studied the crowd. "Had me a chicken hawk pesterin' Mrs. Beadles' hens."

"Did you get him?"

"Ever known me to miss, Cotton?"

"Not hardly."

"Well, good day gentlemen, and good luck." He glanced at the crowd one last time before shaking the reins. "You'll need it."

"We sure will," Dave said, and made a face as he took a sip of the coffee.

"Bad as mine?" Cotton glanced at his mug and back at Dave.

"Worse. I wish you'd get Alice to teach you how to make coffee."

"Me? You're the one who made this witch's brew."

"Yeah, but you don't make it any better than I do." Both men tossed their coffee into the street as Mayor Parker approached, leading his horse.

"I think everyone's here who plans on going. So, we can get started anytime you're ready, sheriff."

"Why can't I get it through your head? We're only chasing one man, not a band of cattle thieves. And I don't need an army to catch him, either. Besides, Dave has worked as my deputy for three years. He could more'n likely get the job done by himself, if the truth were known."

"Well, there's no reason to argue, because we're all going, and that's that." The mayor gave a nod of finality.

"That thousand-dollar reward Jim Larkin's putting up for Karen's killer wouldn't have anything to do with it, now would it?" Cotton raised his eyebrows as he struck a match and lit his pipe.

"Yes, it would. That's a lot of money to all these men, including me." The mayor made a sweep of his arm. "Everyone here has as much right to it as you and Dave do."

"Sure they do," Dave said with a snigger, "but half of them wouldn't know what to do if they were lucky enough to catch Slim, and the other half ought to be locked up themselves." He nodded toward a group huddled around the watering trough, smoking. Frank Barnes glanced up from the cigarette he was rolling and grinned.

"You wouldn't be talking about us, now would you,

Deputy?"

"Take it anyway you want, Frank." Dave stepped forward, but Cotton clamped a strong hand on his shoulder.

"Not now, son, we've got other fish to fry."

Frank had served time for selling firearms and whisky to the Indians before coming to Leon. Considering the amount of money Frank always seemed to have, Cotton had a notion the man was back in the same rotten business, but he had no way of proving it. He had never seen Frank or his friends do a lick of work. Instead, they hung around the back room at the pharmacy, drinking eighty-proof cough medicine and playing cards. To top it off, they were bullies. Every time there was trouble, he could count on one or more of them being involved.

"That's right, sheriff. You can save your pretty deputy, if you want," Frank said. "But someday you ain't gonna be around, and one of us is gonna have the pleasure of teaching him a thing or two." Dave tried pulling away, but Cotton tightened his grip.

"Maybe, but it could be the other way around, too." Cotton shoved Dave back inside the office and closed the door as the men laughed. "Come on, let's get ready to ride."

Chapter 4

"They're sure as hell gonna slow us down and get in the way." Dave stood in the stirrups and shaded his eyes against the sun. The posse was scattered rag-tag across the countryside. A good portion were still drunk from a meeting in front of the courthouse. The mayor had announced the need for a posse, and repeated Jim Larkin's offer of a thousand-dollar reward. Keith Johnson had already fallen out of his saddle and sprained his ankle, and they had left Toby Sorenson three miles back, puking his guts out. It was Frank Barnes himself who had produced several bottles at the meeting and passed them around. Instead of arresting the whole town, Cotton decided it was better to ignore the illegal contraband after watching the mayor and judge share one of the bottles.

"We'll have to make sure we stay ahead of 'em to keep them from covering Slim's tracks, but I'm afraid if we leave them behind someone's gonna to get hurt."

"I wouldn't worry myself too much about one of them gettin' hurt," Cotton said. "They'd deserve it."

"I'm not. They can shoot each other all to hell for all I care. It's them hurtin' or killin' someone else I'm worried about."

"Or shooting one of us." Cotton grinned. "I'd recommend

staying out of the brush and in the open 'til you're sure that most of them have sobered up. Then I still wouldn't trust Frank Barnes and that group he rubs elbows with. They'd probably plug you anyway, just for the fun of it."

~   ~   ~

They only covered ten miles the first day, and camped under some small oaks by a creek. After handing out tasks to some of the more reliable of the men, Cotton took Dave with him to the edge of the campsite to go over plans for the following day.

"About half of these men won't last another day." Dave took out the makings and began rolling a cigarette. "No one's seen Toby all afternoon."

"Good. No great loss. Probably still laying under that bush heaving his toenails up." Cotton propped his boot against a rock and started packing his pipe.

"Still wish it was just you and me. Took us half the day just getting these clowns in line enough to ride out of town, let alone hunt a killer."

"Yeah, but you need to remember you're dealing with farmers, store-keepers, and a few drovers. Outside of a few who fought in the war, most of them's never been part of anything like this. You can't expect them to have much discipline."

"You're probably right, but this guy might be making good time. We'll never catch him at this rate."

"Maybe we won't catch him right away, not as a group anyway." Cotton grinned. "But we eventually will when this bunch tires of the chase. If worse comes to worst, we'll call in some outside help. We'll catch him one way or the other."

"It just goes against my grain watching them falling all over each other and covering up Slim's trail." Dave took a drag on his cigarette.

"I know, but let's forget it for now. What I want is for you to ride ahead tomorrow and pick up his trail. Don't report back to me unless there's a problem, or you know you've found where he's headed. Now, we'd better get some sleep and try to get an early start."

Chapter 5

They were up at dawn and on the trail by six o'clock. Dave spaced himself about a half a mile ahead of the others and, although Slim's trail was almost two days old, he soon found it. He would have been caught up in the excitement of the hunt except for the nagging feeling that something was wrong. The killer was apparently making no effort to conceal his tracks. After establishing exactly where the fugitive was headed, he rode back to report to Cotton, and found his boss in a heated argument with Joe Parker.

"What are you trying to do, kill us all? We've already covered nearly twenty miles, and it's not quite noon." The red-faced mayor mopped sweat from his forehead with a handkerchief.

"I warned you in the beginning, we're out to catch this man, not have a Sunday picnic," Cotton said firmly. "Our killer took off sometime night before last. Y'all took most of yesterday just getting out of town. And don't forget, he's got a mighty fast horse."

"Speaking of which, look at our horses." The mayor waved his arm in the air. "They're more tired than the men, and we're half dead."

"Well, you'll just have to keep up, or go home."

Major Mitchell

"We'll all be on foot if you keep pushing us like this." He shook a finger in Cotton's face.

"If I might interrupt," Dave said with a grin, "I've found his trail just over the next rise."

"Like I said, keep up or go back home," Cotton yelled. "Saddle up, and let's go."

Dave grinned at how eager the half dead men were to get back in the chase. The thousand-dollar reward, it seemed, was just over the next rise and they quickly forgot their fatigue.

By mid-afternoon Slim's tracks looked even fresher and Dave was confident they were gaining on him, but the fact that Slim seemed to be sticking to the road still bothered him. He had chosen the trail itself, rather than riding parallel forty or fifty feet to one side to let the grass and brush cover his tracks. Slim seemed to be traveling at a casual trot, and not varying his direction of travel, which seemed strange for a man on the run. There were times when Dave was able to follow the trail while galloping his own horse. In some of the areas where the road narrowed, and the grass grew thicker, he walked his mare, but seldom did he have to travel slower than a trot. As the afternoon sun beat down, Dave found himself having to spend as much time waiting on the posse as he did looking for tracks. The times he dismounted and walked beside his horse, he could hear Cotton urging them onward.

Late that afternoon, Dave rode ahead, losing complete contact with the posse. He searched the ground and finally sat down under an oak tree on a small rise about fifty feet from the road. Fifteen minutes later Cotton rode up to him.

"Taking a little rest?" The sheriff leaned forward in the saddle.

"No, he's gone."

"What do you mean, gone? Who's gone?"

"Slim, our killer, he's gone," Dave said, calmly rolling a cigarette.

"Damn your hide. What are you talking about?"

"He stopped here and rested," Dave pointed to the tracks under the tree, "then headed down the trail toward Geuda Springs. Then along came a couple hundred sheep who

21

entered the trail right over there." He pointed. "It'll take some time to find him again."

"Might as well make camp here tonight." Cotton squinted as he studied the countryside. "Damn those sheep anyway. He's stayed on the road this far, what makes you think he's going to change now?"

"Wouldn't you, after having your trail wiped out? Anyway, my guess is he's over the initial shock of the killing, and things are gonna be different from now on. I've got a feeling he's not as dumb as he's led us to believe, and we're in for a real ride."

Chapter 6

By the following morning, the posse diminished considerably when sixteen men turned back. The remaining group spread wide across the trail looking for sign. It was about noon when Cotton was startled by a shout from the other side of the road in a small ravine.

"We caught him, by God. We got the bastard!" One of the men was waving his hat in the air.

Cotton spurred his horse down the rocky slope in time to see a frightened young man on top of a horse surrounded by the posse. He had his hands tied behind his back. One of the men was holding a long rope and knotting a noose in one end. Cotton reined his horse to a stop, throwing gravel across their boots.

"What in hell's going on here? Untie his hands." Cotton swung his foot over the pommel and dropped to the ground.

"We caught him, and now we're gonna hang this murdering pig. Then we're gonna collect the reward." Frank Barnes laughed before giving a raspy cough.

"Knew it was gonna come to this sooner or later," Cotton mumbled as he stepped away from his horse.

"You know Frank," he continued in a loud voice, "I've never had any real reason to arrest you or run you out of town, but I should have made something up. Untie that boy and let him go."

"The hell you say."

"I didn't do nothing, mister. Honest I didn't," the youth said as tears rolled down his dusty cheeks.

"You're not hanging anyone, Frank. And, I'm not going to repeat myself again. Let him go."

"Just turn your back one minute, and we'll save the town a lot of money on a trial." At Frank's urging the other men dropped the rope over a tree branch and put the noose around the young man's neck.

"I said, you're not hanging anyone." Cotton pulled his pistol. "Now, take that rope off his neck."

The crowd thinned as Cotton and Frank stared at each other. Dave walked his horse to the edge of the circle and dismounted. He casually drew his own gun and shrugged. "I thought you might need some help."

"Look, sheriff," Smitty said. "If you want the credit for catching him, you can have it. I just want the reward."

"I'm not talking just to hear myself. Take the rope off." He raised the .44 higher.

Someone toward Dave's right made a quick move for his gun, but Cotton fired before he could clear his holster. The bullet brought a small puff of trail dust from the center of the victim's vest and pitched him backwards. Almost instantly another gun boomed and Cotton felt a rending pain as a bullet caught him in the left shoulder, spinning him off his feet. Dave fired and the blast knocked Smitty backward over a log.

Frank cursed as Dave pointed his gun at him and yelled, "Don't even think about it."

"Oh, God. Oh, God," Mayor Parker cried as he held the reins of the frightened horse. "Someone help me." Fred Walker ran to pull the rope off the young man and help him dismount while others milled around in shock, staring at the dead men.

"You damn fool," Cotton gasped as he struggled to his feet. "You're responsible for two dead men and this hole in me."

"Me?" Frank acted surprised. "All I did was catch your

24

killer. You started all the shooting."

"Shut up, Frank," Dave yelled. "That's not the Larkin horse, and he doesn't look anything like the stable hand."

"Well, if he ain't the killer, then why'd he run when he seen us coming?"

"Seeing you and your bunch charging with your guns drawn would make anyone run," Cotton said. "I would have run myself."

"Gentlemen, please," Mayor Parker said. "We've got a real problem on our hands. The killer is still on the loose, and our posse is shooting each other. You can't go around killing each other like this."

"I can if they try to hang everyone they run across," Dave said. "You men are gonna have to bury those bodies. Mayor, you can try to patch Cotton up enough so we can get back into town. I'm disbanding this posse as of this minute."

"You can't do that," Parker said with nods and murmurs of support.

"He can do what he damn well likes," Cotton said weakly. "With this hole in me he's in charge. If you don't like it, take it up at the next Town Council meeting."

"Frank Barnes," Dave called loudly as he stepped away from the mayor. "I'll take your guns now. All of you," he said with a sweeping motion toward Frank's friends. "You're all under arrest for attempted murder."

"The hell, you say?" A grin crept across Frank's face as he casually moved to his right. His friends, a heavy built man called Hawk, and a small-framed individual known as "Mex", glanced at each other and shrugged. Mex tucked his thumbs in his gunbelt and strode to his left. Hawk smiled when Dave turned and walked toward his horse. The smile vanished when he pulled a shotgun from his bedroll and pointed it a Frank's head.

"That ain't too nice," Frank said, holding up one hand and unbuckling his gunbelt with the other. "I've never liked you either, but I'd never use a scatter-gun on you." Frank's friends followed suit, tossing their guns at Dave's feet. "Now, I really owe you," Frank continued. "Smitty was kin of mine, and no one takes my gun and gets away with it. You're a dead man. I'll see to it."

"You can try if you like." Dave turned to the youth that Frank had been trying to hang. "What's your name, boy?"

"Pete, Peter Martin."

"Where are you from?"

"A farm outside Geuda Springs. I was headed toward Leon to visit my Aunt and Uncle. We heard my cousin died."

"What's your Aunt and Uncle's names?"

"Larkin, Jim and Beth. I've got another cousin too, his name's John."

"Yes, yes, I know them," Dave said gently. "That's why we are out here, trying to find the man who killed Karen. As Deputy Sheriff of Leon, I'd like you to come into town and fill out a report on this incident. Will you?" A look of bewilderment crossed young Pete's face. "I'll help you."

~   ~   ~

They made camp in hope that Cotton would be strong enough to make the trip to Leon in the morning. Dave took Pete aside and questioned him about the farms and houses located around Gueda Springs, and places where someone running from the law might take refuge.

"Gueda Springs ain't too big. Most of the town can be seen easily from our front porch," he laughed. "Nearly all of the farms lay right along the road, 'cept one or two little ones. They're over yonder located about here," he said drawing a map in the dirt. "Our place, and most of the others, sits here in the big flat area near the town. These little farms sit in a little valley in these hills. Old man and old lady Clemson live in the first place here. A woman, her little girl and her crippled husband named Jamison live in the second place, right about here," he said putting the final dot on his map.

26

Chapter 7

Otis Felts sat on his heels staring at the scene below him. The posse had been trying to hang a teenage boy, then there was shooting and two men lay dead. He had turned back to see if he was being followed, but he hadn't expected to see this.

"Musta been after me, but why were they trying to hang that boy?" he mumbled. "Better sneak down there tonight and find out for sure."

Otis waited until after the evening meal, when the men were sitting around the campfire talking and drinking coffee. He crept silently in a circular pattern down the slope, pausing behind small bushes, until he was close enough to hear their conversation.

"I don't care if you're king over these United States, you can't say I'm guilty of trying to murder this here boy. We all thought he was our killer," said the big man with a beard.

"Look, Frank, I'm not going to argue with you. Even if he was Slim, you couldn't hang him without a trial. That's the law."

Otis grinned and shook his head. They didn't appear to be very efficient. They didn't even know what he looked like and had tried to hang another man. He decided to lay in his vantage point awhile longer and listen as the two argued. Some of the members of the posse were glad the chase was over and were happy to be going home. A few others sat quietly drinking coffee without saying anything. He raised his eyebrows when someone mentioned a thousand-dollar reward Karen's father had offered for his capture. That meant there would be a lot of people looking for him. The young deputy broke off the argument and sat down by the white-haired man who had been shot in the arm. Otis noticed he also was wearing a badge and decided he must be the one in charge, or at least he was until he'd gotten shot. He crept closer to hear better, and paused again behind a bush. They were less than ten feet away now, and when light from the campfire shone on the older man's face, Otis recognized him as Cotton, the friendly sheriff he had met on one of his visits to town.

"What's your plans now?" Cotton said.

"Get you back to town so the Doc can patch you up. Then put Frank and his band of idiots behind bars."

"Then what?" The young lawman looked perturbed. "You hadn't really thought that far ahead, had you?"

"No, I thought you'd know what to do."

"What if I don't make it? Men die from smaller wounds than this. Just listen, and learn," he said, cutting off the protest. "I might be laid up for a while, and you'll have to take over. And the fact is, you can't get young Pete there to sign a complaint against Frank without his parents' permission. Wire the sheriff in Gueda Springs, Barry, William Barry, and tell him to get that boy's parents over here to sign a complaint. You can't hold them very long without it."

"I can lock them up for shooting you."

"No you can't. Smitty did the shooting, and he's buried over yonder. You saw to that yourself. When it comes to a hearing, if you don't have a signed complaint, all you can charge Frank with is being the same jackass he's always been. Get hold of the boy's parents."

Otis lay quietly until the men were asleep. Then, slipping silently up the slope the way he had come, he decided to make dry camp right where he'd left the horse tied.

"Well, Roan, old boy," he whispered to the horse as he made a meal out of cold stale biscuits and beef jerky. "Look's like we'll be riding alone tomorrow. They didn't know what they were doing anyway. It wouldn't have been much fun even if they did keep chasing us."

The pain of seeing Karen lying in a pool of blood had already begun to fade with the excitement of the chase. He thought of the many times he'd been tracked in the past, and how he'd learned to elude his pursuers. There had been times when he was starving and had snuck into a kitchen to take a loaf of bread without being seen. He had made a game out of hiding his trail and even on occasions had taunted his pursuers. It had been a long time since he had played that game.

"Well, it's probably better this way. I guess we're getting too old to be playing games, now aren't we?" he said as he closed his eyes. "It's time to find us a place and settle down." Sleep came quickly as the horse munched quietly on the rich grass around Otis' meager campsite.

~ ~ ~

It was almost noon the following day when Otis finally decided to rest. The horse had gone lame and he had been walking most of the day, leading the great animal. The dew had burnt off the grass hours before and a stiff breeze was coming from the west. He looked back the way he had come, and all he could see was the same endless sea of prairie grass tossing in the wind. He was leaving little trail to follow. Finding a decaying log, Otis sat down and opened his bag. He found only one hard biscuit and a small piece of dried beef. He ate his meal while surveying the flat skyline.

"Must be some sort of house over there," he said, with a nod toward the thin line of blue smoke ascending skyward. "Almost directly south, about a mile or two. Don't know exactly where we are, but one thing's for sure. We ain't got no food, and I need a place where I can fix you a new shoe." He rubbed the horse's nose. "What about us going over there and swapping howdies with them folks?"

Chapter 8

Vicky Jamison looked up from her vegetable garden when her daughter's dog began barking. A gust of wind blew dust in her eyes and forced her to use the end of her soiled apron to clear them. She was startled to see the tall, skinny man leading his horse out of the grass toward their small farm. They had gotten very few visitors in two years, and this was the first one that had come in through the prairie toward the rear of their little two-room cabin, and not by the road that led toward Gueda Springs. She dropped her hoe and started toward the house to see what the stranger wanted. Caroline, her only child, toddled along beside her, tugging against her skirt.

"Who he, Mommy? He a nice man? Cuddles, angry, huh Mommy?" She paused to stare at the towhead, wondering how so many words could come from a three-year old.

"Cuddles barks at everyone, honey. Now come on."

She found the stranger talking to Harold, who was sitting in his crudely made wheelchair on their front porch. Though Harold was fifteen years her senior, he had made the most dashing figure she had ever seen when they first met. He was tall and well built. The brass on his blue uniform sparkled almost as much as his smile. They were married when she turned sixteen, against her grandmother's wishes.

"He's a soldier, Vicky," her grandmother had protested, "and he'll be involved with killing." Vicky had come from a long line of Quakers, and believed any act of violence toward another human was wrong. But her love for Harold was strong, and they were soon married. Besides, she had reasoned, the war between the states had ended thirteen years earlier, so there should be no need for him to kill anyone. It was wonderful the way the other soldiers held their sabers to make an arch for them to walk under. That was four years ago. Two years later, friends helped her build the house and barn, while Harold took care of Caroline from his chair. The bullet which was lodged in his spine, fired by an Indian, refused to let his legs work.

"Vicky, this is Mr. Henry Jones," Harold said. "Mr. Jones, meet my wife Vicky and my daughter Caroline."

Vicky eyed the tall, skinny man with a pock-marked face and large buck teeth. His clothes were tattered and he was covered with the dust of many days of travel. He also looked half starved. "Good afternoon, Mr. Jones," she said with a small curtsey.

"My friends call me Hank, ma'am," he said, taking Vicky's hand. Her bottom lip quivered as she smiled. The man's stare went right through her.

"Mr. Jones, ah, Hank, was telling me that his horse went lame out in the prairie. He wanted to know if he could bed down in the barn tonight and perhaps borrow some of our tools to repair his shoe. I told him that you could also use some help around the place, and perhaps he could stay a few days longer to help you. Maybe he could earn a little money to buy some supplies in town."

"As far as food goes, he doesn't need to work. I'll certainly feed him," Vicky said. "But as far as money goes," she shrugged, "I'm sorry, we haven't any."

"That's all right, ma'am," he said with a toothy grin. "I didn't really ask for any money. That was your husband's idea. I'm just worried about old Roan here. He's a good horse and I'd hate to see him get any worse."

"You're welcome to stay and eat. If you'll excuse me, I'll

fix supper." Taking her daughter's hand, Vicky entered the small house and closed the door.

She liked the comfort of their home. It was much like herself...uncomplicated and simple. It consisted of one large room that served as a living room and kitchen, with a small bed near the stove where Caroline slept. A heavy curtain separated the room from hers and Harold's bedroom. Heavy cast-iron pots and pans hung from pegs on the wall above the crude sink board. Her one and only luxury was the second door to the house that led out back toward the garden. As she washed her hands, she could hear Harold apologizing to the stranger for his wife's abrupt manner.

"This crippled condition of mine has been hard on her. When I was a lieutenant in the Army, people respected me and followed my orders."

Vicky closed her ears to the rest. She had heard it repeated many times, and knew every word by heart. Whenever anyone did happen to visit, which was seldom, or when something didn't go his way, anyone within ear-shot got a lecture on how important he used to be, and how insensitive his wife and child had become. If he could only walk again, things would be different. He'd show everyone. She sniffed and swiped at the corner of her eye with a knuckle as she vigorously peeled the potato in her hand.

The first time she had seen that look on Harold's face was at his bedside when the doctor explained that her husband would never walk. Now it seemed that every small incident caused the look to return. *He shouldn't care if some dirty tramp thinks he's important or not*, she thought, and grabbed another potato.

Harold *was* important, and she loved him, but his moods were making it hard on everyone. She arched her back and stared blindly out the kitchen window for a second before dropping the potato into the water and reaching for a third. She shook her head as she thought about his constant chiding of Caroline for not acting or speaking like an adult. He scolded her for not saying excuse me when leaving the table, or leaving a toy on the floor or spilling her milk, all of which

32

were normal things a growing child would do. It had gotten to the point where Caroline hated going near her father for fear of receiving another scolding. Their daughter's fear had caused Harold to accuse Vicky that very morning of turning her against him. The thought of his accusation caused her temper to burn, but she bit her tongue and kept her anger to herself. *If I say anything, he'll only start another argument.* She tossed the last potato into the pan and grabbed the butcher knife.

After the potatoes were sizzling and a pan of biscuits were in the oven, she washed Caroline and herself and changed their clothes. As an afterthought, she took a towel and wash pan along with a bar of lye soap out on the front porch.

"Here you are, Mr. Jones. If you'd like to freshen up, supper will be ready in just a few minutes."

"Thank you, ma'am," Otis said. "You're very kind."

Vicky went back inside feeling remorseful. Mr. Jones was probably a nice man down on his luck. She stirred the pot of beans that had been simmering with a slab of bacon all afternoon. She was also sorry for feeling resentful toward Harold. It wasn't his fault he was crippled.

They used to have fun together. They had danced and gone to parties, and he laughed all the time. She hadn't heard Harold laugh in such a long time. She wiped the corner of her eye with her apron thinking it wasn't her fault either.

Her feeling wasn't due to his being crippled, either. She assured herself of that fact as she turned the potatoes in the pan. Vicky knew she could deal with caring for a crippled husband. What she resented was the bitterness. Harold's anger toward God, and a sense of defeat, had consumed his entire life. It permeated everything inside their home. She also resented that none of the ladies or men from Gueda Springs came to visit like they used to, but she knew the reason was Harold. She paused to blow her nose before pulling the biscuits from the Dutch oven.

~   ~   ~

Vicky washed the dishes and put Caroline to bed by the light of a single kerosene lamp in the center of the table. She listened politely to Mr. Jones' conversation about his life experiences for about an hour, then excused herself and made her way to bed.

After Harold's release from the hospital, Vicky used to try to help him at bedtime, but that only made him angry.

"There are two things you are never going to help me with," he yelled. "Putting myself to bed, and doing my daily duties in the outhouse."

The latter was fine with Vicky, but she had never understood why helping him dress for bed would make him so angry. *Anyway*, she thought as she fell asleep, *there are probably more things he could do, if he only tried.*

She woke to the sound of someone splitting logs outside her bedroom window, and fumbled for a second or two before pulling back the curtain. It was dark with only a tinge of red on the eastern sky. She smelled coffee drifting from the kitchen. She dressed, brushed and tied back her long golden hair, and left the bedroom quietly to the sound of Harold's snoring. She moved the coffee pot off the stove and poured herself a mug. The liquid inside the pot was black as tar.

Hank came in with an armload of wood. His shirt and face had been washed and his hair combed. "Good mornin', Mrs. Jamison," he said with a toothy grin. "Hope you didn't mind me making coffee. I usually get up early."

"No, I don't mind," she mumbled. "It's kind of strong, though."

"I'm sorry; that's the way I'm used to drinking it. Most of the men on the trail, working cattle, you know, ranch hands? They boil it till you can shine leather with what you don't finish off at breakfast." Vicky sipped her coffee as Hank shifted nervously from one foot to the other.

"The coffee's fine; don't worry about it," she said with a smile, and the nervous action stopped. "Well, I guess I'd better go collect the eggs and milk the cow. Caroline will want breakfast as soon as she wakes."

"Now don't worry about that, ma'am," Hank said eagerly. "I can do all those things for you. You just relax and finish your coffee."

Before she could protest, he was out the door and to the small shed they used as a combination barn and hen-house. She watered down her cup of coffee and went outside. Standing back, she watched Hank as he collected the eggs in the basket she had hanging inside the barn. He then cleaned the bucket at the pump and began milking Edith, who didn't seem to mind a stranger doing the chore. Hank talked to the cow and stroked her like a kitten. He then fed the horses and Edith, and took a rake to the barn floor. Vicky could see that he was indeed talented and experienced with animals. He had done in a matter of minutes what would normally take her a couple of hours. By the time she had breakfast ready, Hank was finished cleaning the barn and had washed up.

After breakfast, Hank excused himself and went outside. From her kitchen window, Vicky could see him staring at the prairie, back the way he had come.

"He's running from something," she said.

"Who is?" Harold asked, glancing at her over his coffee mug.

"Hank, the only other person around, except us," she giggled.

"And how would you know that he's running?" he snapped at her. "Are you able to read people's minds, among your many talents?"

"I was only commenting on the fact that he came across the prairie. And now he's out there looking back the way he came, as though he's watching for someone who might be following him." She tossed her wadded dish-towel on the sink-board and went outside, ignoring Harold's apology. He frequently apologized for cutting remarks, only to repeat them minutes later. If it were not for her faith in a loving God, she would long ago have given up trying to make something of their marriage.

"Hank," she said, walking up behind him. He jumped like a frightened animal. "It's all right. I only wanted to know who you are looking for. Is there someone else out there? Are you expecting someone?"

"Oh, gosh, Mrs. Jamison," he laughed. "I didn't hear you coming. No, I was just looking. I don't expect there's another soul out there, except maybe rabbits and snakes. Besides," he began shifting from foot to foot while his eyes seemed to search for something that wasn't there, "you don't want to know who might be out there, or why I come that way."

"Why, is there someone out there who's dangerous?"

"No, no." He shook his head. "It's just that, well, I done some terrible bad things."

"And you thought that somebody might be following you."

"Yeah, it's...."

"You don't have to tell me anything, if you don't want to." Vicky put her hand on his arm. "As long as no one hurts Caroline, or Harold, or myself, I don't need to know what you've done in the past. You're welcome to stay here as long as you want. Besides," she smiled, "we have all done a lot of horrible things that God has forgiven. I can forgive your past."

The nervous dance stopped as he grinned at her. Vicky knew she had found a pliable student to teach her faith to, and the sharing of her faith was terribly important. It was something she deeply missed since Harold's convalescence. When they first met, he would sit and listen to her talk for hours on end about God, and even go to meetings with her. Now he refused to even listen for a few minutes.

Harold was sitting on the porch glaring as she returned to the house. Vicky closed the door with a bang and scrubbed angrily at the breakfast dishes. Through the window she watched Hank run in slow circles shouting, as Caroline and Cuddles chased after him.

"God, I don't care what he's done, please make him stay, at least for a while. He'll be good for Caroline and me. For all of us."

Chapter 9

Normally the citizens of Leon would not even have noticed a stranger riding into town. The arrival of drovers herding cattle toward El Dorado, farmers looking for a place to sink their roots, or travelers simply going west was almost a daily occurrence. They were used to seeing strangers, and most only stopped long enough to quench their thirst in the back room of Adam's Pharmacy and buy supplies at the store. But the sight of the tall buckskin-clad rider on a huge brown and white pinto caused everyone to stop what they were doing and take a long look. It wasn't that they hadn't seen Indians before, because they were living on land that had once belonged to the Comanche, Kiowa and Arapaho before the first white man had ventured into Kansas. But this man commanded their attention. He walked his horse trailing a rope that was tied to the hands of a dirty, hungry looking white man. Tying a white man to his horse was bold for any Indian, but to parade him down the main road in town, leashed like an animal, was insane. Loud murmurs rolled as he passed their way.

"He's got a lot of bark, I'll say that much for him." Mayor Parker shook his head and chuckled. The rider paused to glance around before dismounting in front of the sheriff's office. His shoulder-length hair was raven black, except for streaks of gray showing above his temples. His bronze skin matched that of other Indians, but his most striking feature was the light, dusky-blue eyes of the rider. The mayor studied the man intently as he tied the animal to the railing. The stranger removed his hat and used it to swat the dust from his legs and arms, as he took in his surroundings.

"I'll wager next week's salary he sees everything going on around him at the same time," the mayor said to the group of men who had stopped to stare.

"Yeah, that son of a bitch." The rider shoved his prisoner inside the sheriff's office.

Mayor Parker turned to see Frank Barnes standing beside him. His only dealings with Frank had been a little over two weeks ago, during the posse incident. He hadn't liked him then, and decided he liked him less now. After the attempted hanging of the young boy out on the trail, the mayor had hoped to see Frank and his buddies get hung, or at least spend some jail time. But the parents of the lad had been afraid to press charges, so Frank and his gang had only spent a few days locked inside their cell.

"Do you know him?" Parker asked.

"Yeah, I know him," he said, spitting tobacco juice on the sidewalk. "That's Manhunter, the bounty huntin' bastard. I swore I'd kill that half-breed next time I saw him." Frank's spurs clinked as he headed toward the pharmacy.

Shaking himself, Joe Parker crossed the street toward the sheriff's office, and received another shock as he opened the door. Sheriff Harvey Blankenship was laughing as he clasped the rider in a one-armed hug. Parker had seldom seen Cotton smile, let alone laugh.

"Joe, come on in. I want you to meet an old Army friend of mine. This is Matthew Blue. We rode together for five years. Matthew, this is Joe Parker, the mayor of our town."

After the obligatory hand-shake and nod, the Indian poured himself a hot cup of coffee and took a seat while Cotton locked his prisoner in the cell.

"Damn, it's good to see you, Matt," Cotton said as he tossed the keys in the desk drawer. "Matthew was the best tracker, hunter, guide, and fighter in the outfit. He even saved my life once."

"Looks like you could've used me again," he said, and made a face after taking a sip of coffee. "This is horrible. You make this?"

"Naw, my deputy did."

"He must be trying to kill you. By the way, how'd you get bunged up?"

"He got shot a week ago while standing off a lynch mob," Joe Parker said. "He should be home in bed right now."

"Really? I didn't think anyone would ever out-pull you in a gunfight."

"This little scratch? Aw, it ain't nothing. I'll tell you about it later," Cotton said with a wave of his good arm.

"Nothing? You almost bled to death," Parker said, and proceeded to tell the story.

"Now, Mayor," Cotton waved the story away with his good hand. "I don't want to dispute your word, but I'm not sure I remember it exactly that way."

"Which goes to prove you're not young anymore," Matthew said. "You might be slowing down. There was a time when nobody could get the drop on you." The sheriff's face turned crimson as he knit his eyebrows together.

"You never could hold your tongue, even when I was your commanding officer, could you?"

Parker's nerves relaxed as the Indian broke into a laugh that caused him to spill some of his coffee.

"Dad-blamed Injun. Think you got me again, don't you?" Cotton's scowl broke into a grin as he chuckled.

"Hey, what happened to this berg anyway?" Matthew shifted in his chair to peek through the window. "Last time I was here, there were only a couple of buildings, besides a few houses and some weeds. I see you even changed the name from *Little Walnut* to *Leon*."

"Yes, and we're going to turn Leon into a first-rate city; one the citizens can really be proud of." Mayor Parker tilted his chin in the air as he spoke.

"Hmmmm," Matthew took another sip before placing his

cup on the edge of Cotton's desk. He glanced back out the window. "How many people live here now?"

"Oh, about three hundred or so, counting the closest farms. We're hoping to outgrow Coffeyville and El Dorado in the near future. What's the matter, Mr. Blue," Parker said, seeing the Indian's intent expression. "You act as though you don't approve of our plans."

"Oh, no." He turned the corners of his mouth down and shook his head. "That's just fine, if it's what you really want. But you've got too many people for me right now."

"Matt's never liked having more'n one or two folks around him at one time." Cotton chuckled.

"But, Cotton said you were in the Army. How'd you cope being all grouped together with a bunch of soldiers?"

"I didn't." Matthew took another sip of coffee and grinned. "I was a scout, so I didn't even have to see his ugly mug unless it was absolutely necessary." They were interrupted by Dave Price entering the room.

"Glad you showed up, Dave. I'd like you to meet Matthew Blue. He's a...."

"Yeah, I know, he's a bounty hunter," Dave said. "The whole town is in an uproar. An Indian bringing in a white man, leading him through the streets like a dog tied to a horse."

A thin smile crossed the Indian's lips as he eyed the deputy from head to foot. His manner sort of reminded the mayor of a rattlesnake he had run across once while walking in a dry creek bed north of town. That snake had sized him up the same way.

"Well, I thought about walking and letting him ride my horse, but I was afraid he wouldn't cooperate. He might've run off and left me stranded. Of course, I could have shot him. Would that have made you feel any better?"

"It would've probably made me feel better if you hadn't come to town in the first place."

"Then perhaps I should leave." Matthew grabbed his hat from the rack before turning to Cotton. "When can you telegraph Wells Fargo and collect my money?"

"I'll send the telegram this afternoon." Cotton's voice was icy as he glared at Dave. Mayor Parker cleared his throat a couple of times before speaking.

"I have to be getting on my way."

"Me too," Matthew said. "Thanks for the coffee, Cotton. I'll be seeing you." The mayor accompanied Matthew as far as the hitching rail before stopping to face him.

"By the way, Mr. Blue, there is an old friend of yours in town. A fellow by the name of Frank Barnes. He called you a half-breed and said he was going to kill you."

Matthew raised his eyebrows and gave a crooked grin. "I didn't know he was out of prison yet. They must be letting them out early these days."

"What did you do to him to make him that angry?"

"Nothing much." He put a foot in the stirrup and swung atop the horse. "I suppose he didn't like getting caught."

Chapter 10

It didn't surprise Matthew to find that the hotel in town was full and that he was invisible to the waitress in the restaurant. He paid premium prices for the few supplies he needed at the store and left town. Finding a secluded spot on the bank of the Little Walnut south of town, Matthew made camp. After bathing in the stream, he cooked himself a hot meal and then stretched out to take a nap. It was late in the afternoon when his solitude was broken.

"You're not very observant, letting someone sneak up on you like that." Dave cast a shadow across Matthew's frame.

"Oh, I saw you coming all right," Matthew lifted the hat from his stomach to reveal a gun. "I just didn't figure you were dangerous."

"Why not? The way I treated you back there, you know I don't like bounty hunters."

"I didn't figure you liked much of anyone. But, to answer your question, it's the eyes. You can tell by the eyes." He closed his own eyes and yawned. "Now, what do you want, boy? You're cutting into my nap time."

"Well..."

Matthew opened one eye as the deputy shifted nervously and then sat on his heels and cleared his throat.

"Well, Cotton says I owe you an apology."

42

"And you don't think you do?"

"You're a bounty hunter."

"And you're a deputy. We both do the same thing, but I get paid a little more for my trouble.

Dave's face reddened. "I'm not a hired gun. Most men like you are nothing but killers. They kill people and collect reward money. That's nothing less than murder for hire."

"And you're full of horse manure." Matthew closed both eyes again and yawned. "I don't think you'll find any bullet holes in my prisoner. He gave up peacefully, like most of mine do."

"Peacefully? He said you nearly starved him to death. Kept him running, wouldn't let him sleep or eat. You call that peaceful?"

"Look, boy, he's not a nice man. He robbed a bank and shot a teller who is lucky to be alive. Now I could have killed him and still have collected the reward, but I didn't. And I don't have to justify my actions to you or anyone else. I wasn't welcome in your town, so I came out here, and now, you're disturbing my peace."

"Okay, you're right." Dave lowered his eyes for a second. "As far as the town goes, the sight of an Indian leading a white man with a rope...well, there's too many memories. It's kinda hard for them to accept what they saw."

"That's too bad. I guess they'll have to get over it."

"My father was killed by a Comanche arrow."

"My father, mother, brother and sister were all killed by white men."

Matthew opened one eye and glared before closing it again. "Look, I'm not in the mood to get into some argument about who hates who the most. What happened a few years ago was war. Simply two nations, two races, at war with one another. A lot of people died on both sides, and the stronger nation won." He sat up and studied Dave's face a minute before shaking his head with a smirk. "I don't know where Cotton found you, and I don't give a damn. I don't give a damn about any of it. I make a living catching men who break the law. Now, if you'll leave me alone," he lay back and covered his face with his hat, "I have some serious sleep to catch up on."

"I came out here to tell you that Cotton wants you to come to his house for dinner tonight." Dave paused for a moment. "He's too sick to come out here. Doc won't let him leave town. I guess he's afraid that Cotton's strength isn't built up enough." He waited a minute longer for Matthew's reply, but didn't receive one.

"Well, damn it, are you coming or not?"

"I'll be there," Matthew removed his hat and opened one eye and scowled. "His house is the one with the white fence at the edge of town, isn't it?"

"Yes. How did you know?"

"I saw Alice hanging clothes as I rode in this morning," Matthew covered his face with the hat. "I suppose they're still married."

"Okay, then I'll tell him you'll be there tonight, right around dinner time. You are coming aren't you?"

Matthew heaved a sigh as he removed the hat with his left hand and calmly pointed the gun at Dave's head. "Look, I already told you I'd be there. And like I said, you're disturbing my nap time. I also told you that you aren't really welcome here, so if you don't leave right now, you might not be eating dinner tonight yourself."

He watched the deputy ride toward town at a full gallop before lying back on the grass. He yawned and grinned before covering his face with his hat. A moment later, he was snoring.

Chapter 11

Cotton laughed as tears ran down his cheeks. Dave had just given an embellished account of his meeting with the bounty hunter. His temper rose with his boss' laughter, and Cotton just laughed even harder.

"What would have happened if I'd grabbed my gun? I might have shot him, or he could have shot me. I don't think it's very funny."

"I don't either," Alice Blankenship said as she passed through the room on her way to the kitchen.

They had been married twenty-two years and Cotton still thought her as lovely as the day they were wed. He also valued her opinion on the character of a person, and had learned over the years that her opinion was almost flawless. "Well, you don't think Matthew would have shot him, do you?" he called after her.

"No, I don't. That is, unless he's changed," she said, coming back from the kitchen with a steaming bowl of mashed potatoes. "It's been quite a while since we've seen him, Harvey. People *do* change, sometimes."

"Not Matthew."

"She's right," Dave said. "You should have seen the look in his eyes." They were interrupted by a knock on the door.

"Matthew, come on in." Cotton opened the door wide and

clasped the tall Indian by the shoulder.

Alice ran to greet Matthew, and was engulfed in a bear hug. "Ah, Alice, you're still the second prettiest woman in the world."

"And, who might the prettiest be?" She tilted her head back with mock displeasure. "It's still Prairie Flower, I hope."

"Yes, there isn't any other."

"Well, I don't mind coming in second place to her. She was indeed beautiful." Alice gave him another hug before pushing away. "Now, let me go check on your dinner before I burn it."

"Heard you and Dave had a little run-in today," Cotton said, glancing toward Dave.

"No, not really." Matthew shrugged, and returned to making small-talk with Alice as she set the table.

"Not really? Is that what you call it? You pointed a gun at me," Dave growled.

"You wouldn't leave me alone. Look," Matthew said after a long minute, "there's a real world out there with some bad people. A man could get hurt, botherin' folks the way you did. I once met a man who shot his saddle partner because he was snoring too loud. Then he rolled over and went right to sleep. Say what you need to say, and then leave people alone. It's safer that way."

"And what if I'd pulled my gun?"

"I would have taken it away from you." Matthew turned the corners of his mouth down and shrugged. "Let's eat. I haven't had a home-cooked meal like this in years."

They feasted on fried chicken, hot biscuits, green beans, mashed potatoes and gravy. Alice remarked, after passing the potatoes to Matthew a third time, that he must be half-starved.

"I was," he said with a mouthful of biscuit. "You never ate my cooking, did you? You'd be starved too."

"I'm glad to know you were starving too, and not just your prisoner." Dave reached for the plate of biscuits in front of Alice and got his hand whacked with her butter knife. He leand back with a scowl and she passed him the plate.

"I don't know what's stuck in your craw, boy; we've

already had this discussion. But here's something you should learn right here and now." Matthew laid his fork on the side of his plate as he talked.

"Hunger and thirst are the two forces that drive man. He might crave companionship, or money, or clothes, cattle, or a million other things, but he can live without them, and many do. But he can't live without water and food for very long. You take those things away from him, plus keep him moving so he can't rest, and he will eventually do most anything you want. Even if it means giving up and going to jail without a fight."

"Sounds more humane than killing a man to me," Alice said. "There's too much killing and hurting people going on in this world. First we were fighting the British, next we were fighting Indians and the French. Then, we starting fighting and killing each other simply because one's from the north and the other's from the south. And if that wasn't enough, we started killing Indians again. And now that the Indians finally moved to the reservation, we are back to killing one another. Now, you tell me why?" She whacked the table with her palm. "It doesn't make any sense."

"Most people are against killing," Cotton said as he buttered another biscuit. "But every once in a while, someone gets greedy and wants what someone else has, and they're willing to hurt or kill to get it. Sometimes leaders get greedy, and we have a wars."

He laid the knife on his plate and stared across the table at Dave. "There are a few people who just like killing for no reason at all. But regardless of their reason, it's up to folks like us to catch them in order to protect everyone else. And I don't give a damn if it's you and me, or Matthew here, just so long as they're caught."

"Now, I want you to listen to me closely, because what I'm going to tell you just might save your life some day." Matthew pointed at the deputy with a piece of chicken. "I could have confronted that man the first day I found him, which was about three or four hours after the robbery. But there would certainly have been a fight, because he was desperate. One of us would have been hurt or killed. And why? Because I bulled into a situation that could have been avoided."

"You see, son," Cotton said, "generals have fought wars this way for centuries. You know David, in the Bible, had his men circle entire cities and not let anyone in or out. After a while, those people inside would get so hungry they'd throw down their arms and give up."

"Huh, I didn't know that was in the Bible." Matthew reached for another biscuit. "Of course, I haven't read much of that book in awhile, either."

"I just think it's kind of cruel, starving a man like that," Dave said.

"What's cruel about it?" Cotton gave a curt laugh. "He's alive right now in a warm cell with clean clothes and hot food in his belly. And you tell me Matthew is cruel? He could be dead, which is probably what would have happened if a posse had caught him. He didn't scalp him, he simply brought him in alive."

"Look," Matthew said. "What I do is neither good nor bad. I catch men who have broken the law. If you want to talk cruel, go and talk to the teller he shot. It's too bad my methods bother you, but I'm not going to feel sorry for the man in your cell. I learned my methods from my father and my grandfather, who were Indian, and I also learned a lot from this man right here." He nodded toward Cotton. "He was the best commanding officer in the Army. But the whole issue is, what I've learned has kept me alive, which is more than people will be saying for you some day. I doubt if you'll see thirty. You'd better learn to listen to Cotton, and you'll live longer."

"Well, would anyone like some apple pie?" Alice said. "Or, shall we catch every bad person in the world first?"

~   ~   ~

"Still trying to change the world, Alice?" Matthew retrieved the sign leaning behind the door. The men had

48

retired to the living room for brandy and cigars while Alice cleaned the table.

"Yeah, you shoulda seen them." Cotton scowled as he poured the brandy. "She had Mabel Johnson and Freda Walker and that bunch of hens she quilts with all carrying signs up and down main street like a bunch of clowns." He set the bottle down on the coffee table with a thud. "They even decided to go over to El Dorado and cause them folks trouble too. Dad-blamed women, anyway." He winked at Alice before handing one of the glasses to Dave.

"We're just hoping that women will eventually get some of the same rights that you men have." She smiled as she stacked the dirty plates.

Matthew held the sign up in the lamplight. *Let Women Have Right To Vote, Too* was plastered across both front and back in bright red letters. "Huh, you wanna re-word that? Not all men have that right. They'd really pitch a fit if I showed up on election day wanting to cast my ballot."

"Yes, but they need to change that too." She leaned across the table and gave him a nod. "If we women could vote, I bet we'd change it so you could too."

"Sure, you're right. And I'd give you my vote right now, but I don't have one." He returned the sign to the corner with a laugh.

"Yeah, well, there's probably a lot of things that need to be changed. Here you go, Matt," Cotton said, handing him a glass of brandy.

"Like this?" Matthew lifted the glass in a salute.

"Yes, like that," Alice said. "And you should know better, Harvey Blankenship. You represent the law, and here you are breaking it on two counts. State-wide prohibition on alcohol was voted in two years ago. Besides that, Matthew is an Indian."

"Aw, it was a stupid law anyway. Besides, as far as giving Matt a glass of brandy, I ain't giving it to his father's side. I'm giving it to the part that takes after his mother, and she was white."

"Oh, you men." Alice grabbed the stack of dirty plates

and disappeared into the kitchen.

"Speaking of things that need to be changed, I'd like you to have a try at catching this killer we were chasing when I got shot. It's been a couple of weeks now, and with me laid up, Dave hasn't had much time to go hunting. Every two-bit gunslinger in the area has been out there looking for him and ain't done nothing but cover up the man's tracks." Cotton waited for an answer, but none came.

"There's a thousand-dollar reward on him. And, Dave," he turned toward his deputy, "I want you to show Matthew where we lost his trail. We just might get lucky and find this guy."

"Not interested," Matthew said.

"What do you mean, you're not interested?" Cotton set his glass on the table and leaned forward.

"I'm tired." Matthew put his own brandy glass on the coffee table and sat on the edge of the sofa, rubbing his palms together. "When I caught the man locked in your cell, he was hiding in my old place, where Prairie Flower and Pita are buried. Sitting on that hill, and staring down at their graves...." He glanced up and gave Cotton a half-smile.

"It took something out of me. I've changed. Here." He patted his chest. "I hadn't been there in ten years and it still bothered me."

"I can understand that. It would've gotten to me too," Cotton said. "But this isn't the same man we chased ten years ago. He did almost the same thing to those young people, but he's a different man altogether. I'd like you to catch him. You're the best tracker I know, and it's going to take some doing to get the job done."

"Like I said, I'm tired, Cotton." Matthew leaned back and closed his eyes.

"Look," he went to an old desk to open a drawer and tossed a stack of newspapers on the table in front of Matthew. The headlines on the one facing up read *Local Sheriff Incapable Of Catching Larkin Murderer.*

"There's a whole stack of them if you want something to read," Cotton continued. "Jonathan Williams, a new reporter they hired over at *The Vindicator*," he tapped the paper with his index finger, "he hails from Saint Louis, and he writes a story at least once a week asking for my dismissal. Says I was okay as long as things were nice and peaceful around here, but now that we got ourselves a killer, he doesn't think I'm tough enough."

"He doesn't know you very well, does he?" Matthew laughed. "You were plenty tough enough in the Army."

"Yeah? Well, I need your help. Here, take a look at some of these." He shoved the stack closer.

"No need to. I read some of his work when I was in Wichita last spring, and I doubt anything I could say or do would stop him. He's written a bunch of ten-cent novels about the Indian wars that tell anything but the truth. Besides, I'm not too popular around here." He grew silent as he studied the pattern woven into the oval throw-rug under the table.

"Well, okay then. What about the boy and girl this madman killed?"

"There will always be someone killing somebody somewhere. You should know that as well as I do."

"What are you going to do, then?"

"I've saved up enough money to buy a little place somewhere and retire. That's all I want to do. I would recommend you quit too, Cotton. We're getting too old for this. You've got your little farm. Quit this and grow some corn, or hay. That's the first hole a white man ever put in you, and he did it from the front. I'd say that's a message."

Chapter 12

It took a week for the Wells Fargo draft to reach the bank at Leon. Matthew was glad to finally have the money in hand, thinking of nothing more than leaving town and finding a quiet place to sit and contemplate his future. He had been treated poorly in Leon, where years before he had been welcomed. But that was before he had become the Manhunter. Now, he was shunned by women and children, and men seldom spoke to him unless it was necessary. The only other person outside of Cotton and Alice who had sought his company was the new reporter, Jonathan Williams. He wanted to do a series of stories on the Indian who legally hunted white men. But Matthew had turned him down, and the following day the paper ran a searing article, calling him cold and blood-thirsty. Accompanying the story was a cartoon of a hard-looking Indian chief, holding a lance and leading a white man tied with a rope through the streets of Leon. The article also called for Cotton's dismissal, because Manhunter and the sheriff were close friends.

Cotton used the incident in another attempt to induce him to take up the hunt, and he again refused. "The fact is," said Matthew, "white men don't need guns or Comanche lances to wound someone. They can do that easily with pencils and paper.

Matthew was leaving the bank when he was accosted by a large man on the sidewalk.

"Are you Manhunter?" he demanded in a booming voice that caused people to stare.

"Manhunter was the name given to me by the Comanche. Most white people call me Matthew Blue." Matthew took the man in from head to foot in one glance. He did not seem unfriendly, just abrupt.

"I'm Jim Larkin." He shoved a large, rough hand toward Matthew. His grip was just as hard and calloused as his manner. "They tell me you're the best tracker around. Is that true?"

"I've been told that by some."

"Let me get to the point," Jim Larkin said. By this time a crowd had congregated, making it almost impossible for Matthew to leave the vicinity. "I lost my daughter about two weeks ago, and God only knows why, but no one has been able to find her killer."

"I know. Cotton told me about it. I'm sorry. I heard there were two young people killed."

"I don't want your sympathy, Mr. Blue. I'm sorry about Carl Jenkins, but I'm more concerned about my daughter's killer. I want you to catch him. I've put a thousand-dollar reward on Slim, and I want you to bring him back. He's not real smart, and I don't really care if he's alive, just so we get him. He also took one of my horses. A large roan. Best damned racehorse in Kansas. I'd like it back, too. I'll give you a thousand for her killer, and another five-hundred for that horse."

"He must have some intelligence, if he worked for you."

"Yes, well he was good with animals, I'll admit that. But he goes into these fits every once in awhile. Rolls around on the ground, shaking and foaming at the mouth like he's got rabies. Scares the hell out of everybody. Karen, that's my girl, told me to get rid of him. Said he was dangerous. I didn't believe her. I didn't think he was that crazy." The large man's voice trailed off and he swallowed hard.

"Sounds more like he's got some sort of sickness to me,"

Matthew shrugged. "I met a man in the Army once that acted that way. They had to discharge him. The Army surgeon told me a little about it. He called it a disease and said that it doesn't actually make people crazy, like everyone thinks. He had a name for it, but I can't remember what he said it was. Now, your man might be insane, but again, he might not be. In fact, some believe that people with that type of condition should be revered. They say when they go into their fits they are touched by the gods and given special powers."

"Touched by the devil, if you ask me," Larkin almost shouted. "He murdered my little girl, and I want him caught."

"How do we know he actually did it? Did anyone see him do it? He might have found them murdered the same as anyone else, and ran because he was afraid he'd get blamed."

"Damn it, man. What are you trying to do, take up for this killer?"

"No, you asked me to find him, and I'm simply asking questions." Matthew cocked an eyebrow. "You said he was a simpleton, yet according to the sheriff, he took time to pack a bag with food and took a Winchester with a box of shells. Now, I find he's also taken the fastest horse in the state. On top of all that, absolutely no one has been able to find him. Sounds pretty smart to me."

"I didn't ask for no sermon, or to be belittled in front of the townspeople by a half-breed Indian, no matter how good a tracker you are. Now, I've offered you fifteen hundred dollars for that man's capture and the return of my horse. Are you going to do it?"

"I'll think about it."

"Think about it?" The muscles in Larkin's jaw flexed as his face reddened. "What do you mean, think about it? You want more money, is that it?"

"No, I retired from this type of work a week ago, when I brought my last prisoner in." Matthew kept his gaze locked onto Larkin's eyes. "I don't want to chase men anymore....no matter what they've done. I'm going to buy me a little patch of ground somewhere, and raise horses."

"I'm asking this as a favor. I've never begged a man

before, but I'll do it now, if you want." Larkin's voice quivered. "They can't find him, but I think you can. You find him, and I'll give you enough horses to retire and run that place of yours in style."

Chapter 13

Guiding a bounty hunter was not Dave's idea of a pleasant way to spend a couple of days in the countryside, but Cotton had insisted, and he was Dave's boss. Talking and being friendly was not part of the agreement, so he had decided to talk to Manhunter only when it was necessary. As it turned out, that was exactly what the Indian wanted. They rode for hours without speaking. Finally, it was Dave himself who broke the silence late that afternoon as he brought his horse to a halt under an oak tree.

"Here's where we lost his trail," he said, dismounting. Although two weeks had passed and the road had been heavily traveled, Dave could still make out the tiny hoofmarks left by the sheep. He watched as the Indian studied the earth beneath the tree.

"He stopped here to rest, then rode down that trail ahead of the sheep," Dave pointed.

"Larkin called him a simpleton. For a simpleton, he sure knows how to hide a trail," Matthew said.

Dave led the way on toward the place where the posse had made camp after Cotton was shot. The sun was sinking behind the hills and the temperature had begun to drop, so Dave busied himself with building a fire while Matthew unsaddled the horses.

"You don't like me much either, do you?" Dave glanced toward the Indian.

"Like you? What's that got to do with anything?"

"Well, you're not talking to me, just like I'm not talking to you."

"Now, just when I thought I'd finally found someone who was pleasant to ride with." He grinned and tossed Dave's saddle and bedroll into a heap. "White people talk too much in the first place. They need to learn to keep their mouths shut and to listen."

"All right then," Dave snapped. "We won't talk. I'll take care of the pack-horse, and you can cook."

Matthew laughed as Dave jerked at the leather thongs and gave the pack a shove. The horse snorted and danced away as the pack dropped to the ground. He then tossed the bedrolls on the soft grass near the campfire and stomped off to gather more wood. When he returned with an arm-load of sticks Matthew was on his knees on a tarpaulin, kneading biscuits.

"Coffee's almost ready," he said as Dave dropped the wood.

They ate a meal of bacon, hot biscuits, potatoes, and canned beans. Dave, although still angry and silent through most of the meal, had to admit to himself that Matthew was either a good camp cook, or he was hungrier than he'd thought. He attempted to compliment the Indian and received a simple grunt for the effort, so both men finished in silence.

"Cotton tells me you had a wife and child once. What happened to them?" Dave glanced up from scrubbing his plate over the wash pan.

"Came home one day and found them dead. Some drifter had killed them both." His eyes got distant and he stared into the fire. "She was true Comanche. She had shiney black hair and her skin was soft like velvet. My boy was large and strong for his age. Now, they're gone."

"What happened to the man who killed them?"

"The law they had at the time couldn't seem to find him. I don't think the sheriff really cared that much. They were just Indians to him. So Cotton and I took some time off from the

Army and found him ourselves."

"Then what happened?"

"I killed him."

The Indian grew sullen as he stared into the fire, so Dave decided to leave the matter alone and went to bed. He was still sitting motionless, watching the flames, as Dave covered himself with his blankets and closed his eyes.

Dave decided the man might not be all that bad. He might actually get to a point where he liked him. Cotton had always spoken highly of him, and Dave loved Cotton like a father. But when sleep finally overtook him, he dreamed of red men and white men fighting. The scenes were vivid with booming guns, pounding horse hooves and screams of people in pain. He woke with a start in the cold pre-dawn air, as an Indian with hideous war paint was about to kill him. The Indian was Matthew Blue.

A deep voice made him jump.

"Have a bad dream?" He turned to see Matthew sitting with his blanket pulled around his shoulders. "You were talking something fierce. I reckoned the Devil himself just about had you by the way you yelled when you woke up."

"Not the Devil," Dave said. "You."

"Me?" Matthew glanced up from lighting a cigarette.

"Yeah, you." Dave told him about the dream, and by the time he finished Matthew had fallen back against his saddle laughing.

"I didn't think it was so damn funny," he said as he stoked the fire into a blaze. "You looked pretty mean with all that war paint on."

"Well, if it'll make you feel any better, I haven't worn war paint in years," Matthew said, still chuckling.

"You mean you used to wear it?"

"Hell, yeah. All Comanche boys do when they earn the right. It's good medicine, and protects you in battle or during a hunt. You have certain feats of endurance, fitness, and bravery to complete before you are considered a man. There are also many things you must learn. You have to sit and listen to the Elders and Tribal Council to collect wisdom, and learn the history of the tribe. Every young brave must spend time alone in meditation, talking to the spirits to find his own magic. Kind of like going to school. It's all part of becoming a man. Becoming a brave is like your diploma when you graduate from school."

"Why did you wear it? I mean the war paint. Were you in any wars?"

"What you're really asking is, did I kill and scalp any white men?" His stare made Dave uneasy.

"Yes, I suppose I am."

"In the first place, you wear your paint for other reasons than making war. You wear it when you hunt buffalo and other game. But yeah, I was in one or two battles as a young brave. That is if you want to call them that. The Indian wars," he tilted his head and grinned, "as they are now known, and disease had just about destroyed my people by the time I got old enough to fight." He stood up and grabbed the coffee pot. He swirled the pot several times before tossing yesterday's leavings into the brush.

"The Penatekas used to be the largest band of Comanche, but they lost over half of their population from cholera, brought to them by the prospectors heading for California." He stared inside the pot for a second or two before filling it with water from a canteen and dropping in a handful of grounds. "You wanna heat up that oven while I make some biscuits?"

"Sure." Dave set the dutch oven on the rocks at the edge of the fire before wiping the inside of the frying pan with a rag. "Go on. You were telling me about what happened to your folks."

"Well, the people of the little group I was with consisted of about thirty women and children," he glanced up at the sky thoughtfully, "eight men, too old to fight, and fifteen young men armed with three rifles, a few lances and bows and arrows. We were moving our camp to the hills, hoping to find safety and some game. Everyone was starving." He paused in the middle of kneading biscuits and gazed into the distance.

"How long since you've seen a buffalo in Kansas?"

"I don't think there are any," Dave said.

"You're right, there aren't. Cotton tells me there used to be over thirty million buffalo roaming the plains. Last time I was down in Texas, Quanah Parker told me he thinks there are less than a million left anywhere.

"Anyway, as I was saying, we were attacked by soldiers and militia for being what they called *renegades who were off the reservation.* We returned the fire and ran like hell."

"What do you mean you returned the fire? Didn't you talk to them first?"

"It's kinda hard to talk to a man when he's trying to put a bullet in your gut." He gave Dave a crooked grin. "Here put these biscuits in the oven before we wind up eating them raw."

"Ow, dang it!" Dave let the lid drop with a clang and shoved his fingers in his mouth.

"Gets kinda hot, doesn't it?" Matthew laughed. "Here." He tossed him a rag. "And, to answer your question, they didn't want to talk. They rode down on us firing their guns. Three women, five children, two old men and five braves were lost in a matter of about fifteen minutes."

"Then how did you know they considered you renegades?"

"That came later, after they caught us," he said wiping out the coffee cups and handing one to Dave. "Like I said we ran like hell, and finally made it to some small hills, where we were able to hold them off for the moment. I had one of the rifles. I suppose I killed some white people that day; I didn't keep count. We were trying to stay alive. They attacked us again a couple of days later. This time they had reinforcements. I guess there were about fifty soldiers in all. And I tell you what, we didn't hold them off very long. That whole battle lasted about two minutes at the most. Nearly everyone died, including my mother, brother and sister." Matthew paused and swallowed hard.

"I'd find that story hard to believe, except I remember hearing some men talking when I was about ten years old," Dave said, dropping several slices of bacon into the frying pan. "They were laughing about having killed a whole village of Osage. They were part of some sort of militia. They thought it was kind of funny the way everyone ran when they were being shot at."

"I guess we would have looked funny to them. And to answer your earlier question, we didn't have time to put war paint on, or do ceremony. But I've always believed the real war paint is worn on the inside anyway," he said with a grin.

"What about your father?"

"He died several years earlier. Want some beans? We got some left over from last night." Matthew stared into the pan that had been left sitting all night.

"Yeah, why not? Stick them over there on that side of the fire and let 'em heat up. You were telling me about your father."

"Well, I'd like to say he died as a true warrior. You know, war bonnet, paint, weapons stuck in his hands, but he didn't. He went on a hunt with several braves, and none of them returned. We found them all dead. My father had been shot in the back. Never knew who did that."

"And what happened to the people you were with? How'd you get into...."

"The Army?"

Dave nodded.

"Boy, you're just full of questions. Better check on the biscuits, or we might be eating rocks.

"The Army came later." Matthew paused as he stirred the beans. "The ones that lived were forced onto the reservation to live like peaceable Indians. I was wounded and spent a couple of weeks under the care of a military doctor. We became friends. Dr. Wayne Tisdell. He found out that I could speak English as well as read and write, and when Captain Blankenship, Cotton as you know him, needed a guide and scout, he introduced us. That's how I got into the Army. I never really was a soldier, as Cotton would have you believe. They didn't let us become soldiers. We were paid as civilians working for the government. Most everyone liked me enough, so that no one complained when Cotton gave me a uniform and even had me working as his aide for a while. We spent the next five years freeing land that used to belong to the Comanche, Cheyenne, Osage, and Pawnee from hostile forces, and making this place safe for law-abiding citizens, like yourself."

Dave glanced up to catch a bitter scowl that quickly faded. "But that was fighting against your own people. How could you do that?"

"You do what you have to do in order to survive. Here," he passed Dave a plate with a scoop of beans. "In the Army, I was fed and had warm clothes in the winter. And I didn't have to worry about being swarmed on in the middle of the night by people with guns and knives who didn't like the color of my skin."

Matthew took a long sip of coffee, then setting the cup aside, broke open a biscuit and stuck several pieces of bacon on the inside. "Yes, I killed a few of my brothers while wearing a uniform," he said over a mouthful. "Men who, like me, had left the reservation because they didn't like being told they had to live on a certain block of land and couldn't leave it. We were foolish enough to believe that when the white government promised something, they would keep their word. They had promised that some thirteen million acres of Kansas land would belong to the Indian 'forever.' They changed their minds in 1853 and said we had to move south to the Oklahoma Territory. Not everybody liked the idea.

"The Indians we fought against were already there, starving to death. They were like us, and didn't like seeing their families freeze in winters that were too cold. They didn't like seeing their children taken to white men's schools and taught that their fathers and mothers were foolish, and they must act like white men. Yes, I killed a few of them."

He finished his breakfast in silence. Dave had suddenly lost his appetite and had to force his down. They made a quick job of cleaning the campsite and packing the equipment. Dave was saddling the horses while Matthew circled the campsite on foot, studying the ground. He suddenly stopped and removed his hat.

"Better come and look at this." he sat on his heels and motioned.

Dave knelt beside him to study the ground. There were footprints leading to and from the site.

"About two weeks old," Matthew said. "About the time you and your posse were here, wasn't it?" Dave nodded as he rose to his feet. "Whoever it was, lay right over there," he pointed to a spot behind a rotting log, "and listened to the goings on. Get the horses and let's see if we can't find out who your company was."

They followed the tracks up the hill to a spot where someone had made camp around the same time as the posse. Then, mounting his horse, Matthew started following the tracks backward, the way the mysterious rider had come.

"He went off this way, down toward the road," Dave said.

"I know that. But wouldn't it be more interesting to find out where he came from, and maybe who he is? We can always follow the trail the other way. Besides, if he stayed on the road after you left, his tracks would be gone by now."

They followed the trail for about three miles to a small creek running with amber-colored water. Finding no tracks on the opposite bank, Matthew dismounted and began wading downstream toward the road about three quarters of a mile away. He had only gone twenty or thirty yards before he stopped and pushed his hat to the back of his head. "Hello." Dave jumped from his own horse and splashed through the icy water to join him.

"There you are." Matthew pointed toward some stones where the moss had been scraped clean by iron-shod hooves. "It looks like he left the road and rode upstream to here." He waded further up the stream to find more marks left by the horse. "Let's quit getting wet and mount up. We'll follow him the other way. Now, we've got an idea it's your man you've been chasing, so, let's go find out where he's headed."

"You don't really think he's our killer do you?" Dave asked.

"And why not?"

"Why would he take the time to backtrack and spy on the

very men who are trying to catch and hang him? That sounds stupid to me."

"No, it would be stupid not to." Matthew started his horse into a trot back the way they had come. "One of the first things you need to learn in order to stay alive in this business, is to find out what your enemy is doing. Now evidently, that's exactly what Slim has done. And, come to think of it, he's still alive at the moment. Isn't he?

"A good scout will always be looking behind him, and to each side, as well as to the front. It kept my grandfather alive, and it's kept me alive for twenty-nine years."

They followed the trail back to the campsite and down to the road, where Matthew stopped his horse to stare at the road.

"Hell, no telling which, if any, of those tracks are his," Dave said. "I count at least four wagons, not counting the horses. Most of them were more than likely looking for the same guy. A thousand dollars is a lot of money to folks around here."

"It's a lot of money to everyone. Better watch your back." Matthew frowned. "You might get shot by accident."

"Or on purpose." Dave glanced over his shoulder as they started their horses forward. "Frank Barnes said he was gonna kill me for shooting one of his boys named Smitty. He said Smitty was kin to him, although I doubt it. I don't think that lizard has any relatives."

"He has, and Smitty was a distant cousin of some sort. But if it's any consolation, you're in good company. He swore he'd kill me too. But that was a long time ago, and it hasn't happened yet," Matthew said. "Although I wouldn't put it past him to at least try."

"You know him, then?"

"Yeah, I helped put both him and Smitty in prison about five years ago, for selling guns and whisky to Indians."

They spent the remainder of the day trying to locate the trail. Dave watched as Matthew wandered back and forth across the roadway, dismounting repeatedly to study the soft earth, then remounting to ride further down the road. He seemed tireless, and spotted things that Dave had overlooked, even though he himself was considered one of the better trackers in the area. Everything seemed to attract his attention.

"It will speak to you," he said when Dave asked about his procedure. "The dirt, sand, broken tree branches, bent grass. The earth doesn't like evil men and will tell others where they hide. If you listen, it will tell you how many men rode this way, and how long ago. That's why I said white men talk too much and don't listen. Many white men rode into traps, simply because their voices could be heard from a half a mile away. Sound carries on the prairie, and if the Comanche could hear them, there isn't any reason the man we're chasing can't hear us. Learn to ride quietly and listen to the earth."

Dave grew silent as he tried to emulate the Indian's actions. The man they were chasing seemed to keep the same pattern of following the roadway. Only now, he had switched to riding some twenty or thirty yards to either side of the road, allowing the grass to cover his trail. By mid-afternoon, Matthew dismounted and pointed to a set of tracks near the road.

"One of his horse's shoes has been damaged. See how he limps? Left rear."

Dave leaned close to take a better look. There was a distinct mark down the center of the shoe print. "Yeah, it'll be easy to tell him from the others, now. Must've caught a sharp rock or something." He shaded his eyes and gazed ahead. "How far do you think he'll get with him hurt like that?"

"Hard to tell. Besides, there's no rule that says he can't swap horses." Matthew grinned. "We'll follow this one for now. Come on." He swung back into the saddle. "We've got a couple of hours of daylight left."

The sun had sunk behind the distant hills when Matthew dismounted under some trees and removed the saddle from his tired horse. Dave could hardly move as he followed suit.

"He's left the roadway here and headed out toward the grass land." Matthew nodded toward the endless sea of grass waving in the breeze. "It'll be hard enough to trail him in full daylight. Might as well stop here for the evening."

"I don't know who's more tired, me or the horse." Dave

dropped his saddle and arched his back. "I don't care if Slim rides all night."

Matthew laughed and tossed Dave a canteen. "Here, take a break. I'll get the firewood."

Dave could see why Cotton liked Matthew. He was as tireless as the old sheriff himself. That evening, after a meal much like the two previous ones, Dave slept soundly with no dreams of Indians, shootings, or scalpings.

Chapter 14

Matthew sat silently tossing sticks into the fire. According to the stars, the night was half-spent. He picked up another stick and stared into the flames. The old habit of watching sparks float to the heavens had returned. Sitting on the hillside above the graves of his wife and son had started the cycle all over again. Toss a stick into the fire and watch the sparks fly. Stick after stick as the sleepless hours drug by. The nightmares had also returned. He thought they were dead, like Prairie Flower and Pita. But after ten years and the thousands of miles he had traveled, they still came to haunt him. *Why can't my spirit float away like the sparks, and leave the pain behind?*

As the fire died down to smoldering embers, another vision came to the Indian. He no longer saw the sparks the wind whisked away, or smelled the pungent smoke. The odor of human blood filled his nostrils, and what he saw were the mutilated bodies of his wife and son lying on the floor of his cabin. He felt the deep, stabbing pain in his heart as he buried them again for the millionth time. His mind retraced their steps as he and Cotton followed the killer into the cave where he was hiding. Matthew again felt the cold, bitter satisfaction of seeing the killer beg for mercy as he closed in on him with his own knife drawn. He felt the killer's damp hair in his fingers as he jerked his head backward. Matthew jumped as he heard Cotton's voice inside his head, telling him to stop as he pulled the knife across the killer's throat.

Chapter 15

"Why do you insist on carryin' that cannon around?"

Matthew glanced up from cleaning his Sharps side-hammer rifle. "Didn't know you were awake."

Dave crawled out of his bedroll and threw another stick on the fire. "Ain't it kind of heavy? They make lighter guns, you know."

"Yeah, but it'll shoot twice as far and carries a heavier load than your Winchester." He held up a paper-patched cartridge. ".50 caliber, backed by 140 grains of powder. The ball itself weighs 700 grains. When I hit something, I want it to fall, even if it isn't dead."

"But it's only a single-shot. I can crank off seven rounds before I have to reload."

"Maybe you can. But you'd have to get close enough to hit your target. And if your target happened to have a saddle-gun and wanted to shoot back, you would be within his range also. Then, it's a matter of who's the best shot, or who happens to get lucky." Matthew injected the cartridge in the chamber and laid the gun aside.

"Remember hearing about Adobe Walls, in South Texas, back in '74?"

"Some," Dave nodded.

"Quanah had 700 warriors and fought for three days.

Know how many white men were inside those three buildings? Twenty-eight men and one woman. You would have thought there was no way the people inside Adobe Walls could have survived, but they did. Know why?"

"They were better shots and had thick walls to hide behind?" Dave shrugged as he poured two cups of coffee.

"I'm sure the walls helped, but James Hanrahan, Bat Masterson, and the rest of those hunters all had these." He caressed the stock with affection. "My people couldn't get close enough to use their bows and lances, and the few guns they did have were held out of range. In three days of fighting, the men inside Adobe Walls only lost three people, while we lost a couple dozen."

"Were you there?"

"No, I was already being domesticated by that time." He smiled and sipped his coffee. "Ever wonder where the term *sharps-shooter* came from? It's because this gun is so accurate. One of the buffalo hunters hit a warrior from 1,500 yards. That's nearly a mile. Now, when I heard about it, I decided I was going to get me a gun like that. I'd advise you to do the same."

"Still don't think I'd wanna lug that heavy thing around. There ain't no buffalo around here, and I don't aim to go shooting any elephants either, cause, there's not any of them either."

"Just thought you'd like to stay alive, that's all." Matthew tossed the remnants of his cup into the fire. "Think of it this way. If we were enemies, you could shoot a whole case of shells at me and I wouldn't care, because I'd never let you get within range. But on the other hand, if I can make you run for cover from a mile away, who has the edge?"

"Maybe, but it's still only a single shot."

"True. But one that will kill you a mile away." He hoisted his saddle onto his horse and came back for his bedroll. "I don't ever want to be caught hiding behind a rock again, while someone is shooting at me and all I have is a bow to fight back with. I don't care if you do have your Winchester. If you ever get caught in a similar position, you'll wish you had my gun."

He paused to study Dave before giving the ties on his bedroll one last tug. "Come on, let's go."

Chapter 16

The evenings grew colder and a frost clung to the roof of the house and barn in the early morning hours. It had been four weeks since Harold Jamison had sat in his wheelchair and watched Hank lead his horse into the yard. Now, he sat brooding as he watched Hank and his wife working together and laughing.

Hank had become an asset around the farm, especially since harvest season was upon them. The farm didn't grow much outside of the vegetables in Vicky's garden, but there were the eight acres of corn that would have taken her a week of hard labor, squeezed between her other chores, to harvest and store. She would have also had to cut enough wild grass and hay to feed the animals during the long, hard winter months. Hank worked at these tasks like a possessed man from early morning until dark, smiling all the while.

Harold recognized his problem, although he hated to admit it. He had thought that, although Hank lacked education and refinement, he might become sort of a companion to him in his long hours of confinement in his chair. Harold seldom had any male company, and those who did visit seemed to ignore him and gravitate toward Vicky. He had hoped that Hank might have been different.

What was worse, it seemed that his wife enjoyed the

company of the stranger. At best, Harold had expected Vicky to simply tolerate the tramp, but they spent hours together. She worked side by side with him. They talked, they laughed. *She seldom laughs around me anymore*, Harold thought as he watched them. But two days earlier his bitterness had actually turned into hate. That was when he witnessed his wife giving Hank a hug after they had finished storing the last of the corn into the crib.

Another thing he hated was watching Hank at play with Caroline. Three days before, he was stunned when Hank fell on the steps of the house and started shaking violently and frothing at the mouth. The incident had frightened Caroline to the point of tears. Vicky said she thought Hank had a sickness she had read about while he was in the hospital. Something called epilepsy. And, while many people who had the disease had been confined in mental institutions, as she understood the article, they weren't really dangerous. Harold wasn't so sure.

"Poor man," his wife had said. "I can see why he doesn't have any friends. No one wants him around."

Harold agreed with that last part of her statement. He certainly didn't want him around. And, like the others, thought he should be locked inside an asylum somewhere. But Hank was still here, and spent most of his idle hours running, crawling, playing dolls, and giving piggy-back rides to his daughter.

"If he's not with my wife, he's with my daughter," Harold mumbled as he watched them. "This ignorant bastard is taking my place, and there's not a damn thing I can do about it."

Chapter 17

"This little one needs a wagon," Hank said as he and Caroline lay on the floor playing with animals made of corncobs and sticks.

"I thought of that," Vicky said, drying the supper dishes. "But we just haven't any money to spare."

"Who needs money? I'll make her one," he said with his toothy grin.

"Out of what?"

"I seen some scrap boards out behind the barn. I'll use those."

"And what are you going to use for wheels?" Harold asked with a snort.

"I can make those too. I've done it before." He seemed oblivious to Harold's sarcasm as he moved one of the corncob figures across the floor toward the little girl. "Here comes the horse. Drrump, drrump, drrump!"

~   ~   ~

Early next morning, Harold watched as Hank carried a stack of scrap lumber inside the barn. He could hear him cutting and pounding with the tools that used to fill his own hands. His hatred for the man grew to drastic proportions that afternoon as he watched Hank pulling Caroline around the yard in her wagon, wooden wheels and all. He burned inside, knowing if it weren't for that cursed Comanche bullet in his spine, he would be the one playing with his daughter instead of the stranger.

"Damn it," he swatted at the corner post. "I wonder if there is anything that man can't do?"

"I doubt it," Vicky said. "And I wish you'd stop using that language around our child."

"*And I wish you'd stop using that language around our daughter,*" he mocked her. "Is there anything *I* can do that won't upset you? Maybe I ought to stop existing so you and Hank can be happy together."

"What is the matter with you, Harold? You're acting like a child."

Harold stared into his wife's deep blue eyes. They were cold as ice. He had never seen them that way before. His mind had suddenly gone blank.

"If you won't discuss it with me, then how am I supposed to know what is bothering you?" She spun on her heel and slammed the door as she went inside.

She's my wife. She should know what's wrong. His eyes bounced back and forth from the closed door to the tramp pulling his laughing daughter in the homemade wagon. *She's my wife.*

The bitterness rolled inside his breast like a brooding storm. *I know what she wants. She wants a husband. One that can do all the things a husband can and should do. Work and support her. Buy her pretty things and take her to parties. She wants a man, not some slithering thing that can't even walk. She needs a man that can hold her in his arms and kiss her. Take her to his bed and make love to her. That's what she wants. She'll never admit it, but I know she wants those things, and needs them. Everything I can't do.*

His eyes finally rested on Hank, who was feigning tripping, and falling over backwards in order to make Caroline laugh. *He can. That ugly scarecrow can do all those things.* The very thought of Hank with his wife repulsed him.

He tried pushing it from his mind, but it persisted, and fluttered around inside his head like a housefly, seeking for a place to light.

"Vicky. God, I love her so," he whispered.

Harold's attention was turned from his daughter's wagon as the dog bolted to the edge of the yard barking. He watched quietly as William Barry walked his horse up to the house and slid his massive frame out of the saddle with a grunt.

"Afternoon, sheriff, what brings you all the way out here?"

"Afternoon, Harold," he said, removing his hat and using it to dust his pant legs as he stepped onto the porch. "Afternoon, Mrs. Jamison," he added with a nod as Vicky came out of the house smiling.

"Just out for a ride, and thought I'd drop by and see how you folks were doin'. Don't get out this way much." The chair creaked as he sat down and wiped his face with his scarf.

"Would you like a glass of fresh buttermilk, sheriff," Vicky asked.

"Yes, that would go good on a hot day like this." He mopped the sweat from his face again as Vicky went to get the buttermilk. Harold smiled, remembering how he'd been thinking it was on the cool side for a mid-October day.

Barry drained the glass, wiping his mouth on the back of his sleeve, and handed it back to Vicky for a refill.

"Thanks," he said, watching as she filled the glass to the brim. "Now, tell me, who was that I saw playing with Caroline as I came riding up?"

Harold glanced at his daughter, who was sitting in her wagon playing with her doll.

"That was Hank. He's the man who's been staying here and helping us around the farm for the past few weeks. Now, where'd he go?"

"He stared at me for a second or two when the dog started barking, then disappeared inside the barn." Barry wiped his mouth with the dusty scarf this time.

"I'll go fetch him." Vicky set the pitcher of buttermilk on the porch beside the sheriff and bounced down the steps.

Harold watched his wife glide gracefully toward the barn with the wind tugging at her skirts and making the ends of her hair dance in the sunlight.

"What'd you really come all the way out here for? I know it wasn't Vicky's buttermilk."

"Oh, I don't know." Barry poured himself another glass as he watched Vicky dragging the reluctant farmhand toward the men on the porch. "It ain't half-bad. You ought to drink more of it yourself. It might help your disposition."

"Huh," Harold grunted, knocking the dead ashes from his pipe. "I hate buttermilk almost as much as dull conversation with patronizing people."

Vicky paused as the lanky man dropped his hat and stooped to retrieve it.

"Sheriff, this is Henry Jones. He's been living here and helping us around the farm." Vicky smiled as though she were presenting someone of notoriety.

"How-do." Barry nodded toward the man, who began rocking back and forth from one foot to the other, clutching his tattered hat tightly at his waist with both hands. "Where do you hail from, son?"

"Missouri."

"Missouri? What brings you way down here?"

"Don't know. J-just happened by here. That's all." Henry's eyes rolled from the sheriff to the porch floor, then toward the wagon in the yard with Caroline.

"What's got you scared? Is the law chasing you?"

"Got in some trouble back there. Man said I'd been seein' his daughter, when I ain't never seen her a'tall. Wanted to take a whip to me. So's, when he tried, I taken it away and whupped him real good."

"Did you kill him?" Vicky's voice sounded sort of high and squeaky to Harold.

"Gosh no, Mrs. Jamison. He wus cussin' and shootin' as I lit out on old Roan." Hank waved an arm toward the horse standing in the corral.

"Mighty fine hoss you got there." Barry rubbed the stubble on his chin.

"Yes, sir."

"You vouch for him, Mrs. Jamison?"

"Yes, sheriff. What's this all about, anyway?"

"Nothing to worry you about." He rose from the chair and arched his back. "Got word that some ranch hand killed a couple of young people over near Leon. One of them happened to be ol' Jim Larkin's daughter. He's offered a big reward for her killer, and everyone seems to think he headed our way. I think he's holed up somewhere in Arkansas myself. Town's crawlin' with gunslingers lookin' to make a fast buck. Just thought I'd ride out and see if you folks had been bothered with them tin-horns over-running your place."

"What's the killer look like?" Harold asked.

"Don't rightly know. I got about six different descriptions from the rabble that's huntin' him. And I can't wire Leon since ol' George died." Barry mounted his horse with a grunt. "Dang contraption in his office just sits there rattling away, and nobody seems to know what it's saying. Western Union's supposedly sending someone next week, but that don't help us none right now. Just as soon as I find out, I'll let you know."

"Thanks for the buttermilk, Mrs. Jamison." He turned the mare with a tip of his hat and walked her slowly out of the yard.

"That's scary," Vicky said, picking up the empty glass and pitcher.

Harold watched silently as Sheriff Barry disappeared over the small rise that separated theirs from the other farms. He struck a match against the porch railing and lit his pipe as Hank returned to pulling Caroline in the wagon. He drew deeply, exhaling a cloud that hung in the air and gave him a ghostly view of his daughter. He drew again as the cloud lifted and exhaled another cloud. He didn't answer when his wife asked him if he wanted anything. He didn't hear her. He was lost in his thoughts.

Chapter 18

That evening, after Caroline had been put to bed, Vicky sat down to read her Bible.

"You understand that book?" Hank said, watching her.

"Yes, I believe I do." She smiled warmly. "Have you ever read it?"

"I tried, some. A long time ago. But it don't make no sense to me."

"If you ever want to know anything about the Bible, or God, or life in general, just ask Vicky." Harold laughed. "She knows everything there is to know on those subjects."

Vicky stared at her husband through watery eyes.

"Oh, but I do. I wish I could understand it all." Hank seemed oblivious to Harold's cutting remarks.

Vicky asked him to sit beside her at the table while she turned to her favorite passage in the Book of Saint John. For the next half hour she shared with Hank her faith and love for God. When they were finally done, Hank thanked her and excused himself and went outside.

"What are you trying to do? Convert him?" Harold laughed bitterly. "Don't waste your time. He's nothing but a moron. I doubt if he can understand a word you're saying, and even if he can, he isn't interested in your religion. All he's interested in is your looks."

Damn, I can't believe I said that. He fought an impulse to grab his wife's hand as a crushed look swept over her face.

"Well, it's true!" He raised his voice as her eyes watered, and a single tear mapped its way down her cheek. "I can't do the things a husband's supposed to do with his wife anymore. Are you thinking the same thing about him?"

"Oh, God. Why are you acting like this? What have I done to make you this angry? I'm your wife, Harold. How could you even think such....such things? I've only been nice and loving to him, because I know that's how God wants me to treat everybody. And yes, I do hope he finds God. I wish you...." she turned away to choke back a sob, "you wouldn't make fun of what I believe. He needs love and God the same as you. You used to go to church with me, remember? You used to believe the same as I do."

"And that was before God let this happen to me." He laughed and tossed the blanket that covered his legs onto the floor. "Look at me. Go ahead and take a good look. I'm not a man anymore. I'm a thing. You hear that? A useless thing."

Vicky dropped to her knees and tried to hug him. "God help me, I love you, Harold. I've always loved you. And I always will."

He pushed her away. "Quit your crying. It doesn't affect me anymore."

~   ~   ~

Otis leaned against the side of the house in the dark, having his evening smoke, and listening. *Moron* was what Harold had called him. All this time he had thought Harold liked him, but he wasn't any different than the rest. They were all evil. He could hear Vicky crying through the open window. The one person in the world who liked him, and he was treating her that way. Maybe she loved him. She treated him nicely, anyway.

He walked quietly to the corral, crushing his cigarette on the way. "Come here, boy," he called softly to the horse. "Yeah, I love you too." He nuzzled the horse's neck as it gently pushed against him with its nose.

"I want to know something, Roan," he said, rubbing the glossy mane. "Why would anyone treat a pretty girl like that so mean? It don't make no sense. She's got to be the prettiest girl in the whole world. And nice too. No, it don't make no sense a'tall. I know one thing though. He'd better not make her cry again. No, we won't stand by and let that happen, will we?" He gave the horse another hug.

Chapter 19

A cold wind was blowing as ominous clouds hung on the horizon. Otis threw another log inside the stove and closed the door with a clank. It had been two days since the argument between Vicky and Harold. Caroline was singing softly to her rag doll on the floor while her dog, Cuddles, crept closer to the fire. Otis sat cross-legged on the floor beside the little girl, looking content as he stroked her golden head. Vicky smiled at them as she hung the dish towel on a peg and went to the window.

"Looks like a storm might be on the way," she said. "I'm glad we got all the corn and hay in."

Otis voiced his agreement, but Harold sat quietly sulking. "It's cold in here." He rubbed his arms.

"Why didn't you say something?" Vicky disappeared into the bedroom and returned with a blanket. "Here, let me cover you up."

"I can cover myself!" he yelled as His hand connected with Vicky's cheek. *Damn.* He grabbed for her as she retreated against the table holding her cheek. Before either of them could say or do anything, Otis was in front of Harold, holding a gleaming knife against his throat.

"Hank, no!" Vicky screamed as she grabbed his arm. "Hank, stop! Oh, God, please don't."

Otis studied Vicky's face and calmly put the knife back in his boot. Then reaching out, he tenderly touched the red mark on her cheek. After one more threatening glance toward Harold, he quietly left for the barn. Vicky and Harold stared at each other for a long minute in silence. Neither of them saw Hank the rest of the evening.

~   ~   ~

Vicky lay in bed watching the shadows dance across the ceiling. *God, have I actually wronged both my husband and Hank?* She had needed help with the farm. Hank offered his assistance, and she had accepted. She couldn't see any wrong in what she had done; she thought Harold should have been happy for her. Besides, she was teaching Hank about God, and leading him toward Christianity. But something was desperately wrong. Her husband had almost died because of this friendship.

"God, what is happening?" she whispered out loud. "Help me understand." All she heard was Harold's snoring.

The next morning Hank was gone. Vicky searched the barn and the yard, but he had taken his horse and vanished. She pulled her tattered coat tightly around her as cold rain pelted her cheeks, and returned to the house.

Chapter 20

"The rain's washed away nearly all the sign," Matthew said. "We're more or less on our own."

Dave pulled his old pocket watch from his vest pocket and flipped the cover open. If it was working correctly, it was ten o'clock in the morning. The rain that had soaked the riders earlier had ceased, but drops still hung on the tall grass. Dave's pant legs were soaked and clung to his skin as he joined Matthew who was crouched down, studying the ground.

"My guess is he's on foot by now." Matthew stood to gaze across the plains. "He's walking now. He couldn't have gotten much farther with a mount like that. If he loves horses like you and Cotton say, I doubt if he'd shoot it or leave it out here. He's probably holed up somewhere trying to heal the animal. Wonder where the nearest farms lie?"

"Gueda Springs is southwest from here." Dave shaded his eyes and gazed that direction. "According to that boy Frank tried to hang, a couple of farms lie somewhere between us and the town."

Matthew glanced at the cloud-cover rolling in on the horizon as thunder rumbled in the distance. He pulled his buckskin jacket tight as a gust of wind chilled him. "I reckon we'd better head that way. We just might be lucky enough to find him at one of the farms before that storm hits."

"I thought you were doing pretty good following his trail," Dave said as Matthew put his foot in the stirrup.

"Just a Comanche's luck." He swung into the saddle with a grin. "Come on, let's go."

Dave had to push his horse hard in order to keep up with the Indian as he raced through the grassland. Water mingled with froth on the mare, making its coat glisten. Matthew turned in his saddle and grinned as he saw Dave's horse struggling to keep up, then slowed to a lope. By midday they were walking, and the sun had broken through the clouds. Grass and dirt thrown from the horse's hooves had created cakes of mud on Dave's body and face.

"We'll rest the horses here." Matthew stopped at a small stream bed with a trickle of water in the bottom. "How much farther to town?"

"Oh, about ten, maybe twelve miles, is my guess." Dave knelt and wet his scarf in an attempt to wash his face. "We could've made it in a day and a half, if we hadn't been trailing him. We should be running into one of the farms fairly soon, unless we miss them altogether." They ate a lunch of cold biscuits and dried beef as the horses drank and grazed lazily on the rich grass.

"I've got to ask you a question that's been bothering me," Dave said, choking on the dry bread. "Those men, the ones that killed your mother and family, they were white, weren't they?"

"Yeah, why do you ask?"

"Well, I know you told me about being in the Army simply to survive, but whatever happened to them? I mean, if someone did that to my family, I'd probably hate them the rest of my life. That's why I had trouble coming out here with you." Dave stared as Matthew calmly chewed his biscuit. "A Comanche killed my father. But I'd think you would....I don't know....maybe hate me because of those men."

"You mean, why don't I hate all white people, and go around trying to kill them?"

"Yeah, something like that. I was just wondering why

you don't."

Matthew laughed. "I did hate them, at first. In fact, I guess I still hate the memory. That was the main reason for my becoming friendly with the doctor and being Cotton's scout. I thought I might get a chance to catch the captain alone sometime and do to him what he had done to my family. I guess it wasn't meant to be though. My Pawnee brothers beat me to it."

"What happened?"

"He was stupid. He had been given orders to drive a small band of Pawnee from their land. From what I understand, he decided to wait until the men left to go hunt buffalo. Then, as the plan went, he would have his men sweep into the village and kill all the women and children. He thought the men would leave and join the rest of the Pawnee who had already fled to Nebraska."

"The United States Army did this? I mean we're talking about the government here. Aren't we?"

"It happens, and not just here. The strong conquer the weak. Anyway, this captain had done this before, according to Cotton. It had worked in the past, so he was hoping it would again. Only problem was, the Pawnee had seen them, and knew they were coming. So the warriors left like they planned, only they didn't go very far. They waited out of sight behind some trees along the river. They had also left some men hiding in their village. When the Army came in for the kill, they rode into a trap. Braves poured out of teepees and those hiding in the trees came charging on horseback from behind. Those soldiers were trapped and didn't stand a chance. They all died. To answer your question, I sort of felt justice was served. Yes," he set his lips in a thin line and nodded, "I would have liked to kill that Captain personally, but I never got the chance. That was one of the few times I thought that maybe the medicine of the Pawnee was stronger than that of the Comanche."

Dave shoved the last bite into his mouth and took his time chewing.

"You still haven't answered part of the question. Cotton

claims to be real close to you. Cotton's white."

"Now I see," Matthew nodded. "How can I be friendly with a white man, no matter who he is, after what happened to my family?"

"Exactly."

"See, that's the problem with you." He stood and began to ready his horse. "You throw everyone into one category. You hate all Indians because of what one Indian did to your father. It doesn't make any difference that your father might have killed several Indians in his lifetime. But one Indian did kill your father, and that makes all Indians bad."

"No, that's not true," Dave said.

"Yes, it is. Just look at yourself. You didn't like me when you first laid eyes on me. Was it really because I'm a bounty hunter? Or the fact that a half-breed led a white man down the city street bound with a rope? I think the latter one." He gave the cinch a final tug and let the stirrup fall into place.

There was a moment of silence while both men let their horses drink one last time from the creek.

"Did you know that the land my people used to hunt extended all the way from Kansas to the Mexican border? The Comanche at one time were a mighty nation of almost twenty thousand people. We occupied a range of 220,000 square miles. But now, we are a defeated people. Can I blame our defeat on all white people? No. Can I blame the death of my mother, brother and sister on every white person I meet? Cotton's wife, Alice, never hurt anybody in her life. I can't blame her for what happened. I can't even blame white people in general for what has happened to the Comanche." He pulled his horse up the bank and prepared to mount.

"There's a family of Caddo living not too far from where we are right now. The mother has two small boys. Can you blame them for what happened to your father?"

"No, I don't suppose I can," Dave said, mounting his horse.

"Neither do I hate all white people. I only hate those who cause hurt to others. Those I can hate."

A loud peal of thunder caused both men to look up as the

sun disappeared behind dark clouds. In the distance, a rope of lightning flashed that seemed to extend all the way from the heavens to the earth.

Matthew mounted his horse in one bounding leap. "We'd better go, or we'll get caught in the next downpour."

~   ~   ~

Late that afternoon the two tired riders were outside a small village with one main roadway running through the middle and small clapboard buildings on either side. The hogs in the pen at the edge of town were wading in mud up to their bellies. Wind blew the rain in horizontal sheets that swept under their slickers to soak their pants and run inside their boots.

Dave checked the pocket watch again as water poured from the brim of his hat and splashed onto his saddle. "Five-thirty." He snapped the cover closed and returned the watch to his vest pocket. "I guess we did."

"Did what?" Matthew asked, and tossed the waterlogged cigarette he had been trying to light.

"Missed the farms completely." Both riders glanced to their left as a sheet of lightning lit the blackened sky and thunder rolled. "Might as well go down and see if we can find a place to spend the evening."

Chapter 21

Leaving their horses at the livery stable was easy, but convincing the balding proprietor at the small hotel to give them a room took some doing.

"He's an Injun, and we don't let his kind stay here."

"Look, Mr. whatever your name is, he's with me, and we're here on official business," Dave said.

"That don't make no difference. You can stay, but he can't. He'll have to sleep at the livery or somewhere else."

"My hell, Harry," a portly man who was sitting in a corner spoke up. "It's raining dogs and cats out there. Give 'em the cabin out back. I'd rather stay there anyway. It's better'n what you call rooms inside here."

The proprietor grumbled several obscenities, then made Dave sign the register and pay up front before releasing the key. The cabin was small but comfortable with two cots lining opposite walls. After a hot bath at the barbershop, they ate fried steaks at Rattlesnake Jack's. Matthew's presence drew more protests inside the small restaurant, but those complaining quieted as Dave removed his coat.

"Maybe you should have shown your badge to the man at the hotel. It seems to work here," Matthew said as they chose a table near the kitchen.

"Maybe. What I really felt like doing was slapping him

up beside the head."

"No, I tried that once, and it won't get you very far. Of course, we might've gotten free room and board inside the jail. But the badge would probably work best in the long run. Try wearing it on the outside of your jacket where everyone can see it."

While the restaurant wasn't much to look at, the food was hot and satisfying. They washed their meal down with several cups of hot coffee, and made their way toward the sheriff's office.

"Well, glad to see that Harry finally gave you a room."

"Huh, I guess we owe you a big thanks," Dave said, shaking the man's hand. "I didn't recognize you as the sheriff hidden behind that paper."

"No matter, Harry knew who I was. Sit yourselves down. What can I do for you?" William Barry was a portly gentleman in his mid-forties with a congenial manner that belied his status as a lawman.

"We're here looking for a stable-hand, goes by the name of Slim. He killed a young girl and her boyfriend back in Leon. We have cause to think he might have headed your way. He's a tall, skinny guy with pockmarks and buck teeth. Ugly as sin. Think you might have seen him?"

"I heard about the murders, and I'm really sorry it happened. But no, I can't say as I've seen your man, and I haven't really been looking, since I didn't know what he looks like." Sheriff Barry leaned back in his chair and tapped the fingertips of both hands together as he studied the men.

"What do you mean you didn't know what he looks like? I wired you personally." Dave's chair made a rasping sound on the wood floor as he shifted angrily.

"But you didn't get any answer, now did you? Must've gotten at least one or two wires a day since ol' George died, and nobody's had any idea what that dang thing was trying to tell us. We just got our new operator yesterday." He shifted in his own chair. "Someone could have sent me something in the mail. Stage comes here twice a week."

"Damn!" Dave scowled as he glanced at Matthew.

"What's this guy resemble, anyway? I know you said he's ugly, but I've seen a lot of ugly folks in my lifetime. Ol' Harry back at the hotel ain't no real prize himself."

"Mid twenties, about six feet tall with buck teeth. He has long blond hair and pock marks all over his face."

"Huh, that could be most of a dozen folks I've seen the past few weeks. That thousand-dollar reward has brought us a lot of newcomers. There's some of 'em we don't particularly like having. I've got several of them locked up right now." He rose and opened the door separating the cells from the office area to reveal three men sitting in a crowded cell. "They came in here about a week ago looking for the same man. When they didn't find him, instead of hitting the trail back where they came from they started drinking and raising hell. Wound up busting up the saloon along with a couple of citizens. Now, I know we ain't supposed to have a saloon, but we do. They'll sit here until the circuit judge gets to town, then he can handle the situation."

He closed and locked the door and returned to his desk. "Not all bounty hunters are like you, Manhunter."

Matthew glanced up from rolling a cigarette.

"Yes, I know you, or rather know of you. You mind your own business, don't cause no one trouble, except for the men you're chasing. And, most importantly, you bring most of them back alive and let the law deal with them. I can't say that everyone who wears a badge and calls himself a lawman does that. Ever thought of being a lawman yourself?"

"I thought about it, once or twice," Matthew struck a match on the bottom of his chair and lit his smoke, "but not too many places would want a renegade Comanche for their sheriff. And if they did, I'd have to put up with all the politics, same as you."

Barry laughed. "Yes, you're right. Now, how can I help you boys?" He placed his large hands flat on the desk top.

"That boy, Peter Martin, said there were some farms around here," Dave said. "Our killer might be hiding out at one of them."

"That's a possibility, for some of the more remote farms

no one ever visits. But I've been to every one I can think of, and no one's seen your man. I really don't think you'll find him here."

"Maybe not. But I know that at least two farms he described as lying between here and Leon are kind of out of the way from the rest of them. Did you check them out?"

"Yes, the Clemson ranch, and the Jamison place. But, that was a few days ago, right after I got word about the killings, and that you folks were thinking he might be headed our way. The only new person around is the Jamison's handyman, Henry Jones, and Mrs. Jamison vouches for him. Come to think of it though, he did look something like how you described your man." He drummed his fingers against the desk and stared into the distance. "I'll tell you what," he slammed his palm down with a bang, "I'd like to go back out there with you myself, just to make sure. I never thought of it before now, but it does make sense, seeing as you say he took out across the prairie that way. He just might have stayed hidden and landed there after I'd visited them." Barry frowned as he stared at the falling rain that had turned the street into a river. "Not worth trying today. We'll leave first thing in the morning, weather permitting."

"Do you mind if we ask around at some of the closer farms and ranches?" Matthew said.

"No, but you'd be wasting your time. I know that nearly every one of them has been asked about a hundred times by the crowd that's been coming through here. If they haven't been asked, they at least know about him, and no one's come forth and said anything. On the other hand, I don't think anybody's been out to either the Clemson's or Jamison's except me. At least I never heard that they had, and I hear just about everything around here."

The sound of horses tromping down the rain-soaked road caused the sheriff to look out the window again.

"I guess you had to let those boys go without the Martins' complaints, didn't you?" Dave and Matthew both crowded at the window in time to see Frank Barnes, Hawk, Mex, and three newcomers pass by.

92

"Didn't have anything to hold them on," Dave said. "I still think someone got to the parents and threatened them. They wouldn't even look me in the eye, when I tried to argue with them. Neither would the boy, and he's the one they tried to hang."

"You should have made something up, like stealing your horse or something. Then you coulda hung 'em." Barry turned from the window when Dave laughed and shook his head. "Hell, I'm not kidding, boy. Those yahoos are going to cause folks trouble no matter where they go. You can bet your Aunt Betty's false teeth, they frightened the Martins into not signing. There's some people better off dead, and those men are some of 'em." He shook a finger at Dave and sat down.

"Pete said he heard Frank say he was going to kill you. Is that true?" Dave nodded. "Then, watch your back, because he ain't gonna shoot you to your face."

Turning to Matthew, the sheriff raised his voice. "Manhunter, do us all a favor, will you? If you ever have the chance to track Frank Barnes or any of his friends again, kill them. Okay?"

"If I'd known they would have let him out so soon, I might have," Matthew said. "He threatened to kill me too."

Chapter 22

The following morning the three men were on horseback by sun-up. The ride to the Clemson ranch was a pleasant one. The rain had stopped and the sun shone brightly. The cool morning air smelled sweet with the scent of grass and flowers. Birds sang and fluttered in the trees as they passed, and small animals scurried across the trail ahead of the horses.

Matthew gazed at the endless sea of grass waving in the breeze and wondered why man would want to disturb such a beautiful setting by plowing the ground and building towns. As a young boy he had heard of times before the first white man set foot on the Comancheria. The Comanche hunted the buffalo and moved freely from place to place following the game. Their stomachs were full and their bodies warm. The neighboring tribes seldom gave them trouble, except for an occasional raid from both sides. That was what the old men remembered. But all he had known was war, hunger, and death.

Now, men like Frank Barnes roamed the plains. They were more evil than the buffalo hunters who killed the food supply. These men killed for pleasure and took anything of value. They cared nothing for the Indian or the white farmer, struggling to eke out a living for his family. They left a wake of pain and misery wherever they went.

A feeling of melancholy swept over Manhunter as he thought. What if he was no better than Frank Barnes or Slim. He made his living chasing men, and at times had found it necessary to leave a wake of violence behind him. Perhaps what Little Wolf said was true. "The God of the Comanche had lived years ago, but died of old age." His boyhood friend had believed that was why things had changed. *Maybe so*, Matthew thought as his horse plodded onward.

The Clemson ranch was little more than a clapboard shack with a run-down corral, a few chickens, one old horse and a few pigs. The old man and lady who lived there were past their prime and couldn't properly take care of the place. No, they hadn't seen Slim, but Sheriff Barry was a friend of theirs, so he had a hard time getting away.

It was almost noon when they finally crossed the small rise of ground that separated the Jamison place from the rest of the farms. The little white house sat against the yellow prairie and dark green trees. There was a barn no bigger than a large shed, with a small corral and two horses. A buckboard stood to one side, with chickens running around and underneath. A milk cow mooed and stuck its head over the corral fence to stare at them. A small blonde girl ran and played with a dog in the yard, both getting muddier as the men approached.

"Hello, Harold." Sheriff Barry greeted the thin man sitting in a chair on the front porch. "How are you feeling today?"

"Not too bad. How about yourself, Bill? Who're your friends? You take up running around with Injuns?"

Matthew pretended not to hear the crude question.

"Harold, how rude of you." A small woman appeared in the doorway, wiping her hands on an apron. It was hard to miss the long golden hair that fell to her waist when she stepped from the porch to greet them. It seemed to sparkle with each step as she approached and offered him her hand.

"Hello, I'm Vicky Jamison, and this is my husband, Harold."

"Pleased to meet you, ma'am," Matthew said as he

touched the brim of his hat with a nod. She wasn't much more than a child herself, perhaps late teens or early twenties. But the hand she offered was calloused and used to work.

"This ought to be fun," Barry mumbled to Dave. "I forgot that Jamison here hates Indians more'n a bout of the plague."

"Well, it's true, he is Indian." Harold rolled his chair to the edge of the porch. "Aren't you, boy? My wife thinks I'm rude, but I haven't much use for Indians since one put this bullet in my spine."

"Hello, Lieutenant." Matthew removed his hat and stepped forward. He heard the young woman catch her breath. "Someone told me you'd gotten hurt a couple of years ago and I was wondering what happened. Now I know. The way you dropped out of sight made me wonder if you weren't pushing up daisies somewhere."

"Manhunter! Why if it isn't Cotton's half-breed scout." His face seemed to crack as a huge smile appeared. "My God, I never thought I'd see your red hide around here."

"Harold, how could you be so rude?" A hand fluttered to her mouth as her eyes darted between the men. Matthew had never seen eyes quite like hers before, and had to struggle to keep from staring.

"That's all right, ma'am." He cocked his head to grin. "I was half Indian, last time I checked. My father was Comanche and my mother was white."

"Hell, yeah, I'm still alive. At least half of me still is." Harold rolled his chair closer and offered Matthew his hand. "I see you're out of the Army. I was kind of hoping to find out how Captain Blankenship and the rest of the boys are."

"Just talked to Cotton the other day, and he's doing fine." The light in Harold's eyes brightened as Matthew spoke. "In fact, he lives just over in Leon. He's their sheriff, and Dave here's his deputy." Dave stepped forward to shake the Lieutenant's hand.

"Yeah, yeah, I remember hearing about him becoming some sort of lawman or something."

Matthew felt a tugging on his pant-leg and looked down to see the towheaded child who had been playing with the dog.

"Hi. What's your name?"

"I'm Matthew," he said, squatting to greet her eye to eye.

"Mat-ew?"

"Yes, Matthew. And what's your name?"

"Carol."

"That's a pretty name. And you're one pretty little thing yourself, aren't you?"

"My, but she's one dirty little thing," her mother said, stooping to wipe some of the mud from her daughter's face with her apron. "Her name is really Caroline, but we often call her Carol."

Matthew studied the woman as she worked on her daughter, only inches from where he sat on his heels. The breeze blew a rebel strand of hair his way, almost touching him. *She's perfect,* he thought. *From the shape of her nose to the curve of her mouth. Harold Jamison is a lucky man.*

She glanced up from her child, and for an instant their eyes held. Matthew thought they were almost the color of his mother's eyes, only deeper. *Eyes are the window to the soul,* he could remember his mother saying, and found it to be certainly true in this case. There was depth in this woman. She was no little girl, as he had first thought. She was a woman held captive in a young girl's body. He wanted to touch her, to see if she was real, but broke the spell by caressing her daughter's face with his palm instead.

"What we're here for, Harold," Sheriff Barry was saying, "is they're looking for the man who killed those young folks over in Leon I told you about. We're just checking around, seeing if any of you might have seen any strangers lately. They kind of wanted to talk to your man, Hank. Maybe he knows something."

"Goodness." Vicky shook her head. "Hank isn't here right now, and I don't think we know anything about the murders. I don't see how we can help you."

"We thought you might have seen someone come by your place here, ma'am," Dave said. "Someone looking for food. He more than likely had a lame horse. And he'd be in his early twenties, about six feet tall. Has buck teeth, long blond hair, and pock marks on his face. He goes by the name of Slim."

Harold broke into a hearty laugh as Vicky paled.

"That sounds like Hank, but he's been with us several weeks. He did just sort of wander up here, leading a lame horse." Her eyes darted around at the faces staring at her. "But he's been working here ever since, and I don't believe he would ever kill anyone."

"Boy, oh boy. That'd be great, wouldn't it?" Harold paused in his laughing to cough. "If you had been harboring a killer all this time?" He coughed again.

"My wife's always looking for the good in people, Manhunter." He knocked the ashes from his pipe against the porch railing. "She'll help anyone who'll listen to her talk about her religion, because she believes that God loves everybody." He laughed and made a sweeping motion with his arm. "That's just great."

"Could be worse things than that," Matthew mumbled as he hoisted the little girl in his arms.

"You're the one who asked me to help him," Vicky said quietly.

"I only asked you to feed him and give him a little work, not let him live here." Harold snorted as he shook his head.

"If he's anywhere around here, we'd like to talk to him," Barry said, breaking up the argument.

"He left two days ago. I haven't seen him since." Vicky was visibly shaken.

"Only after he tried to kill me," Harold yelled. He then began to expound upon the incident.

Dave turned toward Matthew, who raised his eyebrows and shrugged. "He might be your man."

"Everyone around Leon just called him *Slim*. Come to find out though, his real name is Otis Felts," Dave said.

"But our friend's name is Hank, Henry Jones;" Vicky said. "You don't actually think Hank could be the man you're looking for? Do you?"

"We don't know yet," Barry said. "He might be, and go by several names. Or, Hank could be just a man down on his luck. We would like to talk to him, though."

"Well, as I said, he's gone, and I don't have any idea where he is. But, in the meantime, why don't you gentlemen come inside? I'll put on a fresh pot of coffee."

~ ~ ~

Vicky filled mugs from the pot while Dave and William Barry found places at the table. Matthew allowed his eyes to survey the room as he warmed his hands above the stove. He nodded his approval at the heavy cast-iron pots hanging on the wall and the small bed near the potbellied stove. He smiled as he opened the back door of the cabin and saw the garden.

"I had the workmen install it special, so I could bring the vegetables right into the house instead of having to go use the front door." Vicky handed him a stack of plates as he returned to the stove. "Could you put these on the table for me? Thanks."

"Thoughtful, having that door there." He slid a plate in front of each man, then three extras at the empty spots.

"You'd be surprised how nasty it gets out here when it rains, or when the wind blows."

"Nope, I can imagine." He took the knives and forks she handed him. "I would have put a door there myself."

Matthew sat across from Dave and picked up the cup of coffee that Vicky had placed beside his plate. He glanced at Harold as he sipped the steaming liquid.

After a meal of corn bread and beans, Dave and Sheriff Barry excused themselves, as it was late and they had better be heading back toward town.

"If it's alright with the Lieutenant and Mr. Jamison, I'd like to stick around a day or two and see if I can't figure out where Slim, or whatever his name is, went," Matthew said. "I don't believe he's gone very far."

"What makes you think that, Mr. Blue?" Vicky glanced over her shoulder from piling the dirty dishes into the wash pan on the sink board.

"If what your husband believes is true, he cares about you

and this little girl. He won't wander very far." He touched the tip of Caroline's nose with his finger. "He's probably not more than a mile or two from this farm, right now."

"What are we supposed to do in the mean time?" Dave said.

"You can wait for me at Gueda Springs. I shouldn't be too long." He grinned at Dave's irritated stare. "Look, it isn't that I don't think you could find him yourself. But it'll be easier for one man to sneak up on him than two, stomping around, making noise. And I promise I'll go get you when I find where he's hiding."

"Alright, I guess that'll be okay." Dave scowled. "But I'd better wire Cotton though, and tell him what's going on. Knowing him, he's probably worried sick anyway, seeing as we've been gone for three days." Dave got up to leave, but turned back toward Matthew.

"There's just one more thing I've got to know. You said that your mother was white. Yet, you told me back on the trail, that she got killed by soldiers. Now, which story's true?"

"Both," Matthew shrugged. "She was with Comanches, married to a Comanche, and dressed like a Comanche. She died like a Comanche." He took a deep breath and exhaled slowly as he studied the expression on Dave's face.

"I know what you're thinking. Why didn't she jump up and yell 'I'm white, I'm white,' when the soldiers rode into our camp? It might be hard for you to understand, but it is possible for a white woman to fall in love with an Indian. The Captain who led the attack, thought like you. I happened to see him while I was recuperating from my wounds, and asked him why they'd killed her. He told me that it was an accident, but he thought it was better that she had died. He said if she had lived, white people wouldn't want her around because she had been a squaw, and he was probably right."

"Thanks for the education," Dave said. "I've learned a lot on this trip of ours."

"You're a good man, Dave Price. Your heart is in the right place. Maybe we can teach each other."

The two lawmen said their goodbyes and mounted their

horses. "Oh, hell, hold on a minute, Dave." Barry turned his horse back toward the porch where Harold was sitting. "Now, it's my turn to ask a question." He leaned in the saddle and spit before taking a hard look at Harold.

"I heard you say once that you hated all Indians. So what makes the difference with him?" He nodded toward Matthew.

"He's no ordinary Indian. That's Manhunter. He saved my life."

~   ~   ~

Vicky accompanied Matthew to the edge of the yard as Dave and Sheriff Barry disappeared down the road. Cuddles ran circles around the two of them, barking and being chased by Caroline.

"You don't really believe Hank could have killed those people, do you?" she said hopefully. "I mean, you never even met him. And outside that one incident with Harold, he seemed so sweet and kind."

"I don't know. That *incident* you mentioned included holding a knife to your husband's neck. Anything's possible."

"I know it must sound horrible, but I just can't believe that Hank could possible do such a thing. Besides, if Harold had told you the whole truth, you might not feel like you do." She stepped close to stare into his face. "You see, the attack with the knife occurred right after my husband struck me." Matthew's eyes darted between her and Harold on the porch. "Now, I know what Hank did was wrong, but I think he was only trying to protect me. As far as murdering those people in Leon....?" she shook her head, "I just can't believe it."

Chapter 23

Matthew watched Caroline rummage through a wooden box she had pulled from under her bed. There was a ball of string, several colorful pebbles, a tin can with pretty colors painted on the lid and several stick-dolls. Finally, she came up with a tattered storybook and climbed into his lap.

"Mat-ew read," she said, holding the book in front of his face. He turned the pages and read the story of a white bunny rabbit while Harold sat warming himself by the stove. Vicky paused in her cleaning chores to watch them.

"You read very well, Mr. Blue."

"Thank you. But this book *is* sort of easy." He grinned. "I didn't run across any twenty-dollar words like *abolitionists* or *congressional* in the entire story."

"No, I don't believe you would have." She giggled and laid her dish towel on the table. "I know you've had a very good education, though. Where did you go to school?"

"Indian school, on the reservation. They taught us everything in English. I guess they thought it would make us closer to being white people."

"It was wasted on most of the Indians, wasn't it?" Harold said. His question brought a moan from Vicky.

"Not really," Matthew said. "Many of the Comanche are making a fair living in cattle and land dealings, now that they have some understanding of the white man's ways. Besides, the Comanche don't actually have a written language that you could put into book form. I guess, if they were going to teach us how to read, English would have been the logical choice."

"That's good to hear," Vicky said. She glanced up from the plate she was drying to give him a smile. "What about religion? Did they teach you that, also?"

"Here it comes," Harold snorted. "She's going to try to save you, Manhunter."

"Yes, they taught us about the God of the white man. Right out of a Bible, like the one you have laying on the table."

"And did you understand it?"

"Yes, if you mean did I understand what it was saying. But, if you'll excuse my saying so," Matthew paused to look her in the eye, "in my opinion, the God they taught us about would have to be a monster."

Vicky paled as Harold laughed. "I always thought you were different from the others," he said. "Now I know I like you." Both Vicky and Matthew stared as he laughed.

"I've been trying to tell my wife that ever since that bullet took my legs. You said it exactly like I feel, only more profoundly."

Vicky laid the plate on the table as her eyes darted across the ceiling. "How could you say that....about God?"

"Let me explain." Matthew's voice dropped low, just above a whisper. "As a child, I knew about your God. My mother was white. She was found wandering aimlessly by a hunting party when she was eleven years old. They later found her parents' wagon where it had fallen over the side of a cliff. She was the only one who lived. She had gotten off the wagon to stretch her legs, just minutes before it went over the cliff. Anyway, she taught me about her God as much as she could remember. Then, of course, I learned about the gods of the Comanche from my father, medicine men, and elders of the tribe. As a Comanche, I believed in their gods. We would pray and do celebration and ceremony before every hunt. He supplied us with meat and water. We were warm in the winter and had full stomachs. Then white men invaded our land. I watched my people as they prayed to their gods to give them victory in battle. What I saw was a stronger nation defeating a weaker one with more powerful weapons and many soldiers.

"Then the buffalo hunters killed all the game. There were long winters with no food or shelter, no matter how many prayers were prayed. So I decided that the god of the Comanche must either not exist or be one who couldn't, or wouldn't, help his own people. I didn't feel that he was a god that deserved to be worshiped." He paused to take a final sip of coffee and adjust Caroline on his lap. She had fallen asleep and her silky hair cascaded over his arm as he allowed her head to tilt back.

"After we were forced onto the reservation, I was taught again about the white man's God in school. We were told he was all-powerful and could help us in any situation. Having been defeated, I believed this; that is, until I watched how our white teachers treated their students.

"The missionary who carried the black book under his arm and talked of God's love in the classroom would take the prettiest girls to his room at night. He ate well and dressed warm while we went hungry and were cold. He beat us if we didn't say we believed like he taught us. He called us names and made us say long prayers. He'd say things like, 'Maybe God will have mercy on your souls, and not damn you to hell like you deserve.' No," Matthew shook his head, "if his God was like that, if he could not change men inside where it counts, I didn't want any part of Him." He jerked up as Vicky burst into tears.

"I'm....I'm so sorry," she sobbed, "and, I'm so ashamed."

Harold ran a trembling hand across his face and grew silent.

~   ~   ~

The nightmare returned that evening as Matthew slept, but it was different. Instead of seeing Prairie Flower and his son on the floor of his cabin, it was Vicky Jamison and her daughter. Everything else remained the same...the rage he felt at seeing their lifeless bodies...the pain as he buried them. He woke, hearing Cotton's voice as he used the knife. He lay on the floor of the cabin listening to Caroline's soft breathing, mingled with the sound of Harold's snore coming from the next room. Where had Prairie Flower and Pita gone?

Chapter 24

Matthew was up before daylight and rode out into the prairie the way Vicky said Slim had originally come. He made a wide circle around the farm, searching the ground for any tell-tale signs of travel. He returned late in the morning to the smell of hot coffee and frying bacon.

"Good morning, Mr. Blue. You were up early." Vicky set a steaming mug in front of Matthew as he took his place at the table.

"Thanks." He lifted the mug in a salute. "I couldn't sleep much. Besides, I'm used to rising before sunup."

"Your timing is very good, for us anyway. We have gotten used to eating breakfast late around here. Harold sleeps in, and it allows me time to get my morning chores done before Caroline wakes up."

"Hi, Mat-ew." Caroline padded across the floor in her bare feet rubbing her eyes.

"Caroline," Vicky scolded as her daughter wormed her way into his lap, "don't bother Mr. Blue before he's had breakfast.

"It's okay, really." He helped her scoot to a comfortable position.

"I'm afraid she's taken quite a liking to you." Vicky turned back to the stove to fill his plate with bacon and fried eggs.

"I kind of like her too." He nuzzled the tiny head as Harold wheeled his chair from the bedroom to join them.

"Find our man, Matt?"

"No, but I know where he's not."

"Guess you got to start somewhere." He positioned his wheelchair at the empty spot at the end of the table and took a long sip from the coffee mug. "Aaaaah, now that proves there is a god." He grinned and pointed to the mug.

"Can't argue with you there." Matthew took another sip. "This farm would kind of make you think that itself."

"Really?" Vicky set two more plates on the table and reached for her daughter. "Come here Carol, let Mr. Blue eat his breakfast." She placed the girl into a chair next to hers, with a glass of milk and a plate with one egg.

"And why is that, Mr. Blue?" she said, folding her napkin and placing it in her lap.

"Why's what?" He glanced up from cutting his egg.

"You were saying that this dinky little farm would cause someone to believe in God."

"Oh." He nodded as he chewed. "If you've ever slept some of the places I've been, then you'd know that this," he pointed his fork around the room, "is a welcome change to the cold, hard ground and smoky campfires I'm used to. The home-cooked meal by itself is enough." He took another hungry bite.

"Huh, some of the Army food we used to eat would make any sinner cry out for God's mercy, ain't that right?" Harold laughed.

"You said it. I think ol' Wally was the worse cook in the whole bunch." Matthew snickered and sipped his coffee. "Did know how to cook up a pretty good mule, though."

"What?" Vicky dropped her fork in her plate with a clunk. The men laughed as she dabbed at her lips with the napkin.

"Mule ain't all we used to eat," Harold said. "Bobcat's not half-bad when it's done up right. And rattlesnake's actually pretty good."

"Now, I know you've got to be kidding."

"I'm afraid not, ma'am." Matthew shook his head. "Your husband and I have eaten most anything, from time to time. Hey," he turned toward Harold, "remember that time Wally cooked up a bunch of buzzards and tried to tell everyone they were turkeys?"

"Ooooh, stop it!" Vicky pushed her plate away as Harold laughed. The conversation continued as the men reminisced of old Army times, battles and days of glory, some of which turned Vicky pale. Matthew was on his fourth cup of coffee when Vicky stopped washing the dishes to face him.

"I know this might sound hypocritical to you, Mr. Blue, seeing as I married Harold when he was a Lieutenant,. but I just can't agree with the taking of human life. I don't care who they are, or what they've done, it's still wrong. And it always bothered me, knowing my husband might have been guilty of doing just that."

"You see, Manhunter, my wife was raised by her Quaker grandmother." Harold gave a crooked grin and set his coffee cup on the table. "Quakers don't believe in raising a hand against anyone, regardless of what he's doing. Had a hell of a time trying to talk her grandmother into letting us get married. She still didn't come to the wedding."

Matthew sat thoughtfully for a moment, drumming his fingers on the table. "Does that mean if someone was trying to kill you, or your daughter, you wouldn't kill him first to save her life?"

"Exactly." She gave a firm nod. "We believe that, if we should die, it is God's will. That a person is only hurting themselves by harming another human being. We believe no one should ever lift their hand in anger to strike another."

"Huh, I'll bet there aren't too many Quakers," Matthew said quietly. Vicky scowled as Harold laughed.

"That's why I can't agree with what you are doing, and how you make your living, Mr. Blue," she said. "Chasing men just to collect a reward that someone else has offered. I know if you do catch Hank, you mean to kill him, don't you?"

"I hope not. I plan on taking him back to Leon and let the

108

courts try him. But I suppose if he puts up a fight, and tries to kill me, yeah, that's a possibility." He raked the chair against the wooden floor as he stood to his feet.

"You see, this is how I believe it really is. That man, whether it is Slim, Otis, or your Hank, whoever he is, killed at least two people we know of. Now if I let him go, he'll probably kill some more people sooner or later, and keep on killing until he's stopped. Let's suppose he puts up a fight, and I kill him. I've taken a human life, like you said. But on the other hand, I might have saved several others. Which is the greater sin? Killing one person, and saving several lives? Or letting that person live, and perhaps being guilty of allowing the deaths of several other people?"

"Since you put it that way, I don't know what to say." Her eyes darted around the room before settling on the floor. "I think we'd be better off leaving it up to God. I just don't see how anyone could kill another person. I know I could never do that."

"Oh, but you could, and probably would, if someone tried to harm your husband or daughter. Believe me lady, you'd fight, and kill them if need be." He nodded his head. "I've seen it too many times not to know it's true. That's the way life is. Even a mother squirrel will fight to the death to save her young. In the end, the strong survive and the weak die."

"I'm sorry, I can't agree with you." She paused. "Perhaps I would. I might, under the circumstances you describe. But I don't think it's possible."

~   ~   ~

That afternoon Vicky watched Matthew as he split firewood. A soft cool breeze blew and the sun was bright and pleasant in contrast to the stormy weather they'd received the past two days. He had removed his buckskin jacket as he worked, and his powerful muscles rippled as he swung the heavy maul. The thin undershirt clung tightly to his massive chest with perspiration as he worked. Vicky had to admit this man was attractive. His black hair glistened in the sunlight.

His copper complexion only added to the mystique. He talked like a philosopher, but moved his powerful frame quickly and silently, like a cat. She knew, from what little Harold had told her, and listening to their conversation, that Manhunter could be dangerous. She hated to admit, that also added to his attractiveness. He must have sensed her watching him, for he turned from his work to smile. Her hand fluttered to her lips and she turned away as he went back to splitting the logs with his powerful swings.

Vicky scurried toward the barn, not really knowing why. She stood in the cool darkness of the building wondering why she had chosen this place. All the chores had been accomplished hours ago. She crept back toward the door to peer at the Indian. The emptiness she felt inside gnawed at her. It had been two years since Harold's injury. Since that time, he had refused to hold and caress her as he had when they were first married. She knew that sex was out of the question, but the absence of tenderness made the loneliness unbearable. She found herself wondering what it would feel like to be held in Matthew's strong arms.

"Oh, God, forgive me." She squeezed her eyes shut and covered her face with her hands. Thoughts like that were sinful, and had to be pushed from her mind. Certainly, Satan must have gotten a hold on her somehow. She would read an extra chapter in her Bible tonight.

~   ~   ~

Matthew's strange dream returned. Vicky Jamison and her daughter had again taken the place of his wife and son. He woke with Cotton's words as before, but somehow they were different this time. He found himself shaking and knew that sleep would flee from him the rest of the evening. He rose quietly and went out into the cold night air to ponder the dream. Words that had been pushed aside and forgotten years ago had come back. The murderer of his wife and son had given up and surrendered after several days without food or rest, but Matthew in his rage had killed him anyway. He was in the process of taking the man's life when Cotton entered the cave behind him.

"You killed him!" Cotton's voice echoed in his head. "He'd given up, son, and you went ahead and killed him. That's murder, boy. That's murder."

Chapter 25

In the morning Matthew tightened his circle around the farm before returning to the house. Again he found himself helping Vicky with her chores, and the remainder of the day seemed to flee with the sunlight. Believing that winter was now upon them, they had stacked loads of firewood on the porch and brought the rest closer to the house. Several times throughout the day he caught himself watching Vicky as she worked. Her small frame was lithe and strong. She was used to hard work, but made each movement of her body seem graceful, and her hair sparkled like polished glass when the sun broke through the clouds. Her smile was warm and friendly. He liked the small freckles sprinkled across her tiny nose, and the way it crinkled when she laughed. Matthew snickered as he remembered Ten Bears, the Yamparika chief, vowing he would never touch a white woman. *Maybe, but Ten Bears had never seen Vicky Jamison, either.* He glanced over at Harold on the porch. *You should thank your God for blessing you so, old friend.*

~ ~ ~

Harold sat in his favorite spot watching his wife as she worked in the yard. She would stop what she was doing every now and then to steal a glance at Matthew as he worked. In return, while Vicky was hard at her labor, Matthew would do the same. He had been jealous of the attention given to Hank, but this was different. Harold sensed a chemistry between these two that frightened him. He had known Matthew to be an honorable man, and his wife was virtuous. But he was not much of a husband anymore, and the demons of fear and jealousy came to torment him. *I might owe you my life, Manhunter, but I'll be damned if I owe you my wife.*

~   ~   ~

Harold grew sullen after dinner and scowled at the stove while Vicky cleaned the kitchen. She had asked repeatedly what was bothering him, but he had refused to discuss the situation, and she finally retreated into silence. Matthew glanced at him occasionally, but gave his attention to Carol. It was only after Vicky asked Harold if he would like an evening cup of coffee that he broke his silence.

"No, I don't want your damn coffee. I'm surprised you didn't offer it to your boyfriend first."

Instantly a chill gripped him, as Vicky stood open-mouthed with the steaming cup in her hand. Matthew's silent gaze engulfed him as he strove mentally to grab the words and pull them back.

Vicky placed the cup on the table before turning toward Matthew. "I'm sorry." Her voice was almost a whisper and her bottom lip trembled. "My husband must not be feeling well this evening." She took her daughter by the hand and passed silently into the bedroom.

"Lieutenant," Matthew said, closing Caroline's book. "You might have been one of my commanding officers in the Army, and you might be my friend right now, but you are a bastard. You had no right to treat her that way."

"And you have no right to stick your nose into my business, you damned redskin. She's my wife, not yours."

"True, she *is* your wife. Now, treat her like you were her husband."

"Go to hell. What's an Indian know about being a husband to a white woman?"

"For one thing, my father treated my white mother a hell of a lot better than you're treating your wife right now. He was man enough to tell us, children included, when something was bothering him. Instead, you've sat pouting like a child all evening. Your daughter shows more maturity than you've shown."

Harold's face flushed as he angrily spun his chair to face him. "If I wasn't in this chair, I'd punch your face in for that."

Matthew cocked one eyebrow and grinned. "Granted, I've only been here for a couple of days, but from what I have seen, she is a good woman, one that most men would die for. I believe you owe her an apology."

"Damn you!" Harold grabbed the coffee mug and flung it toward Matthew's head. It missed by several feet and smashed against the wall, leaving a trail of coffee that rained across the floor.

"Make you feel better? How about if I go get the dog, so you can give him a beating? Or, maybe I can stand real close and let you punch me in the kneecap."

"You sonofabitch. If I had my gun, I'd...." Harold's eyes darted around the room.

"You'd do what, Lieutenant? Shoot your house to pieces? Kill me? Maybe hurt your wife and child in the process? And for what? Because I smiled at your wife?" Matthew chuckled and slowly shook his head. "I can't figure what any of us did to get you swollen up today. And the only thing I've seen her do is to work like a dog, trying to provide a home for you and your daughter."

"I've seen the way she looks at you. And I've seen you staring at her too, when her back is turned. You can't fool me. I know what you're thinking."

"Oh." Matthew nodded. "Because I think she's a beautiful woman? I guess that means she's been unfaithful, does it? I can't answer for what she has or hasn't been thinking, but, I'll tell you one thing I *do* know for sure. Your wife is striking. You knew that when you married her. Men are going to notice her wherever she goes, so, get used to it. The bottom line is, she's still your wife. You just don't know how lucky you really are."

Matthew crossed the room to where his gunbelt hung on a coat peg and drew his .44. Harold stared as he slid the gun across the table.

"Go ahead. It's loaded. Start shooting, if that's what you really want."

Harold's chin dropped to his chest as Matthew towered over him.

"Lieutenant, you think you're not much of a man because your legs refuse to work. But a man only ceases being a man when his mind refuses to work, and he acts like an animal. Tonight, you became an animal. Go to your wife and apologize. Hold her in your arms and become a man again."

"Matt? I...." Harold shook his head.

"Go on," he motioned with his head, "talk to your wife."

Matthew was collecting the pieces of the shattered mug when Vicky came out of the bedroom with Caroline in her arms.

"I'll do that, Matthew," she whispered.

"No, you won't." He reached for the sleepy girl. "I can handle this. You have more important things to take care of."

For the first time in two years, Vicky slept with Harold's arms around her.

Chapter 26

Matthew squatted to study the abandoned campsite approximately a mile west of the Jamison farm. It was no more than a day old, and had been covered so well that any normal person would have passed it without realizing its existence. Only the keen smell of his horse and his trained eyesight had caused him to stop.

"Smart son-of-a-buck, ain't he?" Matthew glanced toward the horse, who nodded and pawed the ground as if he understood. "He certainly isn't an idiot, like everyone's saying." He studied a broken branch dangling from a bush.

"Now, that could mean two things. It could mean that he was careless and snapped that branch as he went south. Or, it could mean that he wants us to think he's gone south, while he went another way. Which one do you think it really means?" The horse snorted and turned north as he took a bite of the rich grass.

"Yeah, I agree. It's going to take a little longer catching him than we thought. That is, unless we want to call out the Army and sweep the countryside." He swung into the saddle and started the horse walking back toward the farm.

"Wonder what's got him stuck here? Most men would have been a hundred miles away by now. You wouldn't have any idea, would you?" The horse snorted and nodded his head.

"Yeah, I'll bet you do. And if I had your common sense, I wouldn't be hanging around here either."

~   ~   ~

"Oh, Matthew, I'm glad you made it back in time." Vicky met him on the front porch and reached for his hand. "We have a visitor I would like for you to meet." He glanced toward a smirking Harold as she pulled him toward the door.

"Fay, this is Matthew Blue. He's the friend of Harold's I've been telling you about." Matthew removed his hat as the heavyset woman at the table eyed him up and down. The large nose, drawn lips, and beady eyes reminded him of a buzzard he had chased from a horse carcass last fall.

"Matthew," Vicky continued, "I'd like you to meet Fay Ikenberry."

"Pleased to meet you, ma'am."

"Mmmm." The woman nodded back.

"Fay heads the Women's Society in our local church." Vicky's glance moved between the two.

"Well," Matthew said after a minute's silence, "I guess you two have things to discuss. I'll keep Harold company outside." He backed toward the door. "Pleased again to meet you, ma'am." He nodded and received the same "Mmmm" in return.

"Whew," he eyed Harold after closing the door. "Bet that woman could kill a skunk with that stare of hers."

"And probably eats them after they're croaked," Harold smirked as he lit his pipe. "That right there," he shook the flame from the match, "has to be the nosiest woman on the face of the earth. You can bet she only came out here to spy on us, and spread rumors about our having an Indian stay here. God, how I wish you had a loincloth and some war paint in that pack of yours. That'd sure scare the hell out of her."

"Maybe I don't have those things, but I can still give her something to talk about." He headed toward the barn and returned with a small bow and several blunt-end arrows. "I've been working on these for Caroline, but I wanted to talk to you and Vicky before I gave them to her."

"Hell, that's perfect." Harold rolled his chair to the edge of the porch and yelled.

"Caroline!" He looked back over his shoulder at Matthew. "Can you teach her to whoop like a Comanche?"

"Just as loud as you are now."

"Great, by gawd. Just great! Caroline!" The little girl poked her head up over the wooden rail in the back of the buckboard. "Now how in Christ's name did she get in there? Caroline, get over here now. Matthew has something to show you." She disappeared, only to reappear seconds later with Cuddles chasing her.

"I think Vicky put a couple of boxes near the back end so she could climb up in there herself the other day," Matthew said.

"Yeah, she's almost as short as Carol. Better move 'em when you get a chance, or Caroline might fall out and break her neck."

"What, Daddy?" She used her hands as well as her feet to climb the steps.

"Look what Matthew's got for you."

"Oh....!" Her eyes grew wide as she reached for the bow.

"Here," Matthew said, slipping a headband over the golden curls. "Now, come here and let me show you how to use the bow." He placed one of the boxes in the center of the yard as a target. It only took a matter of minutes for the girl to be able to hit the target from a distance of five feet.

"Now, you've got to yell. Like this. Aiiiee-yiiiee-yiiee!" Matthew danced a little jig, holding one of the arrows high over his head. "Now, you try it."

"Eeeee-iiiii!" Caroline jumped up and down waving the bow.

"Great, I think you've got it." He could see an open-mouthed Vicky standing in the doorway beside a scowling Fay Ikenberry.

"Now you are a Comanche." He knelt in front of Caroline and placed both hands on her shoulders. "Comanches don't shoot dogs or chickens, or they might lose their bow. And they don't shoot at people either. Do you understand what I am saying?" She nodded.

"And they never shoot at anything their mother and father tell them not to. Now, go ahead and practice." She let out another yell and fired a bullseye at the box.

"My word!" He could hear Fay's indignant voice from where he stood in the center of the yard. "Are you sure you want that creature to turn your daughter into a savage like himself?"

"Matthew is a highly intelligent, well-educated human being, probably more so than most of the people in town. He is not a savage." The sharp edge in Vicky's voice caused Matthew to stare. "And my daughter is not a savage either. Both of them are children of God, the same as you and I. Matthew is simply teaching her about another culture."

"Well!" Fay Ikenberry grabbed her skirt in her left hand as she marched toward her buggy.

Vicky scowled as she watched the buggy bounce down the rough road. "Now, I suppose, she'll tell all of Gueda Springs how we've turned our farm into a camp of savages."

"I think I can stand the gossip, just as long as she decides to stay in town and pray for our souls instead of coming out here to bother us," Harold said.

"Harold!" She pulled her hair back and tied it with a bow. "She was only trying to be nice, in her own way. Besides, we don't get many visitors and I would like some female company once in a while."

"I might take offence at that," Matthew said, taking a seat on the railing behind Harold.

"Take offence at what? My wanting some female company?"

"No, my being called a savage. But on the other hand, I am a little offended that you'd prefer that woman's company to ours."

"Now, why do I doubt that? And both of you know exactly what I mean."

"Well, I personally wouldn't mind people from the

church coming out for a visit," Harold said with a snort. "The pastor, his wife, the deacons; anybody but Fay Ikenberry. With her nose stuck into everybody's business, and stirring up trouble the way she does, I'm not too sure she's really a Christian."

"Harold." Vicky's mouth dropped open. "Fay Ikenberry is the head of the Women's Society in our congregation. And I hate to admit it, but that is the most powerful organization in town."

"Well, hell." Harold cocked his head to glance at Matthew. "I've lived here close to three years now, and I'm just learning what's really wrong with Gueda Springs. Oh, I know she has her name on the roll, and she runs the place," he said with a wave of his hand, "but just think about this. She might be a plant. A spy from the enemy camp. Maybe in reality, she's a secret agent of Satan." He ended this statement by lowering his voice to a hoarse whisper and covering his nose and mouth with his coat sleeve.

"Well, I still think you ought to try treating her nicer." Vicky choked back a giggle. "She is one of the most prominent people in town."

"Me? Who was it that ran her off this time? Did I insult that nosey woman, Matthew?"

"Nope, not that I could see. Neither of us did."

"Okay, okay. I'm the guilty one." Vicky broke into giggles as Matthew shook his head. "But she was insinuating I wasn't a good mother, and she insulted you, Matthew. You should feel proud that I took up for you the way I did."

"Yeah, well, I suppose she could have found a lot of things to say about me." Matthew dug around in his shirt pocket for the makings and began rolling a cigarette. "Did I miss anything? What all did she say when you were inside?"

"Nothing of any value. We talked mostly about things that concern women. Well, she talked, and I mostly listened. When we heard you whoop, we ran to the door. That's when she saw Caroline jumping around and waving that bow with the feather stuck in her hair." Vicky gave a crooked smile and cocked her head to one side. "She said you were turning my daughter into a savage, and that's what made me angry." Both men roared with laughter.

"I told you it would work, Matt. Didn't I?"

"Harold Jamison." Vicky tried desperately to keep a serious face. "What have you done now? Did you do something to insult our guest?"

"No, nothing like that." Matthew tried to compose himself. "Well, he did suggest I put on a loincloth and war paint, but I told him I didn't have a cloth or paint with me." Vicky sat on the steps giggling as Matthew continued.

"Actually, the bow and headdress were my idea. It's a little cold to be running around in a loincloth today."

Harold doubled over laughing and slapped his thigh. Caroline stood wide-eyed at the base of the steps, staring at her father.

"No, no," Harold said. "You might get goose-bumps on your...." Vicky cut him off with a wave of her hand.

"Stop, please, no more." She wiped her eyes with the end of her apron. "Lord, I can't stand it." She fought off another fit of giggles. "Poor woman. I wonder what she's going to be telling her friends."

"Probably that we've got a savage running around in a loincloth and war paint," Harold said. "And that our daughter's running around buck-naked shooting arrows at the chickens." All three burst into more laughter.

"I'm glad you're here, Matthew," Harold said after composing himself. "I haven't laughed so hard in a long time. I wish all Indians were like you. I wouldn't be in this chair. You're a good man."

"I wish all white people were like you and your wife, or Cotton." He took Caroline by the hand and returned to their archery lesson.

"What do you suppose he meant by that?" Vicky said as they watched then in the yard.

"There's a bond between him and a few white people that's not too common." Harold shifted in his chair with a grunt. "Cotton's like a father to him. He saved Cotton's life once, and I suppose Cotton's saved his hide a time or two, also. We were all like that. We had to be in order to stay alive."

"Really?" Vicky shifted her position to study her husband. "You've never really told me about your battles before."

"Well, I didn't think you'd be interested. I know how you feel about guns and shooting, and things like that. So, I never told you."

"That's true, and normally I wouldn't. But I'd like to know anyhow. Maybe it would help me understand how you feel about him." She nodded toward Matthew and shrugged.

Harold opened the leather pouch and tamped fresh tobacco in his pipe as he talked. "We were trapped by some renegade Kiowa. They'd been causing trouble all the way from Colorado to Texas. Most of what they did was small. A stage stop or farm here and there. So no one ever made much of an effort to catch them, outside of sending a few soldiers out every now and then. But then they decided to wipe out an entire wagon train about twenty miles outside Fort Richardson. Killed everyone." He saw his wife grimace, and decided to leave off telling of the torture. "That was about a year before we got married." He studied her through a cloud of smoke as he lit his pipe.

"Anyway, we were part of those three thousand troops Sherman ordered from Forts Dodge, Sill, Richardson and Concho. I supposed you heard about that?"

She shook her head.

"No? Well, no matter. We were supposed to join the others down in the north Texas panhandle and put a stop to their little party, but they found us first. They seemed to come from everywhere. We made a run for some rocks trying to find cover. That's when Cotton got his horse shot out from under him. Manhunter," he took a drag off the pipe and nodded toward Matthew, "had a pretty fast horse and was way ahead of us all. He looked back and saw what happened and turned that pony around before any of us had a chance to do anything. He grabbed Cotton with one arm while doing a pretty good gallop, swung him up behind him, and headed toward the rocks. Those Kiowa would've had Cotton for sure." He paused to stare in the distance and puffed several times on the pipe.

"Anyway, I'd gotten thrown from my horse about that time. I don't know if my horse got shot, or just stepped in a hole, but he went down and I went head-over-tea-kettle about twenty yards or so from the rocks. I don't remember anything after that. They told me Manhunter jumped off his horse as he passed and let Cotton ride on into shelter by himself. Then he carried me to cover on his shoulder with those devils doing their best to kill him." Harold swallowed hard.

"He took a bad hit doing that. No one knew he was wounded until it was over with. If you watch him closely, you'll see him limp every once in a while. I don't mind admitting it. I owe my life to that redskin."

Chapter 27

The chickens clucked and scratched for bugs in the setting sun as Vicky pulled the heavy rake across the ground. *That woman is forever working. She never ceases to find something to do.* Matthew couldn't keep his eyes from wandering her way as he sat on the porch smoking with Harold. Her small frame and movements were hypnotic to him. He had trouble understanding how such a small girl could work hours on end without tiring. He thought of some of the Indian girls he had known, and how hard they worked around the camp. There were many similarities between Vicky and those maidens, except this fair-skinned, golden-haired girl was also refined and educated. She was someone you would expect to find living in a softer environment with others waiting on her, instead of working like a slave.

"She is rather fascinating, isn't she?" Matthew snapped his head around as Harold laughed. "Oh, don't look so embarrassed. Okay, I'll admit I do get jealous, like I did last night. But that's because I'm stuck here in this damn chair and can't even make love to her the way a man should when he's got a wife like that."

He leaned forward and put his elbows on his dead knees while rolling another smoke. He grinned as his eyes took on a softness.

"You know, the first time I saw her, she was just a kid, fifteen and a half years old. But, Jesus Christ, she was the most beautiful creature I'd ever laid eyes on. I knew right then that I just had to have her, so I started going over to her grandmother's house. That was where she was staying. Her mother died, you know. Anyway, you should have seen the hornet's nest I stirred up by showing up there dressed in my Army blues." He laughed and stared blankly at the cracked porch step at Matthew's feet.

Matthew took a drag off his own cigarette and smiled. *The past is a much better place for you than the present, isn't it my friend?*

"Actually, I thought I looked pretty good, myself." Harold sat back and finished rolling his cigarette. "My boots were shined, my brass was polished. I even had on white gloves and had polished my saber. But you'd have thought I was Lucifer by the reaction that old lady had when Vicky introduced us. I was an *instrument of Satan*, and belonged to an *organization designed for the destruction of human lives*. That's what she said anyway. It took me a whole year to talk that old hag into allowing us to get married. Even then, she wouldn't come to the wedding.

"I love her more than you'll ever know." Harold stared at the unlit cigarette between his fingers, and Matthew felt a lump rise in his throat as he studied him. Sitting in the wheelchair with a blanket draped across his legs, Harold suddenly looked old.

"The first few years were beautiful. I never really told her the truth about what we were doing in the military. If we went out and got into a fire-fight with some Indians, I would tell her that we helped some poor starving savages find their way to the reservation where they would have food and shelter, or something like that. It wasn't until she got talking to some of the other military wives that she found out the truth. Then, this happened to me." He threw the blanket back and glared at his thin legs.

"You know, Matt? I can hardly stand for her to touch me

now. It's not because I don't love her. It's because I do, so damned much. And I can't do anything that a man's supposed to do. When she touches me, I feel like this beautiful creature is touching a dead carcass - - - something that a buzzard has been eating. Can you understand that, Manhunter?" He stared at Matthew with hopeless eyes. Matthew nodded.

"This is gonna sound funny coming from the world's biggest Indian hater, but, I know how you feel about her, and that doesn't bother me." Matthew shifted as Harold continued. "Well, yes it does, but, not that much. I've seen the way you look at her and how your eyes get all mushy. I know you better than you think, and that ain't like you. You're in love with her, aren't you?"

Matthew remained silent.

"No matter. I know you are, and like I said, it doesn't bother me that much. It only bothers me that I can't be the man she needs. She needs some one to take care of her and Caroline - - - to be a man and protect her. You know what I mean?" Matthew nodded.

"She works too damned hard, Manhunter. She'll be an old woman before long. God damn these legs." He grew sullen for a moment before throwing the blanket back across his lap with a jerk. He sniffled and wiped his nose on his sleeve.

"You'll think I'm crazy, Manhunter, but I've got a feeling I won't be around much longer." He laughed as Matthew frowned.

"No, I'm not going to shoot myself or anything like that. It's just this feeling, and probably doesn't mean much. But if something does happen to me, will you take care of them for me?"

"You don't even need to ask. You know I'll check in on them when I can."

"That's not what I mean. Damn, how can I say this?" Harold fumbled with a match in an effort to light the cigarette.

"She really cares about you too, you know. I've seen the way she looks at you. I know my wife, Manhunter. And I know she'll stay with me until I'm dead and buried. And,

126

being the type of woman she is, she'll still remain true to me, at least for a while. But, she's a young woman and needs to be loved and cared for like a woman. She needs to be taken away from this stinking hole of a farm. It'll kill her. I want my daughter to have a good education and know how to act around people, not just chickens and cows. She'll need to meet young men someday, and there aren't any out here." Harold took a silent drag off his cigarette as he studied the Indian's face.

"God, how I hate that pan expression of yours. You'd make one hell of a poker player. Know that? None of you Indians show any emotion." He took another drag off the cigarette before tossing it in the yard. "I feel like I've been talking to Cuddles."

Matthew's own cigarette had burnt down to a butt and he crushed it under his boot heel. Harold backed his chair up and beat his pipe against the railing. Then he glanced toward Matthew. "My daughter thinks the sun rises and sets around you. Take care of them for me, Manhunter, I'm counting on you."

Matthew's face twisted as he rose to his feet. "You know what you're asking? She's white and I'm half-breed Comanche. Do you know what that would do to her?"

His boot crunched the soft earth as he bounded from the porch. His first choice would have been to go to the barn and groom his horse, but Vicky had stopped her raking at the sound of his angry voice and was staring his way. He stood frozen for a second, before shifting and walking briskly down the roadway. He studied the falling leaves and sucked the cool air deep inside his lungs. His heart was heavy for this friend. That was no life for a man like Harold Jamison, to be confined to a prison with wheels that only allowed him to exist. He was right. He wasn't the man he was born to be. The Harold Jamison he had known would never have given up, regardless. He would have fought until there was no breath left in his mortal body, chair or no chair. And then, if possible, he would have fought even more.

He had never known Harold as a husband or father. He

had gotten married after Matthew left the Army. But one thing he was certain of, the Lieutenant Jamison he knew would never have asked anyone, let alone a half-breed, to take care of his family. He would have done that himself. He stooped to grab a pebble and toss it at a ground squirrel.

Taking care of Harold's wife would be every man's dream. And even though he had trouble keeping the woman out of his thoughts, he knew it would be impossible. Harold had to know how society would react toward a red man taking care of a white woman and her white daughter. After all, didn't they think it was good when his white mother had died?

It was hard enough for white men who chose Indian wives. They were called "squaw men," and were made to live on the outskirts of society. But a white woman would be made a total outcast. The few whites who might accept such an arrangement, like Cotton and Alice, would certainly not make up for the loss Vicky and Caroline would suffer.

Matthew picked up another stone and threw it at a squirrel scampering up a tree. Vicky Jamison was a pure, honest woman, who deeply loved her God. Manhunter could never degrade her by being her guardian or mate. What was Harold thinking?

As for Matthew himself, he was no better than the man he was chasing. Cotton was the best friend he ever had, but even he said that Matthew had the mark of Cain on him. He had taken a life when it was not necessary. *That's murder, boy.* He scooped a twig and broke it.

At first, he was happy that Cotton had chosen to cover up the crime. *I don't blame you none for cutting his throat. I'd have done the same thing myself. He needed killing. But, the fact is, he's white and you're Indian, so the law won't see it the same way. They'd say he just killed a couple of Indians, and it wouldn't have even gone to trial. It wouldn't even make any difference that he killed your wife and son. No, he needed killing. But we can't let anyone else know about it.*

That was ten years ago, and Matthew had constantly told himself that he was better than the criminals he pursued, but after all the miles he traveled and faces he had seen, Cotton's words still rang in his ears. *That's murder, boy.* No, he could never dirty Victoria Jamison with his sin. Harold would have to find someone else to look after them. He would find Slim the following morning and leave before it was too late.

Chapter 28

Matthew helped Vicky feed the animals by the light of an old kerosene lantern hanging from a rusty nail in the barn. She didn't mentioned his angry words with Harold earlier in the day. She was laughing about Caroline wanting to wear her headband during her nap time, when she turned quickly to bump her head on a low-hanging board in one of the stalls. "Ow!" She grabbed her head and dropped to a pile of hay.

"Here, let me take a look at that," Matthew said as he knelt beside her.

"Oh, I'm alright. I've done that a dozen times. You'd think I'd learn by now."

"Well, let me look at it anyway," he said, brushing her hair away to reveal a small abrasion that was beginning to swell and turn purple. He pressed against the spot with tender fingers to see if there was any bleeding. "Dang it, the light's so poor in here I can't see. Lean back just a little."

She tilted her head and Matthew found himself staring into the same eyes that haunted his dreams nightly. His heart raced as her lips parted. His finger tips trembled as they traced a path across her cheek to her chin. Suddenly the soft hay beneath them was his wedding bed. The hands caressing her face were not the blood-stained hands of the Manhunter. He was sixteen years old and the girl before him was a Comanche princess with velvet skin. He could hear her breathe as she drew close. His fingers parted the golden locks and found their way to the back of her neck. Their lips were but a fraction of an inch from each other when the lamplight against the hair cascading across her shoulder caught his eye. He jerked away to stand with his back toward her.

"I'm sorry. I didn't realize what I was doing."

"Don't be." Matthew felt her hands tremble against his back. His heart raced as she leaned against him. "It's just as much my fault. I don't know why, but I....actually wanted you to kiss me." He heard a huge sob as she turned to kneel in the hay.

"Oh, I'm so sorry for feeling that way. You must think I'm horrible, with my husband being in the condition he is. God has to hate me! But," her shoulders shook as another sob escaped her throat, "it's been such a long time since he's touched me, I...." She shook her head.

He knelt beside her and placed a hand against her shoulder. "Don't." She pulled away. "It's not right. I'm Harold's wife. I'll always be Harold's wife. Please, leave. I've sinned enough."

~   ~   ~

Matthew was silent through most of the dinner, and didn't spend much time playing with Carol either. He found it easier to retreat to the barn with his horse, which he brushed until the animal's coat glistened in the lamp light. His thoughts ran in a confused, tangled pattern. He cursed himself for allowing his emotions to involve him even a little with another man's wife, especially when that man was one he had always respected. What did she think he was going to do when she told him to leave? He was only going to tell her it was alright. He understood. They had done nothing wrong. She was still Harold Jamison's wife. He kicked the hay at his feet.

But he *had* touched her. It was one thing to touch someone on the arm or cheek with no feeling of affection or anger, but what he had felt as he ran his fingers through her hair was something entirely different. He stopped to study a fly caught in the spider's web in the corner of the stall. He had not only wanted to touch her cheek and neck, but he wanted to taste her lips and feel her body pressed against his. It was no good. He had sworn himself to a life of celibacy on Prairie Flower's grave, but Vicky Jamison caused feelings to stir inside him he thought had died with his wife. He began to wonder if he was losing his mind, when the creaking of the barn door drew him from his private hell. The brush fell from his hand as she stepped inside.

"I want you to know, I take full responsibility for what happened earlier."

"Nothing happened."

"Yes, something did, and I could have stopped it." Vicky closed the door. "I really did want you to touch me. I have since the first day you came here. I don't know exactly why, but I have."

"You shouldn't be here. Go back to the house....to your husband." He snatched the brush from the hay and attacked the horse's side. The paint snorted and stamped his feet with a scowl at his master.

"I have to tell you this." She came closer. "I love Harold, and I always will, but it has been hard on me, on us both, not being like a real husband and wife."

"I know." He kept his back toward her. "I feel the same thing. With my wife and son gone," he shrugged, "it's been like a mixture of both heaven and hell being here. One minute I'm realizing how lucky Harold is to have you for a wife, and a daughter like Caroline. But this afternoon, when we were so close, I forgot about Harold. It was wrong and we both know that." He turned with a heavy sigh to stare her in the eye. "I'll be leaving in the morning. Now, go back to Harold. It's dangerous being here like this."

"I know, but I don't want you to go. I want you to stay. You've been good for us. Harold, Caroline, me, all of us." She gave him a quick hug and brushed his cheek with her lips before running back to the house.

Matthew stared at the half-open door before laughing.

"She's the damnedest woman I've ever met." He patted the horse on the rump. "And don't tell me you haven't felt the same thing since we've been here. I've seen you eyeing that mare in the corner stall." The horse snorted and shook his head. "Now, you're lying, just like I've been lying to myself. We're a couple of liars." He grabbed a sack of oats and gave a double handful to his four-footed friend.

"Not only is she the most fascinating creature I've ever seen, but she's just as crazy as I am. One minute she's acting like one of those nuns in that convent down in Texas, and the next, she's warm and very woman-like." He rubbed the horse's neck. "Kinda makes you wanna grab and squeeze her and kiss all those freckles on her nose."

He chuckled and sat on the milking stool to roll a cigarette. "I haven't felt like this since I was a kid of thirteen or fourteen. Tonacy used to make me feel that way. Did I ever tell you about her?" The horse snorted. "Didn't think so."

"We were in the same class at the Mission school. She was about a year or so older than I was. Anyway, she sat right next to me. Every so often, when she got bored with her schoolwork, she'd hike her skirt up over her knees and look at us boys the way only girls can. I'll tell you what, every one of us boys were thinking things that had nothing to do with our lessons." He struck a match and held the flame to his cigarette.

"Mrs. Jamison can bring out the same feelings inside a man, only in a different way. Kinda good and pure-like. Only thing is, she's married to the lieutenant." He took a long drag of his cigarette and blew a cloud that hung between him and the horse. "Something like that can get kinda sticky. Besides, we haven't got time for women, do we?"

He sat in the lamplight, smoking and listening to the horse munching his oats. He'd made it a point to stay away from women after Prairie Flower and Pita died. It was easier that way. He didn't have to be reminded and re-live the pain. But Vicky had brought it all back. The dangerous thing was, it didn't hurt being around her. He found himself liking her company. He crushed the smoke under the toe of his boot and studied the cracks between the boards in the wall.

When he was in Wyoming he had watched a wolf stalk and kill a young doe. The wolf was so graceful and cunning, the doe never sensed the danger until the wolf pounced. Matthew thought Vicky Jamison was like that she-wolf without even realizing it. The feel of her hands against his back and the warmth of her lips on his cheek begged him to stay another day. And tomorrow something else about her presence would beg him again, and again.

He rose from the stool and grabbed his coat from the nail on a post. Tomorrow he would ride out into the prairie and catch Slim. He had studied the man's habits and knew where he would be hiding. He would once more become the Manhunter and forget about Matthew Blue, the educated Indian and Army scout, friend of Harold Jamison. To Manhunter, Vicky Jamison would be just another person. A poor woman married to a cripple, having to scratch out a living on a little farm in southern Kansas. She would be just like so many others he had seen over the years. Hungry, tired, frustrated in her situation. Pretty, yes, but Vicky would be just another woman. He would find the killer, collect the reward, and leave Geuda Springs far behind. That was his salvation. That was what he told himself. He slipped into the coat and shoved his hat down on his head before heading toward the house.

Chapter 29

Vicky lay in bed watching the shadows as the wind shook the oak tree outside her window. The feel of Matthew's fingertips on her cheek and the back of her neck still made her body tremble. She prayed for God to take away this feeling. Harold had not caressed her like that in years. Maybe he never did. It was hard to remember. But Matthew had, and she had loved it.

She rolled her head toward Harold and whispered, "Why?"

She did not mind the long hard hours working on the small farm. She didn't mind having to wait on her invalid husband. In fact, there were few things that really bothered her, but the lack of affection was a mountain she could not climb. Matthew's touch had been intoxicating to her. She had found herself wondering what it would be like, since the first night she watched him caressing Caroline's blond head as she sat on his lap and he read to her. A twinge of jealousy had leapt into her heart that evening. It was small, but it had frightened her just the same, and caused her resentment toward Harold to grow. Her husband had not run his fingers through her hair, or touched her face (except to slap her), and he had not rubbed her tired back in two years. Vicky stared at him in the darkness. *That bullet damaged much more than your legs, my dear. It took my husband from me.*

The Harold she had married had ceased to exist the day the doctor told them he could never walk again. He had grown angry and sullen. The dark cloud that hung over their marriage grew blacker still, and had only seemed to abate slightly with the arrival of Matthew. There were few trials in her short life for which she had not found an answer in her daily Bible readings and prayer, but the lack of affection seemed to shut the doors of heaven to her. The loneliness she felt inside seemed unbearable at times.

She knew her marriage to Harold was holy before God, and to desire affection from another man was sinful. But she had felt Matthew's fingertips on her cheek and the back of her neck, and so help her God she had loved it. His touch made her feel like a desirable woman again, and not a hired hand or housekeeper. She choked back a sob as she thought about the barn. It had taken every ounce of strength she had to keep from throwing her arms around him. She had wanted him to take her in his arms and kiss her. The thought frightened her. But she knew if Matthew stayed here like she had asked him to, she would have to go back for more.

Chapter 30

"Dammit," Otis jumped the fallen log and dashed to the middle of his camp. He grabbed the rifle and what few things he had before throwing the saddle across the roan. He had gone to the creek to fill his canteen when he happened to see the tall Indian walking his horse toward his camp. He untied the horse and led it away without taking time to tighten the cinches, then dashed back to snatch the rabbit roasting over the fire.

"Come on, boy." He grabbed the reins once more. "Easy now. We got to be real quiet." He glanced back over his shoulder as he made his way through the brush. He couldn't see the Indian, but he knew he was there. He might even be watching Otis that very moment.

Don't want no fight with that man. He ain't really done anything again' me, yet. The fact was, Otis had never wanted to fight anyone in his entire life. It was only when he got really angry, or when someone did something that made him lose control, that bad things happened. He didn't have any argument against this man. He had known for several days that he was at Vicky and Caroline's house. The only thing he wanted to do was to keep an eye on things, and make sure no one hurt them.

He had returned three days ago to tell Vicky he was sorry,

only to find those men there. One of them was the Indian who was nosing around his camp that very minute. He recognized one of the others as the young lawman who had pointed the shotgun at the men who were trying to hang the boy. He'd only seen the third one once, but knew for sure he was a lawman. It wasn't hard to recognize the familiar metal star pinned on his vest. He'd considered leaving that very day, but the thought of leaving Vicky and Caroline was too much for him to consider.

These other men have to be from Leon. He pushed through a clump of bushes and gave a tug on the reins. *Vicky wouldn't have ridden all the way to town to tell the law about me holding the knife to Harold's throat. And even if she did, they wouldn't be sending three men out to get me for that. Besides, no one's gonna spend three days looking for me on Harold's account, when I didn't even hurt him. No, they gotta be after me because of Karen.*

He might have to leave if this man continued to hang around, because sooner or later they were going to meet face to face, and he didn't think the Indian was just gonna want to swap howdies. He was surprised that the Indian was that good. He had seemed to know where Otis would be hiding, even after he had moved to several locations. And this morning, he had come directly to Otis' camp.

On his trips to find food, Otis had spied men on horseback carrying guns. He suspected they were looking for him. One thousand dollars, was what they'd said that night. He'd never met anyone worth that much money. He had laughed out loud, realizing that for the first time in his life, people actually wanted him. But a thousand dollars was a lot of money, and Otis thought it was too bad he couldn't turn himself in and collect the reward without getting hung in the process.

Again, he had found himself sneaking up on neighboring farms and borrowing food. *It ain't really stealing,* he kept reminding himself. *It's survivin', and I ain't botherin' no one either.* But he'd never take chickens or eggs from Vicky's farm. They didn't have enough as it was, and Caroline was a growing girl that needed her nourishment. He didn't want her to go hungry as he had done growing up. So he took two chickens and some eggs from a run-down farm house back up the road where an old couple lived. Then he found another farm closer to town where he took a loaf of bread that sat cooling in a kitchen window. There was also plenty of small game in the area that he could snare without the use of a gun, so food wasn't really a problem. Getting caught was, but he had chosen to stay, knowing there was always the chance of that happening.

He'd been lucky, so far. He guessed the reason that most men stayed closer to town was because they liked to drink and gamble. The only one who had a notion as to where to look was this Indian. Otis had been keeping an eye on him. Being an early riser, he'd perch himself high up in an oak overlooking the farm and watch the man ride the brown and white horse out into the grassland. He'd circle the farm searching for signs, and he'd tightened that circle each day until there was nothing left, but Otis himself.

This was the first day he hadn't climbed the oak to watch, and it was the one day he'd come right to Otis' camp. It was an omen. He and the Indian would meet on the field of battle some day. The outcome would be determined by who took the early advantage. He swung into the saddle and clung low as the roan darted out of the brush into the grassland.

Chapter 31

"Damn." Matthew raced back to his horse at the sound of pounding hooves. He had been hiding behind a clump of trees, studying the abandoned campsite. He leaped astride his horse and dug his heels into its flanks. Otis was only a dot disappearing over the next rise by the time he rounded the clump of brush and trees.

"Come on, boy." He leaned low as the magnificent beast opened its stride, but the horse the killer was riding was almost his equal. A mile passed, and he had gained only a little. He drew the Sharps from its sheath and cocked the hammer, as he released the reins and let the horse have its lead. He took careful aim, only to ease the hammer down and pulled back on the reins.

"It's okay," he said as the horse snorted and whinnied his displeasure. "I couldn't take the chance. They were bouncing around too much, and I might have hit the horse. He runs pretty good, doesn't he? No wonder Jim Larkin wants him so badly." He had trouble turning the animal back toward the Jamison farm.

"Yeah, I know. You could have caught him. But that critter's worth an extra five hundred dollars to us. I don't want to chance him breaking a leg or something." The horse snorted his disagreement.

"Besides," he'll be back this afternoon. "Slim's tied to Vicky and that little girl as much as Lieutenant Jamison. More so, I think. He's got to come back in order to keep an eye on them. Then, we're gonna catch him, and I know exactly how we're going to do it." He patted the horse's neck.

The animal wobbled his head back and forth with a snort and trotted toward the farm.

Chapter 32

The air felt cold on Matthew's face and dew wet his boots and pant legs as the paint moved gracefully through the tall grass. The sun had begun to rise higher and cast a pink hue to the clouds that hung in the eastern sky. But none of these things seemed to clear his mind. Yesterday had been a trying day for Matthew. Harold's request and what happened in the barn were too much for him. *That was the last thing I would have expected out of Harold. Hell, I doubt if I'd have done anything like it myself.* And yet, thoughts of Vicky had crept into his mind, filling the void left by his wife and son. The feel of her warm lips and her skin against his fingers had caused his heart to race. "Oh, you're dumber'n dirt."

He reined the paint to a halt as it whinnied and side-stepped a small covey of quail darting from one bush to the next.

"Well, that's where he was hiding." He pointed toward the clump of trees and brush. "I found that hiding spot myself. Now, if you're so smart, you tell me where he's going to hide next. Farther south?" The horse pawed the ground.

"Yeah, that's what I was thinking myself. Let's go see."

~   ~   ~

Harold Jamison sat in his favorite spot on the front porch watching his wife cut firewood like she was possessed. There was no need for more wood. Matthew had already cut, split and stacked enough for an entire winter. But here was Vicky, working the buck-saw as though her life depended on it. The saw bit through the last few inches of wood and the cut end fell to the ground. She immediately laid the saw aside and wrapped her arms around the remaining portion of the heavy timber to hoist it into position. Retrieving the saw, she began again.

Harold knew his wife enough to know when there was something bothering her. What disturbed him most was her refusal to discuss it with him. That was something new. He always knew what was on Vicky's mind, because she told him, whether he wanted to hear it or not. He seldom ever told her anything about himself, at least not the truth, but he knew plenty about Vicky. Her insistence on discussing every little item had nearly driven him insane. There had been times when he prayed for a little peace and quiet. Now, when he found it, it bothered him.

This time it was easy for him to guess what was bothering her. Something had happened in the barn last night, and whatever it was had changed both her and Matthew. The usually talkative Vicky was silent through most of the evening meal, and only spoke when she absolutely had to. And Matthew might not have been noticed at all, except for the small amount of food he ate. Not that they were rude, or anything of the sort. Quite the contrary. They overdid their politeness. But the most telling fact was the way they refused to look at each other. Matthew kept his eyes glued to the food on his plate and only when handing Vicky the biscuits and butter did he chance a glance at her.

Vicky in return, refused to look their guest in the eye. Harold couldn't help but notice the tinge of crimson that crept into her cheeks as Matthew handed her the plate of biscuits. Then, the way she nibbled at her food, and the coquettish blinking of her eyes, reminded him of their first breakfast as husband and wife. That was after he had known her in a way no man had before.

Her actions that particular morning had caused him to worry. She had been silent and shy, as she moved the food on her plate aimlessly with a fork. Being a newlywed himself, Harold was frightened that he had somehow offended his bride, or maybe hurt her, or one of a hundred other things that had popped into his mind. But, he found these fears were for naught when they returned to their room. She was just as warm and affectionate as the night before, even more so. She had just been shy at the newly found desire and passion released inside her body. That seemed a lifetime ago, and so distant. But as he watched his wife at her chores, he thought of that passion, and wondered if it had been once again awakened. The thought gave him a queasy feeling in his stomach.

After supper, Matthew had ignored Caroline's request to read, and had gone to the barn. Moments later, Vicky had followed, offering no explanation. When she returned, she had begun her manic cleaning chores in the kitchen, and they hadn't stopped. Vicky had never been a sloppy housekeeper, but Harold thought their small kitchen was probably cleaner after the scrubbing she had given it than any hospital operating room he had been in. The over-politeness which had suddenly become part of her makeup had started to grate on his nerves. He felt like screaming at her to stop. The thing that bothered him most was the look on her face. It was the look of a young girl in love, and it scared the hell out of him.

Matthew had left early that morning, even before making coffee, which had become his habit. Harold heard the familiar beat of the paint's hooves as it headed out into the grassland. Harold stared at the barn and the small, seductive frame of his wife. Even dressed modestly in the long skirt and high neckline, one could see her small waist and shapely breasts. *God, how I love that woman!* He looked back toward the barn.

"Dammit!" He drove his fist into the post holding the roof over the porch. He had given his wife and child to this Indian to take care of after he was gone, but not *now*. Not while he was alive. *How could he? In my own barn. My wife and my*

144

friend. He hit the post several more times and the pain felt good.

The sound of a horse brought him out of his private hell and back to the present. He watched Matthew dismount at the barn and remove the saddle from his lathered mount. He was only a matter of feet from Vicky during this process, but neither of them spoke or chanced a look at each other. Matthew attended to his horse in silence, brushing his glossy coat and putting the beast into the corral with some fresh grass from the stack inside the building. Vicky was still sawing at her wood as though each piece was Satan, and she was a righteous angel trying to eradicate him from existence. Matthew passed her entrenchment on his way to the house with a touch to the brim of his hat and a curt nod. She in turn glanced at him in silence as he passed and returned to her battle. He gave Harold a brief nod as he passed him on the porch.

"You two fighting?" Harold asked as Matthew returned from the kitchen with a cup of coffee.

"No, what makes you say that?"

"Just the way you two are acting. She's acting too perfect, and when she does that, I know she's feeling guilty about something. And you're as sullen as a Comanche Injun."

"What the hell do you think I am? Irish?" Matthew scowled over the rim of his cup.

"No, but it's not like you, at least not like you've been since you got here." Harold shifted in his chair. "The both of you have been acting strange since you entered the barn yesterday afternoon. What happened in there, Matthew? You make love to my wife?"

Matthew set the cup down hard, spilling some of its liquid. The muscles in his jaw worked as he stood to glare.

"I've beaten men senseless for saying less than that."

"Have at it, if you want. I just asked an honest question and expect an honest answer. Did you, or did you not make love to my wife?"

"Okay, what's really bothering you, Lieutenant?"

"Just answer my question. Did you make love to my

wife?"

Vicky dropped the buck-saw and crossed the yard to stand at the foot of the porch. Matthew glanced at her, then turned back toward Harold.

"Damn you."

"Yes, I'll probably be damned to hell, unless God has mercy on my soul. But that still doesn't answer my question. I gave her and my daughter to you yesterday to take care of if something happened to me, but I didn't give them to you while I am alive. I would not have done that if I didn't trust you. Did you, or did you not, make love to my wife last night?"

"Why are you doing this to her?"

"Because I have to know."

"No, I didn't make love to your wife. I found myself wanting to, for an instant. But she's still pure as the snow. I didn't touch her. I'll leave in the morning."

Harold turned toward Vicky as a sob escaped her lips. She covered her mouth and spoke with a quiver.

"We didn't, Harold. I swear we didn't. If you must know, I...I wanted to. I was lonely. But we didn't. Oh, God, I'm sorry!" The tears came with a huge sob. "I didn't want to feel this way about anyone but you. You know that I love you, Harold. Please forgive me. Please...."

"Do you love him?" Harold asked.

"I don't know. I love you. You know that."

"Are you in love with my wife, Manhunter?" he demanded with his best Lieutenant's scowl, but received a glare that struck fear into his heart. He took a deep breath before repeating his question.

"Are you in love with my wife, Manhunter?"

"Damn you!" Matthew jammed his fist into the same post that Harold had struck earlier. Harold cringed as he heard the heavy timber crack under the force of the blow.

Caroline dashed from the side of the house to throw her arms around her mother's legs, and stared up at her face. "Wrong, Mommie? Hurt? Wrong, Mommie?"

"Come here. Both of you, come here." Harold held out

146

welcoming arms toward his wife and daughter. The anger that had been bottled up inside had somehow vanished. She had been true to him, and that was all that mattered. As difficult as he had been since being crippled, and as lonely as she must be, she still loved him.

Vicky took her daughter's hand and slowly came to him. He took them both, as best as he could, into his arms and held them tightly.

"No, Mommie's not hurt, honey," he said, kissing the top of Caroline's head. "She just got scared, like you do sometimes. But, she's all better now."

"I love you, Harold." Vicky wet his neck with tears. "I always will."

He watched Matthew as he headed toward the barn. He had also been a true friend. Harold knew a lot of men who would not have taken a cripple's feelings into consideration, but he had. Harold Jamison considered himself to be a lucky man. That was when Harold noticed the blood on the porch where Matthew had been standing. His friend was hurt.

Chapter 33

"That was damn stupid of you," Harold said as he examined the swollen hand. "It's your right one too. What's going to happen if you run into Hank out there tomorrow morning, and he decides to put up a fight?"

"Ow," Matthew said as Vicky began scrubbing the wound.

"Quit jerking. It's going to hurt worse if you keep moving around like that. Men!" She shook her head and moved the lantern for a closer look. "I'll never understand them." She glared at him. "Now hold still.

"Well, no wonder. You've got several pieces of my house stuck inside that cut," she said as she went to her cupboard.

"Your house? What are you going to do?" Matthew drew his hand closer to himself as she returned with a small bag.

"Hold out your hand." She pulled a small pair of tweezers from the bag and reached for his hand. His reflexes made him jerk as she began to probe the wound.

"Look," Vicky set her lips into a thin line and crinkled her eyebrows, "you have several large splinters in that cut, and if I don't take them out, your hand will get infected. Then you'll get gangrene and the doctor will have to chop it off. Is that what you want?"

Matthew stared at the floorboards as he slowly slid his

hand toward her.

Harold started laughing. "I've seen him in battles with bullet holes big enough to drive a team of horses through, and you'd never know he'd been hit. Now he acts like a couple of splinters are going to kill him."

"You're no better, Harold Jamison." She pulled a large splinter from the wound, and began probing for another. "You men will fight and try to carry on with broken bones, cuts, and wounds that are bad enough to have you in bed convalescing. But when it comes to small cuts and bruises like this, you act like children. Besides," she paused to pull another splinter that caused her patient to flinch, "I'll never understand why either of you feel you must hit walls and posts when you're angry."

"Well, it's better to hit something than to hit a person sometimes. Actually, I'm glad Matt chose the post instead of me."

"From the looks of your hand, you've been hitting something too." She glanced toward the hand holding his coffee cup.

"Yeah, well," he said, studying the discolored knuckles. "I hit the same post earlier. Only I didn't break it. And I was smart enough to hit the flat surface, instead of a corner like your patient."

"There." She dropped the tweezers into the pan of water and began wiping her hands on a towel. "Four splinters. I think that's all. But if that swelling doesn't go down in a few days, you might want to go see a doctor. I could have missed one or two."

She went to the cupboard and returned with a dark colored bottle. "This is going to hurt." She poured a generous amount on a clean cloth.

"And the first part didn't?" Matthew scowled.

"Hey, where'd you find that? That's my brandy," Harold said.

"It's disinfectant today, dear. Besides, I can find most anything around here, if I want. It's my house." Matthew gasped as she placed the cloth on top of the wound. Beads of sweat popped onto his brow as she wrapped the hand tightly.

"Better not chase any bad men for a few days," Harold said as he handed Matthew the cigarette he had just rolled and lit. "I think I could probably out-pull you sitting in this wheelchair."

"You had better keep seated for a while. You look as though you might pass out," Vicky said as she cleaned the table. "Harold, keep an eye on him while I fix dinner, and let me know if he starts acting strange."

"Hell, how am I supposed to do that? He's been strange since I first laid eyes on him."

"Harold Jamison." Vicky put her hands on her hips. "Caroline, please don't listen to your father when he uses bad language like that."

"It's the truth. In fact, we're both kind of strange, aren't we, Manhunter?"

Matthew laughed as he stood. "I'm fine." He waved off a protesting Vicky, and arched his back.

"Yes, I agree that anyone who's done the things we've done is strange. I mean, think about it. We put on that uniform, knowing we would get shot at. We took a chance that we might lose our lives at any moment, or that we would have to kill someone. We slept on the cold, hard ground and ate food that you wouldn't feed your dog. And all the time we were doing it, we boasted that we were real men. We thought we were better than others who stayed at home to raise a family. After all," he grinned, "we were tough. We're the real men." He flexed his muscles and laughed.

He turned toward the window and grew solemn. "Know what's out there, Lieutenant?"

Harold wheeled his chair to where Matthew was standing. Vicky laid the potato she was peeling on the table and stood behind her husband, watching the grass waving in the wind.

"I don't see nothing but the grass and a few trees. What do you see, Manhunter?"

"About ten miles beyond Leon you'll find a spread with a small run-down cabin. There's an oak tree standing beside a pond, with two small graves lying in the shade. That's where my wife and son are. If I'd been home, instead of scouting for Cotton, they'd be alive today.

"Yes, Lieutenant, you and I *are* strange. And we were wrong. Dead wrong. I lost my wife and son while I was fighting one of our glorious wars. You came home crippled from another. No, we were led to believe a lie, Lieutenant. The army didn't defeat the Indians. The buffalo hunters did. When there was nothing left to eat, they could do nothing else, and went to the reservation." He went to the stove and poured himself a cup of coffee.

"The smart men stayed home and took care of their families. The army was for fools like you and me, only I was the bigger fool." He toasted Harold with his cup. "And that's why you'd better ask someone else to look after your family if anything happens to you."

"What makes you any bigger fool than me?"

"I let my wife and son die while I was fighting the white man's war against my own people."

He fell silent as he sat on the wood box sipping his coffee. Vicky asked several questions about his family, but received no reply. She stared at her husband, hoping for some explanation, but Harold had joined Manhunter in his silence. She did not hear the Indian's voice again until after dinner, when he read to Caroline. The small girl sat on his lap listening, until her golden head drooped and sleep overcame her.

Chapter 34

The shadows cast by the moonlight danced on the wall as the wind rustled the leaves on the tree outside the window. Matthew listened to the moan under the eaves as he lay on the floor and told himself it was only the wind, but he knew better. They were back. The spirits of Prairie Flower and his son had come to join him, but this time they had brought an old friend with them. It was Matthew's own spirit that had died the day he saw them lying on the cabin floor.

He was suddenly standing beneath the oak tree, as his horse lapped at the cool water in the pond. The squeal of his son's voice caused him to turn as the boy ran toward his father. Matthew scooped the child in his arms and held him on his massive shoulders as he walked toward the cabin. A small slip of a girl with long black hair met him on the steps and lovingly slipped her arms around his neck. Her eyes were both wild and tender at the same time, like a deer. The soft, velvet touch of her copper skin excited the hell out of him. As the daughter of a Comanche Chief she was noble. As his wife she was a vixen and a lover. She was mother to his son. But most of all she turned their cabin into a home and brought happiness into his once lonely life. She was his life. He again tasted her sweet lips and held her shapely body in his arms. But then they vanished like the early morning mist and the pain returned.

His arms were empty and the hollow space in his breast grew larger until it consumed him. The spirit of Matthew Blue had gone with them. He died once again, like the thousands of times before when her ghost had come to visit. He was an empty shell, who wandered from town to town, searching for men wanted by the law. He seldom slept indoors or spoke to a human being. He was a ghost who prayed someone would send a bullet into his breast and ease the pain. And yet, he survived. He could not really call it living, only survival.

He had learned to cope with the pain in recent years, until he sat that day on the hillside staring at his cabin. That's when the ghosts returned. Their visits were short at first, and they only came in the lonely dark when men slumbered and the beasts of the night prowled, but after seeing Carol and Vicky, they haunted him during his waking hours when he required his senses. He would not have minded the visits from Prairie Flower or little Pita so much, for he loved them, but the pain had become unbearable, and he longed for the day when he could join them in their slumber.

He envied Harold for being a man who could simply give his wife and child away. Such a man must not feel pain. Or perhaps Harold only hid his pain well so he would not appear to be a coward. Either way, he longed to be like Harold, who had grown cold and calloused, and unfeeling.

They were gone now. The only the sounds left were the crackling of the logs burning in the stove, Caroline's soft breathing and the moan of the wind. But the anguish remained.

Chapter 35

Matthew rose in the silent hours before daylight and stared out the window. The moon cast its soft glow on a rooster perched atop Caroline's wagon in the yard. He found it almost impossible to flex his right hand, and cursed his stupidity. He could have had Otis and the horse both, alive and in his custody before the sun came up. He studied the swollen knuckles. Harold was right. If Otis put up any kind of fight, he'd be in trouble. Instead, he made a pot of coffee and sat on the front steps with a cup until he heard Caroline's squeaky voice trying to wake her mother.

~   ~   ~

"Vicky's got to go to town and buy some supplies. When the winter storms hit, there ain't gonna be much traveling done," Harold said over a mouthful of biscuit. "That road out there's bad enough when it's dry. Wait until it gets a foot or two of mud and ice." He studied Matthew as he cut his egg with a fork.

"Why don't you go with her? You're not gonna be chasing Hank or anyone else until that hand gets healed. You can help her with the wagon, and it'll give you a chance to talk to that deputy who came out here with you."

Matthew grinned as he took a bite of bacon.

"That bullet that took your spine must've snagged your brain, too." Matthew's eyes darted toward Vicky, then back again.

"What do mean by that, Matthew?" Vicky asked.

"One minute he's acting jealous and accusing me of sparking around with you, and now he wants us to spend the day together alone. Doesn't that seem a little strange to you?"

"That's because I am strange, Manhunter. You should know that by now. Go on, take Vicky to town shopping. I could go, but I'd only be in her way. I can stay here and take care of Caroline by myself." He laughed as Matthew stared across the table. Quit acting so scared. You're only going shopping, not into battle."

~   ~   ~

The ride in the buckboard over the rough road seemed short as Vicky chatted happily beside him. Her smile was enchanting and the rosy tint of her cheeks in the cool air enhanced her beauty. Matthew felt a tinge of sadness as they reached the outskirts of Gueda Springs. The next few hours would be taken up with her shopping, while he checked with Dave Price.

Several men and women paused to stare and whisper as he helped Vicky from the wagon in front of Carlson's General Store. He left her to her purchases and headed toward the sheriff's office. One old man whittling in front of Rattlesnake Jack's glanced up and snickered. Two women greeted him with angry glares and turned their backs on him. *Damned white people, anyway. What's got into them?*

"Well, how's the lover-boy doing?" Dave asked as Matthew entered. Sheriff Barry's greeting was even less friendly, as he only glanced up with a grunt, and returned to his paper work.

"And what the hell's that supposed to mean?" Matthew tossed his hat into the corner.

"You know what it means. You're supposed to be finding

a killer, not making love to the farmer's wife."

Matthew took a step forward and jerked him from the chair with his left hand.

"Here, now," the sheriff yelled as he came from behind his desk to separate them. "If you two want to have it out, go outside. I don't want my office messed up. Besides," he glanced at Matthew's bandaged hand, "I don't think you want to go hitting anyone with that stub of yours. What'd you do to yourself?"

"Just a small accident. It'll be alright in a few days. What's this mule-head of a lawman talking about?"

"Well, if you must know," Barry said pouring himself a cup of coffee, "Fay Ikenberry claims to have paid a visit to the Jamison farm, and says you and Harold's wife have a thing going. She says you and Mrs. Jamison are making love to each other, while her poor old husband can only sit in his wheelchair and do nothing about it. She's also been saying that she wants Mrs. Jamison kicked out of the church and some of the men to go out there and horse-whip you. A few of 'em said they would, but I told them they'd probably only get themselves killed if they tried. I'd planned on heading out that way tomorrow, and find out what's really been going on."

Matthew burst into laughter, while Dave scowled.

"Well, what have you been doing? I've been sitting here on my butt, like you and Cotton told me to, and I haven't heard a word. Have you even looked for Slim, or not?"

"First of all, I don't like your tone." Matthew seated himself next to the door and propped his feet up in one of the empty chairs. "But yeah, I have been looking, and I know where he is. I would have had him today, if I hadn't done this." He poked his bandaged hand in the air. "He's still out there near the farm. He actually never left. Whatever else I do with my time is none of yours or anyone else's business. And if you want to try horse-whipping me, you'd better be wearing a gun."

"Well, you can answer me this one thing. Have you been sleeping with Mrs. Jamison?" Barry leaned across his desk to stare him in the eye.

"No. And you and this whole town can go to hell."

"Fair enough, that's all I wanted to know. You can deal with the talk of the townspeople however you want. It's Mrs. Jamison I feel sorry for." Barry began shuffling through the papers on his desk. "She's a fine woman who's already been through ten kinds of hell, and this kind of talk will only cause her more hurt."

"That's all you wanted to know?" Dave tossed his hands in amazement. "I want to know what the hell he's been doing while I've been sitting on my butt."

"Well, get off your butt, then," Matthew snapped. "I already told you what I've been doing. In the meantime, you could've spent some of your time nosing around yourself. He's got to have food. I doubt if he's been coming into town to buy it at the store. Did you think to ask around to see if any of the people have had anything come up missing lately?"

"He's right." Barry handed Dave a piece of paper. "Mrs. Collier said someone took several loaves of bread right off her kitchen table a couple of days ago, and they never heard a sound. Also, old Carl Andrews said that he's sure he's had a couple of his chickens come up missing. I told him it was probably a fox, but he claims he's killed nearly every fox in Kansas. It might be a good idea to talk to them."

"Alright, first thing in the morning," Dave mumbled. "Only Cotton told me to wait here for you, and that you'd be checking in with me from time to time."

"That's what I thought I was doing." Matthew snickered as he leaned to warm his hands by the stove. "No, I'll admit I haven't caught your man yet. I almost had him yesterday, but he ran, and I was afraid of hurting that horse, so I didn't shoot. But, like I said, I've got a good hunch where he is. And if it'll make you feel any better, come on out to the farm. Give me a couple of days, so I can move my hand, and I'll give him to you.

"And, as to what I've been doing with the rest of my time, I've been working my butt off. I've spent most of my time cutting firewood and stacking it near the house. I just couldn't see making her do it all by herself, especially while I'm eating their food and sleeping in their warm house. I've been sleeping on the living room floor, I might add."

Barry chuckled. "Yes, and I'd probably do the same. Seems to me that some of these church folks who like to talk could have been out there cutting some of that wood themselves. They know he's crippled and she has to do everything by herself as it is."

"Let me tell you about that lady's visit." Matthew leaned back in his chair as he told the tale of Fay Ikenberry's visit, leaving out few details. Dave was laughing just as hard as the sheriff when he finished the story.

"God, I'd have given a month's salary to have seen that old bag's face." Barry wiped his eyes against his shirt sleeve. "She's caused more people grief with her tongue than a hundred Comanche arrows."

"Looks like the horse-whipping party's here." Dave nodded toward the window. They watched as a dozen or more men and women approached the jail with Fay Ikenberry leading the pack. Matthew opened the door and stepped out to meet them. He was quickly joined by Dave and Sheriff Barry as Reverend Nelson came running and stood between the crowd and sheriff, trying to catch his breath.

"What's going on here, Parson? Plan on holding meetings in the jail, now?" Barry said.

"No, I think some townsfolk want you to run what they consider an infidel out of town." He turned to give a quick nod toward Matthew. "From what I hear, they believe he's brought sin into our community and soiled one of our best citizens."

"That's right," one of the men yelled. "Now, if you don't run him out, we're going to teach him a lesson of our own." He mumbled something too low for them to hear, and a young redheaded youth holding the whip stepped forward.

"I'll agree that there's plenty of sin in this here town, but as far as I know, this man didn't cause it. He didn't have to. It was already here." Barry moved between the youth and Matthew. "Now, there ain't gonna be no whipping while I'm sheriff, and if I hear of any of you trying anything like this again, so help me God, I'll shoot your leg off."

"Now, listen here, sheriff...." the spokesman started, but stopped as Matthew joined Barry's side. A loud murmuring went through the crowd and then silenced as Matthew raised his hand.

He removed his hat and pretended to study the band as he talked. "Let me ask you a question first, before you beat me and run me off. Have you personally asked Mrs. Jamison if any of what you've heard is true? She's right in the store, over there." He pointed toward the wagon with his hat. A few members of the mob glanced at each other and murmured, while others shifted their feet.

"No, I didn't ask her," the man said. "I thought it would only cause her more embarrassment."

"Really? I don't see how that's possible," Matthew said. "Her name's already ruined in this town by your vulgar talk."

"Now, wait a minute."

"No, you wait," Reverend Nelson said. "It seems you've already tried and convicted not only this gentleman, but Mrs. Jamison also. You and this whole town, from what I hear are accusing them of adultery, and all that on the testimony of one woman." Fay Ikenberry had worked herself farther back in the crowd and was trying to hide behind one of the men.

"Now, I can understand why you'd get your feathers ruffled over the thought of an Indian being friendly with a white woman," Matthew said with a snicker, "yet, even now, you haven't asked me if it's true. And I don't think it's possible that you've asked Mrs. Jamison any questions either. Better yet, you haven't taken the time to go out to the farm and ask Mr. Jamison if these charges are true. Have you?"

"No, I'm sorry to say they haven't," the Parson said angrily. "I thought I had taught them better, but I guess I still have a lot of work to do."

"I'd like you to come out to the farm and ask Mr. Jamison enough questions to satisfy their curiosity. Then, I'd advise as many of these townspeople as possible to offer an apology to Mrs. Jamison for soiling her name."

"I will. I'll ride out to the farm, first thing in the morning.

And if what you say is true, I'll do better than that. I'll announce over the pulpit on Sunday morning how wrong they are. I hope I can count on your being there, Mr. Manhunter. But if what they are saying is true, I'll personally run you out of town."

"I doubt if there's any danger of your doing that, and I doubt if you will be seeing me inside your church, Parson." Matthew shook his head. "Any church that condemns its members and ruins their names, without even asking if the rumors are true, is not the type of a church I would want to attend."

"Yes, I can understand your feeling, and I agree with you. I had hoped my congregation was a little different, but it seems I was mistaken. I will talk to Mr. Jamison as you suggested. And I will admit right now, in front of all these people, that I, as a minister of God, have somehow failed to teach some of the basic fundamentals. I hope God will forgive them, and I hope you will too, Mr. Manhunter."

"I don't think it matters much one way or the other," Matthew said, and turned away.

The Parson spied Fay Ikenberry as the crowd began to disperse, and scampered to take hold of her arm.

"I wish to talk to you in private, Sister Ikenberry. We have some serious things to discuss." The woman paled as he led her toward the church.

"I think you handled that very well," Dave said.

"I simply told the truth. I've found the truth always seems to work best," Matthew said. "By the way, I owe you an apology. Some of what you were saying before the angry Christians showed up was true."

"What part was true? Don't tell me you have been sleeping with Mrs. Jamison."

Matthew scowled and shook his head. "No, but I can see that anyone within a hundred miles of her farm is never going to believe different. What I meant was I haven't spent as much time looking for Slim as I could have. That part is true. I've spent most of my afternoons doing chores and visiting with Harold. We had a lot of catching up to do."

"Sorry." Dave licked the paper on the cigarette he had been rolling. "I guess it's hard to believe a man could live in the same house with a woman like her, and not consider messing around some."

"I didn't say I haven't thought about it. Why's it so hard to understand that Harold Jamison is a friend of mine, or that his wife might be true to her husband, no matter how young and beautiful she is? Anyway," he placed a hand on Dave's shoulder, "I'll admit to not having caught our killer. Give me a couple of days before coming out to their place, and I promise we'll go out and get him together...." his voice trailed off as Vicky Jamison stormed out of the store empty-handed to climb in the seat of the wagon.

"Looks as though she might have run into some more angry Christians," Sheriff Barry said and started toward the store.

Chapter 36

Vicky was perched in the wagon seat with her teeth clenched, staring at the road leading out of town. Dave saw where a tear had mapped its way down her face, but after a quick study, he guessed it to be more from anger than anything else.

"Need some help, lady?" Matthew cheerfully offered his hand to help her back down.

"Matthew, oh…" She glanced at Dave and Sheriff Barry and tried to smile. "Good afternoon, Mr. Barry, Mr. Price. How are you today?"

"It looks like we're doing better than you are." The sheriff chuckled. "Run into some angry Christians inside the store?"

"Yes, I believe I did. I could not get waited on. And then, then a woman said....ooooh, I can't repeat what she said." She clenched her fists and glared at them. Dave thought she grew more beautiful the angrier she got. "Let's just say, she said some horrible things. Simply awful. Get in Matthew, I want to leave this town."

"But you didn't buy the things you said you needed." He surveyed the empty wagon.

"They wouldn't sell me anything. They called me…well, I can't say what they called me. Mr. Carlson finally told me, after he decided to speak, that he did not want my kind inside his store. Now, will you get in? I'll eat lizards and beetles before I purchase anything from this store again."

A heavyset woman who had been present at Matthew's speech covered her mouth with her fingers and dashed inside the store as a crowd began to gather.

"You are not going to feed your husband and daughter lizards and beetles," the sheriff growled. "Now, get down and let's go back inside. I believe George is gonna sell you what you need this time."

He was already inside the store by the time Vicky was able to climb out of the wagon. The crowd parted, and a few men who had witnessed the meeting in front of the sheriff's office doffed their hats as she passed. A heated exchange of words ceased as Matthew opened the door for her to enter.

"M-Mrs. Jamison." George Carlson looked pale. "The sheriff has just explained the mistake everyone has made. I-I'm sure sorry."

"Mr. Carlson," Vicky held her head high, "I have already explained to Mr. Barry that I would rather eat lizards and beetles than purchase anything inside your store. You have a dirty mind, and any bug I could find would probably be cleaner and healthier than what you'd sell me."

"Gosh, I'm really sorry you feel that way, ma'am, but...." the store-keeper's voice trailed off as Matthew leaned against the counter to study him. He caught his breath as Matthew removed a hunting knife from its sheath and began to cut small bits from a piece of jerky and pop them in his mouth.

"Let me tell you a true story," Matthew said between bites.

"This ought to be good," Dave said and plopped down on a pickle barrel to watch. The crowd backed away at the sight of the huge knife.

"I remember a brave once by the name of Two-tongue. Now, Two-tongue wasn't always his name. He used to be called Low Dog, because he ran hunched-over kind of like a dog. But he had a habit of saying things that were not true. Now, you've got to understand that, to a Comanche, lying is about the worst thing a person can possibly do." He cut another piece of jerky and popped it into his mouth.

"Anyway, he said some things one day that caused a lot of trouble. It almost split the village. We finally discovered Low Dog had been lying, but a lot of people had been hurt. My father happened to be Council Chief at the time, and took a knife kinda like this one and split Low Dog's tongue right down the middle." He held the jerky high and sliced it lengthways from top to bottom with the sharp knife.

"His judgment was that if Low Dog spoke with two tongues, he should have a tongue that resembled a snake's."

The heavyset woman gasped, "That's horrible." Several men burst out laughing.

"Now, if I was you, and I thank God I'm not," Matthew wiped the blade and returned the knife to its sheath, "I would help this young lady with her purchases. For all the trouble and embarrassment you and some of these folks have caused, I think you oughta give her a little extra help, like say, a discount, or maybe even some free groceries."

"Yes, sir." George Carlson stumbled as he rounded the counter. "Now, Mrs. Jamison, if I can see that list of yours, I'm sure we can fill that order right away. I might even be able to do as this gentleman suggested and pitch in a little extra for you and your family."

"Sheriff, are you going to stand there and let that horrible Indian extort our storekeeper like that?" The heavyset woman stood only inches from Barry's face and glared.

"I didn't see Matthew do anything wrong, Mable. All I saw him do was to tell George a story. I kind of enjoyed it myself. Now, if Carlson wants to give Mrs. Jamison a discount on her bill, that's his business. Or if he wants to give her the whole blamed wagonload because of the pack of lies y'all have been telling, I still can't see how that concerns any of us. Now, have a good day." The sheriff tipped his hat and ushered the on-lookers out the door.

Matthew pulled up a barrel and sat next to Dave as the storekeeper loaded large bags of flour, cornmeal, potatoes and other items from Vicky's list into the wagon. Dave, along

164

with several other men, offered to help, but stopped after seeing the Indian's disapproving glare. Dave sat back on the pickle barrel and watched as George Carlson finished the task by himself. Matthew helped himself to a cup of Carlson's coffee from the pot on top the wood burning stove, before snaking one of the five cent cigars out of a jar.

"What was wrong with helping the man load the wagon? You would've been getting out of this stinking town faster."

"Perhaps I don't want to get out of town faster. Maybe I like this town. It's a nice town in a lot of ways. It may have a few narrow-minded people, but in all, it's a real nice place." Matthew took another sip of the coffee and studied Dave's face.

"Besides," he set the cup aside, "if you constantly help someone fix their mistakes, they never learn the consequences of their actions."

"Now, let's see." George Carlson wiped his brow and studied the list. The blood once again drained from his face as Matthew towered behind Vicky.

"That's all free. Yes, that's right. It's payment for all the trouble folks in this town have caused you."

"That's very kind of you, Mr. Carlson," Vicky said, rummaging through her hand bag. "But I am quite capable of paying for these items. Now, if you'll just tell me...." She stopped, seeing the man was about ready to faint. She jerked around to see what he was staring at, and slowly closed her bag as Matthew shook his head.

"No, as I was saying, it's all free. Consider it payment for the trouble, ma'am. And I hope you good folks don't hold this little incident agin' us." He tried to laugh, but it sounded more like a sob.

"Do come see us again."

Vicky walked numbly through a crowd of mixed expressions. Dave had to fight two eager males in order to help her into the wagon, as Matthew spoke briefly with the sheriff.

"You'd better get moving," Barry said as Matthew climbed into the seat beside her. "Looks like rain." Matthew grabbed hold of his hat as a gust of wind tugged at the brim. The dark clouds on the horizon seemed to be boiling as a flash of lightning ripped the sky.

"I think you're right. Looks like we might get wet." Matthew grinned. Then, with a nod toward Dave, he added, "I'll see you in two days, and we'll go collect the guest you and Cotton have been wanting to meet."

With a click of his tongue, and a shake of the reins, the team started moving. Dave watched until the wagon was out of sight, then stared at the empty road awhile longer.

"Damn." He shook his head and laughed before turning to help another man carry George Carlson, who had collapsed face-first with a thud, back inside his store.

Chapter 37

They traveled more than a mile before Vicky broke the silence. "Why did you treat him that way?"

"The storekeeper?"

She nodded.

"Because I wanted him to remember this day. He needs to learn not to believe every bit of senseless gossip. I don't want him treating you or anyone else that way again."

"I will admit I didn't like being treated like an adulteress, or one of those women who work in the boarding house at the edge of town." Her voice was barely above a whisper. She turned to stare at him. "But, was it all a lie? I mean, I do have feelings toward you. Some of it may be true, Matthew. At least for me."

He shook the reins in silence as the buckboard rattled and bumped its way over the lumpy roadway. A covey of quail darted in front of the team as a rope of lightning lit the sky. It was followed by a loud clap of thunder that caused Vicky to jump. Her heart raced as Matthew helped her with her coat, and pulled her closer as small drops of rain began to sting her already frozen cheeks. She pushed back a damp curl that had spilled from beneath her bonnet as the wagon came close to jolting her out of the seat. She again caught her breath as Matthew's arm tightened around her shoulder.

"Are you alright?"

"Yes, I'm fine. Cold, but fine."

Was she? A sudden urge to cry swept through her as she thought of George Carlson in the store, and his terrible accusation. George Carlson deserved the treatment Matthew had given him, and much more. But to her own shame, she did have feelings toward the man beside her. And the fact that he was possibly the only real friend her husband had in the entire world made her feel even worse. Yet, he was a hard man. He had more than likely killed several people. She truthfully knew little about him, but, his very presence drew her in a way she could not explain. She felt her chin tremble as she choked back a sob.

"Hey, are you sure you're alright?"

"Yes, I'm just catching a cold, I think."

She could hear her grandmother's voice inside her head, *You just told a lie, and that's another sin, Vicky.* She buried her face in her hands, trying to stop her brain from working. She had a desire for a man who was not her husband, and probably a pagan to boot, and now she was lying. What must God think of her? Her sins loomed like a mountain in front of her. She cringed as a tree not far off the road exploded, split by lightning.

"Here, now. Here." Matthew pulled hard on the reins trying to hold the horses in check.

She was sure the next bolt would strike her dead. *God please forgive my evil desires.* The wagon lurched forward over a rough spot in the road as the heavens seemed to open and swallow them in sheets of wind-blown water. The stinging drops blinded them, making progress difficult. Matthew stopped the wagon long enough to pull an old blanket from beneath the seat and drape it across Vicky's already drenched head and shoulders. He then urged the team forward.

The tired animals labored in the thick mud as the wheels dug deeper and tossed small balls of mud at the soaked passengers. One of the globs of mud hit Vicky in the face as she turned to look at the old abandoned barn Matthew was pointing at. She managed a laugh as she wiped at the mud with a corner of the blanket. Matthew turned off the roadway and guided the wagon through the open door. The roof had half the shingles missing and offered only partial protection from the rain, but most of the siding was still intact, and gave some protection against the driving wind.

Matthew scooped her from the wagon seat and carried her to a pile of straw. She was stiff and her teeth chattered as she watched him clear an area in which he put a handful of the straw. She jumped as he kicked at one of the rotten stalls and began breaking it into pieces. Moments later, he had a small fire going and brought her closer to the warmth.

"You're soaked and as cold as ice." He pulled the wet blanket from her shoulders. "Here take my coat."

"What about you? Aren't you cold too?" She sneezed and sniffled as he wrapped the buckskin jacket around her shoulders.

"Yes, but I'm used to being cold. And I don't want to have to explain to Harold how his wife caught pneumonia." He threw another broken rail onto the fire and began rummaging through the wagon. He came back with an extra tarp, which he placed over her shoulders before sitting beside the fire to warm his hands.

"Come here, Matthew." She held up a corner of the tarp. "There's room enough for both of us under here. You're freezing."

She giggled as he stared at the tarp. "Come on. I promise not to bite you." He scooted to her side. She placed the tarp across his shoulders and pulled him close to her body. "Now, doesn't that feel better?" He nodded.

"Here, let me see your hand. Oooh." She gave a shudder as she took his bandaged hand in hers. "You're cold as ice. Look at you." She felt his cheek and other hand. You're the one who's going to get sick. You should have said something sooner." She pulled him close, hugging his body with both arms, and rested her head against his chest.

"There, does that feel better?"

"Yes, but you're not much warmer." He gently removed

the rain-soaked bonnet from her head and laid it on the straw. His hand trembled as he tenderly brushed the wet curls away from her cheeks and pulled her closer to his body. His breathing became rapid as she squirmed, burying her face into his chest.

"I don't know why, Matthew Blue," she stared up at him, "but, I find you terribly attractive." He didn't answer as she studied the curve of his lips and nose.

"You don't have to look so offended. I didn't mean it as an insult." She giggled and shifted her body in order to put both hands on his shoulders. The action almost placed her in his lap, with her face only inches from his.

"What I meant was, you stand for everything I find offensive. Guns, violence, chasing men." Her eyes darted around the decaying barn until they landed on the fire. "Maybe even killing. But, I'm still attracted to you." She sighed deeply and smiled.

"I know I still love Harold, and I always will. But my love for him has changed from what it used to be. It's....it's more like loving a brother. Does that make any sense to you, Matthew?"

He nodded.

"I know this sounds strange, me talking like this, and I hope you don't think I'm a bad person, but I believe in being honest. I've got to tell you, so you can help me fix it. I don't think I will ever stop loving Harold. He's been a large part of my life, but, we haven't really been husband and wife for a long time. Since I met you, I've found my feelings toward him changing, and to tell the truth, it frightens me. I don't know who you are, or what you've done. I only know you get paid to chase outlaws, and I can't love another man, because I'm a married woman. Am I making any sense?"

"Perfect." He nodded. "I understand." He gently brushed the damp curls from her forehead and kissed it the way he did Caroline's every evening.

She snuggled closer, feeling warm now, and relaxed. A smile crept across her lips as she thought about Caroline. *This is the way he holds my daughter when he reads to her. Well, not exactly. She actually sits in his lap, and I'm just leaning against him. But, close enough.* Her breathing became slow and even as he held her and gently stroked her hair. In a few minutes, her mind began to drift and she was asleep.

Chapter 38

Matthew sat stone-like, listening to the rhythm of Vicky's breathing. It seemed impossible to him that such a woman could find a man like him attractive. He thought of his progression from Son Of Plenty Horses, the young Comanche who killed his first buffalo at the age of nine, to Matthew Blue, the educated Indian and Army scout. Matthew Blue was the name the teachers at the reservation school had given him because they had had trouble pronouncing his Comanche name, and because of his blue eyes. And, of course Matthew was a Christian name.

He was certain that if Vicky knew his past, she would be repulsed by his presence. How could a gentle girl like this even know what the Manhunter was, let alone allow him to hold her the way he was doing now. He must tell her some day, and he knew that day would come soon. He knew where Otis Felts would be hiding, and he and Dave would ride out to get him. Then she would know. If by chance they didn't have to kill Otis, he would tell her who he really was, and then she would hate him and send him away, but that would be better than coming between her and Lieutenant Jamison, even in a small way.

Matthew had no idea how long they had been in the barn, but he woke her when the fire had burned itself out, leaving only a few red coals. The rain had died to a gentle mist. Wrapping Vicky tightly in the tarp, he carried her to the wagon and hoisted her to the seat.

"You know something?" he said taking his seat beside her.

"What's that?"

"There isn't much to you."

"I beg your pardon?"

"Well, you're only a slip of a girl. You're kinda small, and you don't weigh much."

"I'll accept the part about my weight as a compliment, but I'm hardly a little girl, Mr. Blue."

"I only meant that, it's amazing how little you are, when I've seen you do a man's work without complaining. Don't forget, I've worked right beside you hauling firewood."

"Thank you. I'll accept the whole compliment now." Her smile caused her nose to crinkle.

~   ~   ~

Travel on the muddy road was slow and difficult. The sun had set, and it was almost pitch-black by the time they arrived at the farm. Harold's mood matched the storm outside. He watched Matthew carry the supplies from the wagon with the eyes of a possessed man as he slouched in his wheelchair.

Vicky, on the other hand, was cheerful as she began to fix supper and care for her daughter. After a hot meal, Harold's mood began to lighten as Vicky told him of the day's adventures in town. Matthew noted how carefully she wove the story, leaving out certain parts that might offend or upset her husband, and only telling the parts that would make him happy. He understood that every creature eventually acquired skills to aid them in survival. Not everyone, however, used their skills. He had known some people who might be breathing and taking up space, but not really living. They never fought for their rights or the rights of others. They only whined when they were pushed aside or had privileges taken from them. When they finally ceased breathing, few people actually missed them. They were not bad people, simply useless.

Then, there were others who should be exterminated. They lived like vampires, sucking the life out of those around them. They never added anything to society, but thought they had a right to take what someone else had labored for. They weren't even honest thieves, like the ones who had their names and pictures on wanted posters. They hid behind their piety, in cities and towns across the nation. They sent their children to school and went to church. One might think they were normal, everyday citizens, but they were a deadly menace to society, claiming things they never earned.

Vicky, on the other hand, was like an artist applying paint to a canvas. The incident in the barn became no more than what it had been intended to be, shelter from the rain. There was no mention of their conversation, nor was there a mention of them covering themselves with the tarp and holding each other for warmth. Did this make Vicky Jamison a liar? He pondered the question as he sipped his coffee and listened to her. No, he decided Vicky Jamison was not one to lie, regardless of what the consequences might be. What he was witnessing was a survival technique she had developed, living with a man consumed by jealousy and bitterness. Vicky was not a liar, she was a miracle worker. Harold's mood changed with each word. What started out as a bitter evening, turned into a pleasant exchange between family members and a friend. She smiled warmly when her husband said he wished he could have seen the storekeeper's expression as Matthew demonstrated the cutting of a liar's tongue with his knife.

They said goodnight to each other and Vicky paused long enough to look at Matthew as he stood in the living room with his bedroll.

~   ~   ~

Sleep escaped the Manhunter that evening. He shivered in his blankets as the wind rattled the door and rain pelted the window pane. It was not the cold that made him tremble. He was a man born under the elements and had chosen a lifestyle which often required him to be cold, or hot, or thirsty. It was the feel of a small warm body pressing against his, and the smell of her clean damp hair and soft skin that had set his nerves on edge. Harold Jamison's wife felt good in his arms. Her words and laughter kept ringing in his ears. *Stop it, Matthew*, he shouted silently to himself. *You couldn't have her even if she were free.* Another scene floated across his mind as Cotton's words echoed off the walls of the cave.

"*That's murder, son. That's murder.*"

Chapter 39

Matthew rolled out of his blankets before the first rays of sunlight broke the sky. His hand was still swollen, and pained him when he made a fist. *You are dumber'n dirt, Matthew Blue.* It didn't seem to be getting much better, and Dave would be there tomorrow, raring to catch their killer. He strapped on his gunbelt in the darkness and tried drawing the heavy .44 several times, but found himself awkward and clumsy. He finally gave up after dropping the gun on the floor with a thud.

"Hi, Mat-ew. What you doing?" He turned to see Caroline sitting up in bed and smiling.

"Hi, pumpkin. Did I wake you?"

"Uh-hun. What you doing, Mat-ew?"

"Oh, just seeing if I can draw my gun."

"Why, Mat-ew?"

"You know, I don't really have any idea." He hung the gunbelt beside the door. "That's kind of a silly thing to do, when I could be spending my time with a beautiful girl like you." He pounced on the bed and started tickling her. They stopped their play as a disheveled Vicky jerked the curtain back and glared at them in her nightgown.

"Hey, you two. It's the middle of the night."

~   ~   ~

He spent much of the morning sitting and talking to Harold while Vicky continued her battle with the oak log in front of the barn. Then he played with Carol and Cuddles in the yard and gave the child another archery lesson, during which she insisted on being fully dressed with leather headband and feather.

Parson Nelson and his wife, Linda, arrived in their carriage mid-morning and Vicky stopped her attack on the fallen oak to invite them inside for tea. Matthew did not join them, but chose rather to entertain Caroline and her dog on the front porch, while Vicky and Harold talked with the minister. Matthew chuckled as he heard Vicky through the open door, admonishing her husband for calling Fay Ikenberry a profane word.

He had just decided to head for the barn, when Reverend Nelson joined him on the porch. The minister sat in one of the empty chairs and wiped his face on a white handkerchief, looking pale and beaten.

"It didn't go too well in there for you, did it?" Matthew said after a long minute. He leaned against one of the posts to study the pastor.

"No. Well yes, it did." He looked up with a grin. "I would gladly take a tongue-lashing like I got from you yesterday, or the one Harold just gave me, if every time I found that a member of my congregation was innocent of malicious accusations. I have always believed that Victoria was a fine woman, and I'm happy to find out that I wasn't wrong."

"Well, Parson, I'm happy for you," Matthew said. "I'll say one thing, though, those church members yesterday had a hell of a way of showing their true colors. But, that doesn't surprise me none."

"You don't like me very much, do you Mr. Manhunter?"

"No, I can't say as I do." Matthew studied the crow perched in one of the oaks at the edge of the yard. "But I wouldn't take it personally. I just don't have much use for men of your stripe, that's all."

"And, why is that?"

"Because I haven't met one of them who really lived as though that book they tote around means very much."

The Parson hung his head a second or two before speaking. "I'm sorry to hear you say that. I do my best to live like Christ would want me to. I'm not really a bad person, but, just like every one else, I'm not perfect either, Mr. Manhunter."

Matthew couldn't help but laugh out loud. He wrapped his arms around the post and faced the barn. "I don't know what Jesus Christ would expect out of you, but, I doubt that he would have acted the way your members did in town."

"No, I don't believe he would have either. That's why I'm here. To make amends and ask for forgiveness."

"Well, I can't see why you're feeling sorry for something someone else did, but I'm sure Mrs. Jamison will forgive them. That's in her nature." Matthew allowed his eyes to drift back to the crow as it took flight and landed in the nearest tree. "But don't ask me to. I'd find it awful hard to, after the way I've seen your type treat people."

"So, that's it. Tell me then, just what have you seen?"

"I don't think you really want to know."

"Yes, I do. Please tell me."

"Okay." He locked his gaze onto the man. "Perhaps you can tell me, Reverend. Would Jesus treat people the way we were treated at the mission on the reservation? Would he think Indians were human, or animals?"

"I have no idea what you are talking about. How were you treated?"

"We went hungry while the missionary and his friends gorged themselves with food and grew fat. We were cold while they sat in warm houses by nice fires for which we furnished the wood. We were told we were less than human. Perhaps a little better than dogs, but still less than human. And God, this loving God they spoke of, just might, if we were obedient, have mercy on us and not send us to hell. If we questioned any of their teachings, we were beaten. We were forbidden to speak our own language. It didn't matter that

178

most of us could not understand English. That was the language we had to use. And you'd better not make a mistake, because that meant you weren't listening, or were disobedient. It didn't matter if you couldn't understand what they were saying, you were wrong, and you got beaten.

"The headmaster, Reverend Blessing, received his training from Richard Henry Pratt at the Carlisle Indian School back east. His philosophy was to *kill the Indian and save the man*, which meant, we had to dress like white people, talk like white people, eat like white people, and smell like white people. But, we were still Indians. When we were not in school, we worked in the fields and got paid nothing. At night, while the boys slept, these men of God took the prettiest girls to their rooms and slept with them. If they got pregnant, they were sent back to their families to have their babies.

"We went to school during the day to learn what good white people should know. When we graduated, we were still Indians and no white people would give us jobs, so most went back to the reservation to be rejected by their own families. We dressed like whites and had been taught white man's customs. The girls, especially, didn't want to live like Indians in the dirty teepees or huts. We had been taught to eat Mission food. As bad as it was, it was still better than the food provided to our families by the government. We didn't even worship the same God as our mothers and fathers. Yet the God of the white man was mean and vicious, so, many, like me, decided to have no God.

"Back on the reservation, we had no jobs, no food, and no God, and in many cases, no mother or father. And, yes I do know about Quanah Parker who is getting rich in Texas with large cattle deals, but believe me, he and a few others are the exceptions. Most of the people I attended school with either killed themselves or turned to alcohol.

"You wanted to know, Reverend. That's why I don't have any use for men like you." Matthew snapped his head around as someone sobbed. Vicky was standing in the doorway beside Harold and Linda Nelson with her hand over her mouth, as tears streamed down her face.

"I....I'm glad you told me." The reverend cleared his throat. "I had no idea. I've never been a missionary to the Indians, although I have visited a few missions. The ones I saw were run by kind, loving folks, who cared about those they ministered to." He paused to clear his throat again. "I heard rumors about some of the others, but I only took them as that, rumors."

"George?" Linda Nelson said, "don't you know Reverend Ferguson, the head of the Missions Department in charge of the reservation ministry? Why don't you write him a letter, telling him what Mr. Manhunter said? Better yet, why don't you ask if he won't come out and talk with Mr. Manhunter himself?"

"Yes, I'll write him today, as soon as we get back to town." The parson stood and offered Matthew his hand. "Thank you for sharing your experience with me. It has been an education." Matthew shook the hand in silence.

Reverend Nelson and his wife said their goodbyes to Harold and Vicky, and climbed into their carriage. The parson grabbed the reins, but paused to stare at Matthew on the porch.

"I do hope you will join the Jamisons in coming to Sunday service. You might find it a refreshing change from what you have experienced in the past."

"I might. I won't say I won't come, but, you'll have to do something for me, if I do."

"And what might that be?"

"Take that cross off the building and nail an empty coffin in its place."

"Why is that?"

"According to your book, this Jesus is supposed to have risen from the dead, right?"

"Well, yes. Why?"

"Then, take down that thing that killed him, and show that he's alive."

The parson burst into laughter as he shook the reins. "You might have a deal, Manhunter. You just might have a deal."

~   ~   ~

After lunch, Vicky put Caroline down for her afternoon nap in the bedroom, and began cleaning the kitchen. Harold decided to join his daughter for a siesta. Matthew had just perched himself on the railing to have a smoke when Vicky glided out onto the porch and closed the door noiselessly. She studied him with amusement in her eyes.

"You can't run from me all day, you know," she said softly, and crept closer. "You'll have to face me sooner or later."

His pulse quickened as she inched closer. Her face was close enough for him to see the different hues in her eyes.

"Well?" She cocked her head to one side with a grin.

"What are you saying?" His voice was a hoarse whisper. "Your husband and daughter are right through that door. Your...." He left off with a sweeping hand gesture and Vicky burst into a fit of giggles.

"Matthew Blue, what in the world are you talking about? I only want to doctor your hand."

"Oh." He lowered his gaze as his face flushed.

"Come on, now." She took hold of his good hand and led him to the kitchen table.

Damned woman, anyway. Outside of Prairie Flower, he couldn't remember any female causing him this much trouble.

Vicky had twists to her he didn't think he would ever understand. Of course, men weren't supposed to understand women, especially one that was married to someone else. Vicky was Harold's problem, not his. At this minute, Matthew really wanted to be in the barn, caring for his horse. Instead, he had allowed her to take hold of his hand, smiling like a vixen, and lead him to the kitchen.

He could see Harold lying on the bed with Carol as he followed her to the table, and wondered how that child could sleep in the same bed with a father who snored so loud. Vicky pulled the curtain closed and went to the sink. She returned with a wash basin and pitcher of water.

"Sit down, silly boy." She smiled and went back to the

cupboard for her bottle of disinfectant. Matthew scowled, but did as he was told.

"Let's see if we can remove this bandage first. Hopefully, there won't be any infection." She placed his hand in the basin and poured water over it.

"Hey, that's warm. It feels good."

"I thought you might like it heated." She sat across from him and propped her elbows on the table, then cradled her chin in the palms to study him.

"No, keep it soaking," she said as he started to lift his hand from the water. "It'll make it easier to remove the bandages." She studied him awhile longer.

"You're one strange man, Matthew Blue." She lowered her voice as her eyes darted toward the curtain and back again. "One minute I'm frightened of this rather large, fierce looking Indian, who's going to ride into the wilderness and arrest, or maybe murder Hank. But the next minute, I see this gentle person playing with my daughter. Then, my emotions are taken for a rough buggy ride. You've stirred feelings inside me that I haven't felt since I fell in love with my husband. And right now, I'm looking at a frightened child who doesn't want me to take the bandage off his boo-boo. Incidentally, I should add, this child got his boo-boo by punching a post. Rather silly don't you think? Anyway...." She took a deep breath and sighed.

"Anyway, what?"

"I beg your pardon?"

"You said 'anyway,' but never finished."

"Oh, nothing."

Her eyes seemed to penetrate him and he shifted to look out the window.

"So, tell me, Mr. Manhunter, Matthew Blue, Comanche Indian, soldier, warrior, the one who crushes the evil and defends the weak. Which one are you? Or, are you all of them? I would like to know. I've never met a more complex person in my life. Which one are you, Mr. Blue?"

He remained silent as she began to remove the bandage from his hand. The wet cloth pulled easily from the wound to reveal the swollen knuckles which Vicky carefully studied.

"Well, looks like you're lucky. I don't see any infection." She released his hand. "Let's see how much movement you have." Matthew made a fist and relaxed his grip, then repeated the action several more times.

"Does it hurt?"

"Yes." He stared into her eyes.

"Where?" She held his hand in her left palm, and gently pressed down on the knuckles with her fingers. "Here?"

"No, in here." He covered his breast with his left hand. "I think I've wounded my pride worse than my hand."

"Oh, you silly." She giggled and rose from the table. "Here I am, trying to be a good nurse, and you're making fun of me."

"No, I'm not making fun of you. I'm making fun of myself. I'm terribly sorry for what happened. Staying here with you and Harold, and little Carol, has made me long for something I've always wanted. Something that, I don't know...it's hard for me to explain. I don't even know if I really know what it is. It's, just hard." He grew silent and stared at Caroline's toy box with its toys scattered around the floor.

"I know." She pulled a chair close to him and spoke in a whisper as she began to apply more of Harold's brandy and clean bandages to his hand.

"You were right, you know. It is dangerous, you being here. I told the truth the other evening. I did want you to kiss me. It's been so long since Harold and I....." She looked up as her face turned crimson. "Why am I telling you this? I'm so embarrassed. I don't even know why I told you what I did yesterday." She started to leave but Matthew held her hand tightly.

"I think its better," he said, looking at the half-bandaged hand. "Thank you."

"You're quite welcome."

He held on to her hand as they sat silently for a moment staring at each other. Her lips parted as she leaned closer and touched his cheek with her free hand. Matthew felt as though he were in a different world as he slipped his left hand through her golden curls and around the back of her neck and gently pulled her forward.

"Help me, Matthew. Help me fight this feeling. I don't want to sin against my husband." Her lips were moist and trembled as she spoke.

"I give you back your kiss." He gently brushed her cheek with his lips and rose from the table.

"I'll leave now. I know where Otis Felts is, and I'll take him to Dave. I'll try not to hurt him." He picked up his bedroll from the corner and paused at the door.

"It's better this way. I will only cause you and your family more pain if I stay."

~   ~   ~

It was approximately half an hour later when he heard the barn door creak and soft footsteps behind him.

"How is your hand?" A beam of sunlight slipped through a crack between the board siding and sparkled on her hair.

"The hand's fine." His brushing became rapid and the horse snorted and stamped his feet.

"It's a wonder that animal has any hide left, as much as you brush him." Matthew allowed the brush to fall as she stepped forward and allowed her shawl slip from her shoulders. "They're still asleep and I got lonely. Hold me, Matthew. Please hold me."

His heart raced as she slipped into his arms. He did not question the right or wrong of what he was doing. He simply sat on the hay and pulled her close as she wept softly.

"Dear God, I don't know what I'm doing. I don't know why I'm even here. I only know I don't want you to leave, Matthew. Can't you stay at least this one more night? Harold will want to know why you left, and I don't want to have to tell him," she said as he caressed the back of her head.

"Sometimes I think I'm going crazy living out here. No one comes to see us anymore, because Harold has run everyone away at least once. Sometimes there will be days on end when he won't talk to me. That's why I liked Hank staying here. And that's why I think I'm attracted to you. You're just the opposite of Harold. You're kind and thoughtful. I don't want you to go."

He held her until she stopped crying. She took a deep breath and let it out slowly. "Thank you." She rose like a lady and brushed the straw from her skirt before returning to the house.

Matthew sat in the barn until darkness overtook him. He vowed on the grave of his dead wife that he would die before he hurt or violated this woman or her family. She was pure and innocent up to this point. If he allowed this fire inside his chest to burn out of control, he would never be able to look her or Harold in the eye again.

He picked up his bedroll and walked toward the house, still not sure whether the flames had already reached that point.

Chapter 40

Vicky knew that she had sinned; perhaps not physically, but she had thought sinful things. There was no doubt in her mind that God was displeased with her and that in some way or another she must pay. Tears trickled from her eyes to wet her pillow as she listened to Harold's snoring. He had seemed unmoved by the events of the evening. He watched without saying a word as Matthew returned with his bedroll from the barn. He didn't even question the piece of straw he had picked from her hair as she served him his dinner. She wanted to scream, *Well, accuse me of something, so I can explain*, but he only smiled and enjoyed his meal.

When she was a child. there were times when she was able to picture God, Jesus and the angels on her bedroom ceiling. No such vision came this evening. There was only the blackness of the night.

Her loneliness felt overwhelming. In the days following Harold's injury, she had been able to find happiness by busying herself with her child and chores, but lately, much of what had brought her contentment seemed empty and futile. Even the arrival of Hank had brought welcome change. The joy the tramp had brought into Caroline's life had thrilled Vicky's heart. And Matthew? What could she say about Matthew? Her heart felt like it would burst.

Suddenly, the years of Harold's bitterness seemed like a weight around her neck. The wounds to Vicky's heart were deep. She had prayed daily for God to heal them, yet they remained. She wanted the old Harold back. Was that too much to ask?

She had actually laughed when the doctor at Fort Hayes warned her of Harold's inability to have sexual relations with her. He stuttered and cleared his throat a dozen times while trying to explain.

"I'm sorry sir, but I don't think that will pose a problem at all. We already have one child, and I do have my faith, so I'd not worry if I were you."

She had fully believed it would be an easy problem to overcome. She was determined to be fulfilled though hard physical labor, fervent prayer and Bible reading. After all, had she not been cautioned by her grandmother, only days before her wedding, that sex was only to be used to create children, and not to be enjoyed? If this were true, then surely God would take the desire away completely. Up to now, it had not seemed to be much of a problem. But thoughts and feelings that she thought were dead had crept into her mind. She blamed herself for having watched Matthew as he worked. She could see him that very moment, as his muscular arms glistened with perspiration every time he swung the maul. Then things had gotten worse. She allowed her fingers to caress his buckskin jacket hanging by the barn door as she spied him from inside the building.

The hardest part was seeing how tender he was with Caroline. He never yelled, no matter how trying she was. Even his scolding was gentle, while Harold had become harsher by the day, and Vicky craved to be treated with tenderness. She found herself wanting to feel Matthew's hands on her face and body as he caressed her daughter's head. Now that she had felt the touch of his hands, and his lips against her cheek, so help her God, she knew she wanted more…much more.

She let her hands gently map their way over her body. It was still young. Her hands, arms and legs were strong. Her stomach was firm and flat. She was sure that inside her, her womb was healthy and capable of having more children, which she desperately wanted.

More tears wet her pillow. Such thoughts were sinful and would only bring judgment. She was a grown woman with responsibility. She had a daughter to raise and Caroline would certainly need a healthy, godly mother to guide her. But she might have already gone too far, for surely God could hear her thoughts and know what kind of war raged inside her breast. Such sin could only hurt her, and bring pain to innocent people, including her daughter and husband. After all, she reasoned, it wasn't Harold's fault he was the way he was. Her grandmother had taught her well that God would always require reprobation for sin, and Vicky was sure this sin would separate her from the ones she loved. Certainly from this Indian.

Chapter 41

Dave closed the door as he stepped from the smoky heat of Rattlesnake Jack's into the cool night air. The streets of Gueda Springs were dark except for the yellow light seeping from a few windows. Music from an old piano drifted from the saloon accompanied by some raucous laughter. Fay Ikenberry's visit to the farm and the subsequent gossip had indeed stirred the community. Gossip always spread like wildfire in small communities, and was harder to put out. Even after Matthew's visit, and the scene at the General Store, there were still people who believed Fay Ikenberry's lies, and she had not been subdued by the reverend's tongue lashings either.

Dave admired Reverend Nelson's efforts to curb the talk after his visit to the Jamison farm, but his work had only had varying degrees of success at best. If the matter had come to a vote, Dave knew, the community would be equally divided. The half that really knew Victoria Jamison would stand behind her, while the other half, those who insisted on believing rumors, would say she was a slut who had been sleeping with a dirty Indian. Neither of these things were true. Vicky Jamison was a fine woman, Dave thought, and while Matt might be half Indian, he certainly wasn't dirty. Dave stopped outside the saloon to light a cigarette.

He would certainly be glad when they caught Slim and went back to Leon. He would go to the Jamison farm in the morning. That was good. He was tired of waiting. The longer they waited, the more the rumors persisted. He also knew he had to leave town soon before he did something he was sorry for. It wasn't what they were saying about Matthew that angered him. The Indian could take care of himself. But such talk could damage Mrs. Jamison and her family permanently. Dave had already threatened to shoot one such gossip monger earlier that day in the bar. He pulled his coat tightly and bracing himself against the cold wind as he headed toward the hotel at the far end of the street. He didn't actually hear the gunshot, but felt a sharp pain in his back as he was propelled from the sidewalk to land face-down in the muddy street. Then, everything went black.

Chapter 42

Harvey Blankenship buckled his gunbelt and checked the loads in the Colt. "You're not well enough to go hunting those men. Can't you please listen to reason?" His wife had never begged him for anything before, and the tone of her voice caused him to stop.

"I've got to, Alice. We've been married twenty-two years now, and you've been a larger part of my life than I'd ever admit. I know better than trying to scold you, but, those men who shot Dave didn't ask how he was feeling before they pulled the trigger. And I don't think they give a hoot how I'm feeling right this minute, either." He holstered the gun and put his hands on her shoulders.

"Dave's just barely alive, according to that telegram. He might even be gone before I can get there. I love you, but you know it's my duty as a lawman to do something about it."

"She's right," Mayor Parker said. "They have a sheriff in Gueda Springs. Let them handle this."

"This is only half their problem." He slipped his heavy coat on. "Dave's my deputy and he's my responsibility. I want you to wire Barry and tell him I'm coming."

"And what will you do if you see Frank Barnes or his men?" Alice scowled.

"Kill 'em."

Harvey hated to leave her that way. He only looked back once to see her standing at the corner of their yard watching him go. "God," he urged the horse into a trot, "let me come back to her in one piece. And help me catch those bastards. Help me kill them before they hurt anyone else."

~   ~   ~

Late the following day, Harvey needed help getting off his horse. "My God, old timer," said the man at the livery stable as he helped him to a chair. "Which one you trying to kill? You or your horse?"

He couldn't answer. The two-day ride in the cold, driving wind was hard on his aging body. Every muscle and joint ached and he felt feverish. His hands were numb, even inside his gloves. Someone, he couldn't remember who, helped him to the hotel and checked him into a room. After warming himself by a fire and downing a snifter of brandy, his senses returned somewhat. Still feeling feverish, he took a hot bath and tried to eat a steak dinner, then washed it down with another snifter of brandy and went to bed. It was mid-morning when he was awakened by loud pounding on his door.

After procuring his colt, he stumbled forward, still in a fog, and opened the door. The portly frame of William Barry pushed its way inside. He was followed by the doctor, whom Cotton guessed to be in his late thirties. He promptly made Cotton sit on the edge of the bed so he could take his temperature and listen to his heart.

"You can wire his wife and tell her he's going to live." The doctor glanced at Barry and closed his bag with a snap.

"But as for you," he pointed a finger in Cotton's face, "you're going to stay in town and keep warm until I say you can leave. You're getting too old, and your heart's too weak, to be out in the freezing rain chasing gunmen."

"Just who in the hell...." Cotton stood, but a gentle push from William Barry caused his knees to buckle and he landed back on the bed. Cotton had never met this young man before, but he knew he was right. He'd never felt weaker.

"Either you listen to me, or you're going to kill yourself and make your wife a widow." Cotton held up his left hand in a sign of surrender as the doctor hovered over him.

"What about Dave, my deputy?"

"He's in bad shape, but alive and kicking," Barry said. "I've already got three men out looking for Frank Barnes and his bunch. Everyone in town knows what they look like and will tell me if they show up around here again. So you'd better listen to what Doc says, and take it easy. You couldn't even sign the register when I brought you in here last night."

"That was you?"

"Yes. Old Jonas at the livery sent a boy to my house to find me. He didn't tell me it was only a busted up lawman needing help. So, I ran like hell, thinking Frank Barnes had returned, but all I found was you.

"You know," Barry said as Cotton got dressed, "maybe Doc's right. We're both too old for this business. Have you ever thought of retiring while you can still move?"

"Some," Cotton mumbled as he washed his face.

"I have. The only thing that bothers me, is that young men like your deputy don't have the experience they need, and might wind up dead before they can get it. Of course, we might be dead before we can teach them what they need to know. There's always that possibility."

~   ~   ~

After breakfast, they headed over to the doctor's house to check on Dave Price. The sign over the front door read *Dr. Wilmar Truman, M.D.* Dave was sitting up in bed, being fed hot oats by a pretty girl in her early teens.

"Well, I can see I didn't really need to worry about you," Cotton said. Dave tried to laugh, but grimaced with pain instead.

"This is my daughter, Susan," Dr. Truman said. "She insisted on caring for your deputy personally."

The girl blushed and started to leave, but Cotton held up a hand. "No, don't stop feeding him. That's probably the only way you'll ever get him to eat a decent meal. We know where to find him, and we'll talk later."

"I didn't listen," Dave said in a hoarse whisper. "You, Matthew, Barry, every one told me to watch my back. I didn't listen."

They retired to the dining room where Mrs. Truman served coffee and small, freshly baked cakes. "I think he's going to live now," Dr. Truman said. "Two days ago, I wouldn't have given you a penny for his chances. Though I don't think he'll be chasing any bad men for awhile."

"Boy, we make a sad lot, don't we?" Cotton shook his head and laughed. "A wounded deputy, two old broken-down lawmen, and an Indian bounty hunter wandering around, God knows where. And to top it off, we have Frank Barnes and his gang, and a killer on the loose."

"I know where Manhunter is." Barry sipped his coffee. "He never left the Jamison place. Dave was supposed to meet him out at their place yesterday, and seeing as our Indian friend hasn't come asking why Dave didn't show up, I'm beginning to wonder if some of those rumors weren't true myself."

Cotton had always judged a man by his eyes, and Barry's eyes were hinting at more than he wanted to know at the moment.

Chapter 43

Matthew had risen before sunup and readied his pack for the hunt. By noon, he decided that Dave had misunderstood his instructions. He felt good about himself this day. His hand felt much better as he cleaned and loaded the Sharps. Next, he cleaned and loaded his Colt, and practiced drawing the gun several times. Satisfied that he was at least tolerable, he hung the gun back on the peg inside the door, and went to feed his horse. By midafternoon of the following day he was pacing the porch like a caged bear. He had just made up his mind to head into town when he saw them coming.

"Where the hell's Dave," he growled as Cotton and Barry slid from their saddles at the porch steps.

"He's lying back in town with a hole in his back. We came out here, wondering where in the hell you were." Cotton put his hands on his hips and glared.

"He's what?" Matthew stepped off the porch to face them.

"Seems while you were out here, doing whatever, Frank Barnes and his bunch decided to plug Dave in the back." Barry spat on the ground and wiped his mouth on his sleeve.

"Is he alive?"

"Yeah, and...." Barry started.

"Good," Matthew raised his voice as he drew close to

Barry, "but for your information, Dave was supposed to meet me here early yesterday. When he didn't show, I figured he'd just gotten the days mixed up. I was about to go hunt him up when I saw you coming."

"Now, don't get so het up." Cotton grabbed Matthew's sleeve and pulled him back as Barry grinned.

"Yeah, he's still alive." Barry took a bite off a plug and matched Matthew's stare. "He ain't gonna be no damned good for awhile, but he's alive." He spit into the dust at their feet. "If it'd been me, I'd a been there yesterday afternoon, asking why he didn't show."

Matthew clenched his jaw and stared off in the distance.

"How do you know it was Frank Barnes?" Harold wheeled his chair closer to the steps.

"They didn't try to hide it none. One of 'em even went back inside the saloon and finished his drink before leaving town. They was gone before I could pull my boots on and get there."

"That's just horrible." Vicky held Caroline in her arms. "Matthew?" she said as he pushed his way past her into the house. "Matt?" She tried grabbing his sleeve as he appeared seconds later, carrying his bedroll and Sharps, with the Colt low on his right hip. He could hear Barry's voice as he headed toward the barn.

"Well, guess that answers one of my questions. Got anymore of that buttermilk, Mrs. Jamison?"

~   ~   ~

He'd stayed at the Jamison farm much longer than he'd anticipated. Much too long. Matthew led his horse out of the stall and tossed the blanket and saddle on its back. Where was the Manhunter? He somehow had gotten lost these past few days, and only Matthew Blue remained. He pulled the cinches tight, then gave them a tug, and tightened them again. Dave wouldn't be lying in Geuda Springs with a bullet in his back if he had done his job. He slipped the bridle over the horse's mouth.

"You're not coming back, are you?" The familiar voice came from behind him. The sunlight from the open door danced in her hair as her eyes seemed to engulf him in a violet pool.

"No." He looked away. "I have to go. Dave's been hurt and I should have been there. I should have left long ago."

"I'm really sorry for Dave. I hope he gets better. I knew you would be leaving anyway, very soon." He turned to see a tear trickling down her cheek.

"Goodbye, Mrs. Jamison." He touched the brim of his hat and nodded. "Thank you for your hospitality."

She was still in the barn when he led his horse into the yard. Caroline ran to meet him and he scooped her into a bear-hug. "I've got to go away for awhile. You be good for your mommy and daddy, you hear?"

"Uh-huh," she nodded. He stopped at the porch where the three men waited.

"I'm ready." The lawmen rose silently and mounted their horses.

"Going to go hunting?" Harold said.

"Yes, I've stayed too long. I've got a killer and a couple of skunks running around somewhere, remember? I'll play hell trying to find them all now."

"Not you, Manhunter. You'll catch 'em all. Hank and the bastards who shot your partner." Harold laughed as Matthew slid into the saddle. "Where's Vicky? You're not leaving without saying goodbye to her, are you?"

"No, we've already said goodbye. She's in the barn, looking after the chickens, or something."

"Well, goodbye Manhunter." He smiled sadly. "And good luck."

Chapter 44

Otis had built a small lean-to of limbs and reeds taken from the bank of the creek where he camped. He knelt beneath it now, turning the stick that held a rabbit as the small fire smoked and crackled, sending sparks heavenward. The smell of cooking meat told him that he would soon be able to stop the gnawing inside stomach, but he didn't believe he would ever be able to stop the hunger in his heart. He had left the Jamison farm early the next morning after holding the knife to Harold's throat, and returned Thursday morning to find those men there. He had retreated back into the grassland. The following three days were much of the same. He would slip through the brush, each time taking a different route, only to find that the buckskin-clad Indian was still there. The situation was beginning to anger him. He belonged there, not that other man. Cutting and stacking the firewood should have been his job. He scowled as he turned the stick to brown the other side of the rabbit.

He should have killed the Indian the day he had ridden into his camp. He could have retreated into the bushes long enough to draw him into a chase, then turned and shot him with the rifle. He'd thought about it several times since, and most of the time he was happy he had not pulled the trigger.

How long ago was it since that dark-skinned man had

shown up at their house? Three, four, or maybe five days ago? Otis couldn't remember. All the days on the prairie seemed the same to him. He decided to wait one more day to see if the stranger was still there, and if he was, it wouldn't matter. He'd go in anyway.

~   ~   ~

Shortly after daybreak, Vicky entered the barn to milk the cow and collect the eggs. She was feeling blue, and she knew that Harold must have guessed how strong her feelings toward Matthew really were. Although he had begun to treat her with a new kindness and love that had been foreign to him the past two years, the sadness in his eyes only made her feel worse. She did not hear the footsteps, and only when a shadow passed over her did she realize she was not alone.

"Oh, Hank!" She jumped to her feet and backed away. "My God. What are you doing here?"

"I came to see you." He stepped closer. "Is he gone? I don't see his horse."

"Is who gone?" She backed into the cow, who kicked over the milk bucket.

"The Injun with the buckskin jacket. What was he doing here?"

"Yes, he's gone. He was looking for you. Why are you here?"

"Like I said, I came to see you." He took another step as she backed away. "Why are you scared of me? There was two other men here, too. Did they say anything about me?"

"Yes. They said your name is really Otis Felts, and that you killed two young people in Leon. A young boy and girl." He took another step and she dropped to her knees shaking. "Oh, God. Don't hurt me Hank."

"I wouldn't hurt you for the world, don't you know that?" He sat cross-legged on the straw and ran a grimy hand through his matted hair. He looked much the same as the first day Vicky laid eyes on him. "No, I'd never hurt you or Carol. I love you both too much."

"It can't be true, can it? Tell me you didn't kill those two kids."

"Yes I did," he said and she slumped forward with a sob. Hank sprang like a cat, throwing an arm around her shoulders. "There, there, now. Don't you fret none. They deserved it. Both of them." He gently laid her back on the straw and began petting her golden hair with his grimy hand.

"You poor girl. You don't need to be scared of me, 'cause I couldn't hurt you no more'n I could hurt Carol, or my horse." Then he told her the story of what happened at Leon while caressing her head. Vicky's body began to jerk and wretch, as she rolled to one side and threw up.

~   ~   ~

Harold saw them coming from the barn and hurried toward the bedroom to retrieve his gun from where it was hidden under his shirts in the bottom drawer. He smiled as he felt the weight of the .44 caliber pistol and caressed the smooth walnut grips. It had been a long time since he'd held this tool that had been such a part of his life. Too long, he thought as he opened the chambers to check the loads. *Dammit, Vicky!* She had emptied the gun before putting it away and he had no idea where she had hidden the bullets. *Too late, anyway. They're inside the house.*

"Harold?" Vicky's voice floated from the other room. "Hank has come back to apologize." Harold carefully replaced the revolver in the drawer and rolled his chair to the doorway.

His wife was visibly shaken as she stood beside Hank in their living room. Caroline, who had been playing with her rag doll on the floor, ran to hug Hank's legs. He scooped her in his arms with a toothy grin. Harold swore under his breath, wishing his daughter had been outside somewhere, playing.

"Haven't seen you in quite a while, Hank. Where have you been hiding yourself?" Harold rolled his chair into the room.

"Over yonder." He motioned with his head. "How'er you

doin'?"

"'Bout as good as can be expected, these days. Want some coffee?" Harold rolled his chair toward the pot-bellied stove.

"Yeah, sure. That'd be nice. It's sure cold out there. Ain't had no coffee since I been gone. Shore do miss your cookin', Mrs. Jamison." He balanced Caroline on his knee after seating himself at the table. He accepted the cup from Harold's hand, and began to relax with each sip of the strong brew. Harold thought it might be just his imagination, but the man started looking a little more like the Henry Jones who had lived at their farm for most of a month.

Harold spent an hour talking with Hank about the cold weather, the harsh winter he was expecting, and generally making small talk, while his wife cooked breakfast. Hank held Carol on his lap and chattered away as though he'd never been gone or held a knife to Harold's throat. There was no mention of the two people he had killed in Leon, or exactly where he had been hiding. Harold marveled at how a man who had done such things could eat the way he did. He cleaned his plate and requested Vicky to cook more eggs, which she did. Harold had been acquainted with battle-hardened soldiers who could not eat their fair share for days after experiencing the horrors of war. Yet, nothing seemed to bother Henry Jones. Harold himself only picked at his food and Vicky said she wasn't hungry.

Finally, after Hank seemed to have satisfied his hunger, Harold decided it was time to broach the subject they had been avoiding.

"What are your plans now, Hank? Where are you heading?"

The man stared at him blankly, as though the question had never crossed his mind.

"You know you can't stay here," he continued. "Those men were looking for you, and I'm sure they'll be coming back."

"I....I....I know." He hadn't stuttered a word until Harold approached him with the difficult decision. "It's....it's just that

I'd hoped you wouldn't ha....ha....hate me so...."

"I don't hate you, Hank," Harold said calmly. And he suddenly realized that it was true. *I don't hate you, you miserable bastard. I feel sorry for you.*

"You frightened us, with the knife. But I don't hate you. I'm sorry you are having this trouble, though."

"M....Mrs. Jamison?" Hank turned toward Vicky.

"I don't hate you either, Hank." She had been staring out the window blankly. Now, she turned, and Harold felt his stomach churn as his wife walked slowly toward the pitiful creature and hugged him.

"I don't hate you. I love you like a brother." Harold set his cup on the table in disbelief as the killer broke and sobbed like a baby in her arms.

"God, I'm sorry. Please forgive me. I'm sorry." He had no way of knowing if Hank was praying, or if he were simply asking Vicky to forgive him. Maybe both, he decided. After Hank quit crying, he wiped his eyes on his dirty shirt sleeve and sniffed several times.

"I got to go now. Thanks for the breakfast."

"Could you wait for awhile?" Vicky said, and Harold's heart almost stopped. "I would like to pack you some food, and maybe a warm blanket."

Hank smiled and sat quietly while she wrapped dried fruit, biscuits, dried meat, and several other items. She bundled them tightly in oil-skin, and put them in a flour sack, beside her grandmother's wool blanket.

"We had fun together didn't we?" She smiled as she handed him the sack. "I truly enjoyed working with you. You were good company for both me and my daughter, and I do hope everything works out for your good. I meant it when I said I love you like a brother." There was a moment of silence while another tear trickled down Hank's cheek.

"You know what you'll eventually have to do, don't you?"

"No, what's that, Mrs. Jamison?"

"Before you can really find peace with God, or yourself, you'll have to turn yourself in." Harold almost panicked. His wife had gone too far this time, as Hank began his nervous dance, rocking from one foot to the other.

"I....I....I can't do that. They....they....they will kill me."

"Not if you can find Matthew. He's the one in the buckskin. He's the one Harold calls Manhunter. He's a good man, and he promised not to hurt you if you didn't fight him. I don't know what the others will do."

"Bu....bu....but even if I....I did go with him, they'd still ha....ha...hang me," he said.

Harold held out his arms and allowed Caroline to crawl into his lap.

"I don't know, they might hang you," Vicky said. "But it's the only way you'll find peace. You know that, Hank. You can't keep running from place to place, like a frightened, hunted animal. Don't you see?" She took hold of his shoulders and forced him to look at her.

"You're worth more than that. You mean too much to me, to my husband, and my daughter."

Hank continued his dance as his eyes darted from place to place. Finally, Vicky gritted her teeth and shook him.

"What's the matter with you? Why can't you understand what I'm trying to tell you?"

Harold tightened his arms around Caroline when she started to whimper. Hank stopped his little dance to study Vicky, who now had tears wetting her own cheeks. She was still yelling at him.

"If you keep running, they'll hunt you like an animal. Someone will kill you out there, somewhere, and we'll never know what happened to you. Do you want us to grieve over you forever? Don't you love us at all?" He quietly brushed back a loose strand of her hair.

"Hank, listen to me. God will forgive you, if you ask him to. I have already forgiven you. Don't you understand at all? You have to go back and make things right." Still more silence.

"If you're frightened of what might happen, go find Matthew Blue, and bring him here. I'll go with you to Leon."

Hank touched her cheek lightly, smiled at Caroline and

Harold, and walked to the door.

"Oh God, Hank," Vicky said. "You're breaking my heart. I love you like my brother. Don't you feel the same toward me, just a little?" He left without saying a word.

Vicky fell into Harold's arms. He held her and whispered his first prayer in years, thanking God for his wife and daughter, and because Hank was gone and had spared their lives. He also said a little prayer for Hank, because his wife cared so much about him. Perhaps God would have mercy on his lost soul and fix it like Vicky said. That would be nice. He kissed her cheek.

Chapter 45

Frank Barnes sat astride his horse studying the little white house with a stream of smoke flowing from its chimney. A small barn with a corral stood opposite the house, separated by the muddy roadway leading from Gueda Springs. A man sat on the porch in a crude wheelchair, watching a small blond-headed girl pull a homemade wagon in the yard. The road ended approximately where the girl was playing.

"You sure this is the place?" Frank eyed Hawk as the rest of his men inched their horses closer.

"Can't be no other," Hawk said. "The man at the livery said the Injun had been staying at the Jamison place, and that it was the last farm on this road."

"Well, I don't see him, or his horse."

"Maybe he left," the Mexican said. "He could have heard about the deputy in town, and went back to see."

"Yeah, that's a possibility for sure. I'll say one thing for him, he lives a charmed life. It was much easier to shoot his partner than it is to even find him. Damn, but I want to see his hide in hell."

"From what I hear, they're saying he's mighty sweet on the lady and that little girl down there." Hawk nodded toward the farmhouse. "Why not take one of them, and let the Injun come to us, instead of us chasing him all over Kansas?"

Frank stared at his right-hand man without answering, then eyed the child playing in the yard. "Hawk, I've never given you a proper share of the take, have I? I'll have to see what I can do about it. You boys wait here."

~ ~ ~

Harold looked up at the sound of a horse trotting through the mud. A large bearded man dismounted and approached him. "Is an Indian called Manhunter around here?"

"He was. Left yesterday for town. A friend of his got hurt. Who's asking?" Harold did not like the looks of this man.

"I'm an old friend of his, and I've been looking all over hell for him. Someone said he might be staying here. Is the lady of the house around?"

"No, she's not." Vicky had taken the wagon early that morning to visit Mrs. Clemson and would be back any moment, but Harold was not about to divulge that information.

"Huh, too bad. I'd of liked to swap howdo's with her. Hear she's a right fine looking woman." He took a cigar out of his shirt pocket and licked it before putting it in his mouth. "I see you're laid up. What happened?"

"Took a Comanche bullet in the spine. What did you say your name was?"

"I didn't." Frank lit the smoke and turned toward Caroline, who had ventured closer to eye the stranger. "Hello, little girl. You're sure pretty. Bet you take after your mother, 'cause you're a whole lot better lookin' than your daddy." He laughed. "You got big blue eyes, and yeller hair. How would you like to sit on my horse?"

Carol nodded her head as Frank patted the saddle.

"No, I don't think she'd better do that," Harold protested, but Frank grinned as he reached for the child.

"Aw, come on. He's more gentle than I am." Frank hoisted her to the saddle. He then put his foot in the stirrup and swung up behind Harold's daughter. "Besides, I'd like to borrow her for awhile."

206

"You can go to hell," Harold yelled. "Put her down."

"Yes sir, I probably will go to hell, right along with a bunch of other folks. But, you see, I can't seem to get in touch with Manhunter like I want, so I'll just borrow your little girl here, and maybe he'll come looking and I'll get to see him. Tell him Frank Barnes was here and I'll make sure to leave a nice trail for him."

Harold's threats and curses fell on dead ears as he watched them disappear over the rise. "Carol!" The stranger had ridden off, taking his daughter with him.

Chapter 46

Matthew was standing beside Dave's bed staring at the young man.

"I think he'll be fine," the doctor said. "Like I explained to Sheriff Blankenship, I wouldn't have given him one chance in a million when I first saw him, but he's tough. I believe he'll be up and around in no time."

Matthew watched the pretty girl shove a spoonful of hot soup into Dave's mouth. The tender look in her eyes revealed the obvious.

"You take good care of him." He laid a hand on her shoulder, and she looked up. "And do you both a favor, will you? When he gets well, marry him. Make him stay home." Her mouth dropped open as she turned her face toward the wall. "Make him get a job in a store, or become a doctor like your father. He's too nice, and too important to die."

Dave coughed as he tried to laugh and Matthew returned to the parlor.

Mrs. Truman was busy serving coffee. "I believe my daughter is smitten with your young friend, Mr. Blue." She handed him a cup and saucer. "She won't let anyone feed him his meals, much less do anything else. He is quite capable of feeding himself, you know. He seems like a nice young man. I do hope he gets healthy again."

"He'll be alright," said Wilmar Truman, stirring his coffee. "I guess Susan could do worse than liking a deputy."

"He's a good boy," Cotton agreed, while he studied Matthew's face. He set his cup on the table and folded his hands. "It's not your fault, Matthew. They would have tried to bushwack him even if you had been here. They may have shot you both. You can't blame yourself for what they did."

Matthew took a sip of coffee as he studied Sheriff Barry. "May I ask something? Why didn't you send someone to tell me about Dave when it happened, instead of two days later?"

"I was busy, boy," Barry growled. "You could have taken him with you last time you were in town, instead of making him wait two more days. Or I suppose you could have actually been spending your time right here in town, and riding out during daylight hours. Then, we wouldn't have had all that talk going around town, would we?" Cotton's eyes bounced between them several times.

"Now, I don't pretend to know where you were, or what you were doing, and I ain't a gonna ask, neither. But, dammit, boy, I had a shot deputy on my hands, and I was looking for the men who done the shooting. That boy in there was actually your responsibility, not mine. I just don't have time to run around and wait on you like you was President Garfield or somebody."

Matthew nodded as he studied the cup in his hands.

"Sorry, boy. That's just the way it is," Barry added with a shrug.

"No arguments here." Matthew shook his head. "You're right all the way."

"What's your plans now, Matthew?" Cotton asked.

"Find Frank Barnes, and don't ask me to bring him back alive." The room grew quiet.

"I'm not. But I'm going with you. There's six of 'em. You'll need help."

"You can't go," Dr. Truman said. "You're not well enough. You'll get out there in that cold and get sick again. Next time, you might die."

"Don't tell me what I can or cannot do." Cotton's face

grew red. "I'm healthy as my horse."

"Which was about dead when you came in the other night." Barry laughed. "Doc's right. Let me go with him. We'll bring the whole gang back one way or the other."

"No." Matthew set his half-empty cup on the table and rose to his feet. "I need to go by myself. This is my fight. I should have kept Dave with me. It's my fault he's hurt, and I'll take care of Frank personally."

~   ~   ~

It was growing dark when Matthew left the house. He'd spent the afternoon talking with Dave. Now it was time to get to work. He paused to stare at a large crowd gathered in front of the sheriff's office. The mud-caked wagon with a tired team looked familiar. A young boy ran toward him yelling for him to hurry.

"They got her girl!"

"Who's girl?"

"Mrs. Jamison's."

Matthew reached the steps in full-stride and shoved his way through the crowd. He found a disheveled Vicky caked with mud from her hurried ride in the buckboard. She was talking rapidly to Barry and Cotton as tears streaked the mud on her cheeks. She saw Matthew and bolted into his arms.

"God, oh God, Matthew. They've taken Caroline. They took my little girl."

"Who? Who's taken her?" He grabbed her shoulders and held her at arms length.

"A man named Frank Barnes. He said he wanted to see you. He took my little girl, Matthew. He's got Carol."

He spun without saying a word. The crowd at the doorway parted as his boots rang against the walkway.

"Wait a second," Barry yelled. "I'm gettin' a posse together, and we're leaving tomorrow at first light."

He crossed the street and walked swiftly to the livery. It was deathly quiet when he rode out of town. The only sound to be heard was the wind and the tramping of his horse's hooves in the soft mud. Cotton and Barry were standing on the porch in front of the sheriff's office. He could hear Cotton's voice as he passed.

"Feel kinda' sorry for those guys when he catches up with them."

Chapter 47

Matthew sat on horseback under a cottonwood, rolling a cigarette. A cold, misty rain drenched the countryside, slowing his travel. He had been following the tracks of six horses heading northeast, from where they had left the road. The horses must belong to Frank Barnes and his men. Few men had left town in that number in the past few days, and none that he knew of, outside of Barry and Cotton, had come this close to Harold and Vicky's farm. The thought of the warm, cheerful farmhouse brought a smile to his lips. He let his mind drift toward Caroline and her energetic play with the bow he had made for her. He also remembered Harold, with his many moods and changes, but the tragic look on Vicky's face as she stood in the sheriff's office quickly snapped him back to the present.

he men who left those tracks wanted him dead. They had also shot his friend, and now they'd taken Vicky's baby. There was no doubt in his mind they'd discard Caroline's body when they were through with her. All this just to get at him. *Why didn't they just step out into the street and call for me, like a true warrior? God, I would gladly have met them all. Help me find them before they hurt that little girl.*

He nudged the horse forward, then paused where the tracks turned north through a clump of trees. After a careful study, he made a wide circle and dismounted, then studied the tracks on the opposite side, making sure all six horses had exited the trees with their riders.

"Okay, if you've got any ideas, I'd like to hear them. We've got to figure they won't give us Carol without a fight." He started the horse forward once again.

"You know," he patted the horse's neck, "if we get through this, we're going to go back to our place where Prairie Flower and little Pita are buried. You've never drunk outa that pond, have you?" The horse shook his head as they plodded on.

"Didn't think you had. Well, I'll tell you. It's one more good drink of cold water. It's fed by a spring coming right out of the rocks. Yes sir, we're going to go there and raise horses. I might even find you a pretty little mare, like the one Mrs. Jamison has. How'd you like that?" He turned the horse back to the right as they climbed a hill.

"Yeah, I've got a feeling Prairie Flower would like it if we returned. It's time her and Pita got to rest in peace."

Chapter 48

Frank Barnes sat in a small abandoned cabin watching rain drip through the cracks in the ceiling. Although a fire crackled in the fireplace, the cold wind blew through the open chinks between the logs and beneath the door, and he was freezing. He had felt good when he shot Dave and the deputy fell in the mud. *Now he knows how Smitty must've felt,* he had thought as they rode out of town.

"Cold," Caroline whined as she shivered.

"Can't you shut that brat up?" One of his new men scowled at the little girl. Frank looked up from the cards he held as Hawk answered from his bunk.

"Why don't you shut up and throw a log on the fire?" Hawk didn't like Latrobe, and Frank knew that sooner or later his right-hand man would end up killing him.

It had been a whole day since they had taken Caroline, and still there was no sign of the Manhunter. Frank lay awake all night, positive the Indian would show. The constant care of a three-year-old child was beyond the capabilities of these trail-hardened men who had no children of their own. Any charm there might have been in having her had long since turned sour. Now, they mostly wanted her quiet and out of their way.

"Hungry," she whined again.

"Here," Frank handed her a cold biscuit. "Now, shut up."

"Why don't we leave this hell-hole and go south where it's warmer?" Mex said rubbing his numb hands before the fire. "I got friends in Mexico who's got warm beans and tortillas cooking right now."

"Because I'm not done yet," Frank said sullenly. "I've got one more score to settle. I want that half-breed bastard, Manhunter. I owe him one."

"Yeah? Well, we don't. We started out on this trail with you to get that thousand-dollar reward on Slim, not freeze our asses off, or get ourselves shot while you settle some score with an Injun."

Frank stared at Lefty. He was also new to the gang, and young. About seventeen or eighteen was Frank's guess. He didn't really know for sure, but he thought Lefty had a lot of bark on him, so he'd let him come when they left Leon. He'd never put much stock in a person who carved notches on the grips of his pistols, but Lefty's gun carried eight. He had heard of a man called Lefty down Las Cruces way, who had killed a gambler named Stevens who was known to be some shakes with a gun. Witnesses said Stevens had not even cleared leather when Lefty shot him twice. But all that aside, Frank had never let anyone talk to him like that before and he wasn't bound to let this kid start.

He dropped the cards and bolted from his chair. His back-hand brought blood from Lefty's lower lip as it caught the youngster by surprise. Lefty grabbed for his gun, but stopped when he found himself staring into the barrel of Frank's .44.

"Don't ever smart-mouth me again." He slowly holstered his gun and walked back to the table.

"We'll do both. I don't think Jim Larkin cares who he gives the money to, just so long as he sees Slim dead, and gets that horse back. Fact is, I think he misses the roan more'n his daughter."

"Well, it's been most of a month now, and we ain't seen him or the horse. How do you suppose we're gonna find him?" Hawk said.

"All we've got for our efforts is frostbite and empty stomachs," Mex said. "I haven't had no tequila since we started."

"They're right," Lefty said, wiping the blood from his mouth. "All we have left is enough hardtack and jerky for a couple of days. We're almost out of coffee too."

Frank knew if he didn't do something quickly, he'd lose every member of the gang. Their loyalty was only as good as the money in their pockets. He also knew his own tobacco pouch was almost empty. He shuffled the cards as his gloomy mood deepened.

"Hell, he ain't going to do nothing," Latrobe growled. "We might as well shoot the girl and do what Mex says. Head south."

"You shoot no girl." Mex jumped to his feet. "I never shoot no childs. Besides, I know a man who runs a cantina in Juarez, who'll give five hundred in gold for a young gringa chica like her."

"Sell her, like a slave?" Hawk sounded disgusted.

"Why not?" Lefty said. "You ain't gonna' take her back to her mama, are you? It'd be better than letting her starve to death out here, wouldn't it?"

"We'll leave first thing in the morning." Frank let the cards trickle through his fingers. "And there was nothing wrong with our plan. Manhunter and Slim both were supposed to be sweet on that woman and the girl. I would've bet anything they both would've been here by now. We left a trail her daddy could've followed in his wheelchair." He scooted away from the table and poured himself a cup of coffee.

"We'll head out at first light, just like Mex says. If Slim comes after the girl, we'll kill him and head for the Larkin's ranch. We won't even have to go into town. That way we can miss running into that sheriff. As soon as we get the reward, we'll leave the girl at the Larkin's, or someplace along the way. We'll just say we found her wandering around, somewheres along the trail. Happens all the time out here. The Larkins will give us enough supplies to get a ways south. And if we happen to run into that manhuntin' bastard along the way, I'll kill him myself."

~   ~   ~

They pulled out before daybreak in a heavy mist that turned into sleet, stinging their faces and numbing their fingers inside their gloves. Frank fell into line with the rest, as Mex took the lead. Caroline rode in front of Hawk, wrapped tightly in a blanket. The Mexican started them heading in a northeast direction.

"It's better this way," he said to Latrobe's protest. "If anyone is following us, we allow them to think we're heading back to Leon. Most of the time, a posse will run ahead and try to cut you off. But after going that way a few miles, we're gonna turn in a wide circle," he motioned with his arm, "riding about a quarter of a mile off our original trail, that-a-way." He pointed southwest and laughed.

"From here, we'll head to Mexico, where there will be tortillas and chilis and tequila. And the chicas? You have never seen such beautiful women my friends. Their dark eyes and brown skin and their breasts? A man could die amongst such beauty and still be happy."

Frank closed his ears. He was still brooding over his failure to pay Manhunter back for five years of his life.

It was almost noon and the sun had failed to break through the clouds. The sleet had stopped, only to have the rain return. Frank's toes were numb inside his soggy boots, and he began to think hell itself might be better than this. *At least it would be warm*, he thought. Mex stopped, holding up his hand to silence them before dismounting by a small grove of trees.

"We rest here," he said and started gathering sticks for a fire. The men agreed, and scrambled to find shelter beneath the trees. Hawk broke open several forty-four casings and poured the powder over the damp twigs and grass in order to light the fire.

Frank checked on the child, who had started coughing.

Her blanket was soaked and her hair hung in matted strings down her forehead. He felt sorry, for a short moment, for having taken her. But he only had to remember the reason behind the abduction to quickly decide it was worth any pain he might have caused her. It didn't matter anyway, he reasoned. If she got sick and died, they could leave her body in the bushes and not be bothered with finding someone to take her in. He heard a cheer, and turned to see the crackling flame and smoke from the fire.

Hawk moved Carol close to the flames and changed her blanket to a dry one as the Mexican began brewing coffee. The warm fire seemed to lighten everyone's mood, except for Frank's. He scanned the flat horizon with a scowl. "Two days with a stinkin', cryin', brat," he mumbled. "Where'n the hell are you, Manhunter?"

Chapter 49

The cold wind and rain seemed to have little effect on Matthew as the brown and white horse plodded through the mud. He was very near to the men he was chasing. He could sense it. His horse suddenly stopped with a snort and shook his head.

Matthew could see the smoke coming from a line of trees about two hundred yards ahead. "Well, looks like we've found what we've been getting wet for." He patted the horse's neck and dismounted.

He had followed their obvious trail to their cabin. There had been no effort on their part to cover their tracks. They wanted him to find them.

That first evening, under the cover of darkness, he abandoned his boots for moccasins and leggings, then stole silently to the cabin. Finding a spot near a window he listened. He could hear Carol's uncomfortable whining. He had thought seriously about waiting until they were asleep, and stealing her away that very evening. But on second thought, he decided that would be foolish. If he were caught, fighting inside the cramped quarters would have jeopardized the child's safety. He made his camp under some oaks a mile from their cabin and began his waiting game. They would move sooner or later and he would have a better chance in the open.

~   ~   ~

He rubbed the horse's nose. "You wait here, while I go have a look-see."

He slipped the Sharps from its sheath and proceeded forward on foot. Finding a vantage point behind an outcropping of rocks about a hundred yards from the fire, he surveyed the activity of the men. They were ill-prepared for such a journey this time of year, and were huddled around the fire half frozen. Caroline wandered a few feet away to study a ground squirrel she had spied. She looked frail and frozen herself, wrapped in a dirty saddle blanket. He listened to her raspy cough and decided he could wait no longer. He had to take her now. He returned to his horse and put the Sharps back into its sheath. It would be useless for what he had to do. Removing his hat, and taking only his pistol and a knife, he tied the horse to a clump of bushes near the rocks, and disappeared.

It was easy for him to crawl silently through the tall grass to within a few yards of their campsite. Matthew smiled as he thought how stupid they were. They knew he would be following them. But then, how many white people in the past had been caught unawares by Comanche warriors in situations that could have been avoided. They had also known they were in enemy territory, but somehow, they had thought the red man would expose himself and fight like a white man. He'd often thought that if the Comanche were as large in number, and had the weapons the white man had, the war between them would have certainly gone the other way.

He paused long enough to survey the camp once more. The men were gathered tightly around the fire trying to warm themselves, while Carol had wandered even further from the circle. *That's it, baby. Keep going until you're out of their sight.* How easy it would have been to kill them all at that very moment. He fingered the Colt in its holster then fought back the urge. It would only take one stray bullet to kill the girl.

He crept to the horses tethered on the opposite side of the trees. Slipping between them with a soothing touch and a quiet whisper, he cut the ropes that hobbled them. When the last one was free, he led the Mexican's horse away from camp and the others followed. They hardly made a sound in the soft earth. He glanced back toward the fire. No one had noticed the missing horses. They were still greedily trying to warm themselves while Carol froze. When he was about fifty yards from the camp, Matthew swatted the horse he was leading. It bolted, and the others followed with shrill cries and pounding hooves.

"The horses!" one of the men yelled as Matthew disappeared into the tall grass.

"Damn you, I told you to tie them up." Frank's voice was loud and raspy.

"I did. They must have broken free."

"All of them? You idiot!"

Matthew didn't wait to listen. He was running silently through the grass in a circle to get to Carol. He stopped at the edge of the clearing long enough to locate the men. They had gathered where the horses had been tied. Caroline was staring toward the cursing men. Matthew stepped into the clearing and put a finger to his lips to silence her. She stood frozen as he crept toward her.

"Hell, Frank. The rope's been cut."

"Manhunter!" Frank's voice rang loud and clear as Matthew grabbed Caroline. He dove into the bushes.

"There he is, and he's got the girl. Get him."

Matthew ran as his grandfather had taught him, his body almost parallel to the ground to hide his retreat in the tall grass. He ran a zig-zag pattern, only sticking up his head long enough to get his bearings. It would be difficult for Frank or his men to take careful aim, the split-second he was exposed. First, to the right. Then, several spaces to the left. Back to the right again.

Carol screamed as guns boomed behind them. The bullets sent pieces of brush sailing through the air. He bent closer to the ground as he darted toward the clump of shrubs that hid his horse. More shots were fired sending some of the bullets dangerously close as he made the last few yards. He dove behind a rock just a few feet from where the Pinto was standing. The horse snorted and bobbed his head.

"Don't stand there. Go get him!" Frank's angry voice could be heard between the gunshots.

"Stay right here, baby. I'll stop the bad men from getting you again." He kissed Caroline on the head and set her on the wet grass. He pulled the buffalo-gun from its sheath and knelt behind the rock.

The men were stumbling through the mud in their clumsy boots when he fired his first shot. The boom from the gun brought a scream from Carol as one of the men was lifted from his feet and sent sailing backwards. He slid another round into the chamber and fired again. The second shot broke another's leg and he fell screaming. Frank scrambled for cover as Matthew reloaded and fired. The round kicked up mud as it missed its mark and Matthew cursed his poor aim. The remaining men either ran for cover or chased after the horses.

Matthew reloaded his weapon and waited. He glanced down as Caroline latched onto one of his legs like a burr, crying.

"It's alright, baby. It's alright. They won't bother you again."

He chanced a look over the rock as Frank fired from behind a tree. His round from the hand gun fell far short of its mark. Matthew returned the favor and the .50 caliber Sharps sent bark flying from the tree. He heard the bandit curse, so he fired again. This time, a low-hanging branch near the puff of smoke from Frank's gun fell to the ground.

"Come on, baby. That's enough noise for now." He held Caroline in his arms as he led the horse away from the rocks. His first desire was to stay and finish what Frank Barnes had started, but that would have been too dangerous for Carol. *There'll be another time*, he told himself.

Mounting, he held the child in front of him and sent the horse into a trot. He could still hear Frank's curses and wild gun-shots as he rode away.

~   ~   ~

It was mid-afternoon and the paint plodded tirelessly onward, leaving deep imprints in the mud. The rain had stopped, but the wind brought a damp chill that caused Caroline's teeth to chatter. He still had not seen any pursuit from Frank or his men. He would have made better time if he didn't have Caroline to think of. Her cough and thin clothing worried him.

Slowing the horse to a walk, he chose a small depression, hoping it might shield her from the biting wind. The cold had a numbing effect on his brain, and he didn't realize the buzzing noise that passed his ear was a bullet, until he heard the loud crack of the rifle.

He flattened himself across the neck of the pony, shielding Caroline, and yelled. The horse burst into action, sending a shower of mud into the air. He had somehow let Frank Barnes get close enough to reach them with rifles. All he had been thinking about was getting this child home to her mother.

He glanced back as his horse raced forward and saw four mounted men gaining ground quickly. His pony was laboring hard in the thick mud, while they were on higher ground where the surface was harder. Matthew turned his mount to the left in an attempt to gain drier ground, only to have the animal slip in the muddy bog and go down. He fell hard, blinding himself in the mud. He could hear Caroline crying as he struggled to his feet. Raking the mud out of his eyes, he looked again. They were much closer now. Only two hundred yards away.

Grabbing Caroline, he mounted his horse again and dug his heels into the animal's flanks. The pinto burst into labored action, limping and breathing hard. Matthew knew he could not last much longer at that pace and started searching for a place to make a stand. He could see a cabin a quarter of a mile away and made for it. As they drew closer, he realized it was the same one in which Frank had held Carol hostage the previous evening. Another shot came dangerously close and he again lay flat, pressing Carol against the horse's neck. Another bullet kicked up mud in front of him. He looked back. They were still gaining; only a hundred and fifty yards now. The horse was gasping for air. Matthew pulled the Sharps from its sheath and gripped it with his right hand. The cabin was closer now. He glanced back. They were still gaining. The horse burst into the clearing in front of the cabin.

He held Carol in his left arm and threw his right leg over the pommel. Landing on his feet, he mounted the porch in one leap and shoved the little girl through the door. "Run," he yelled and turned for one more look. The next bullet sent him flying through the open door.

Pain gripped his body as he struggled to reclaim his weapon. He glanced at the hole high in the left side of his chest as blood dripped on the floor.

"So, this is how it ends for Manhunter." He choked back a chuckle. "But why in front of the girl?"

Sliding along the floor, he positioned himself where he could see out the door. They had slowed their horses to a walk and were stopping not fifty yards from the cabin. Caroline sat in the corner of the cabin crying.

"Oh man, that hurts." The burning inside his chest caused him to squeeze his eyes shut.

The men had started walking their horses toward the cabin. He painfully pulled the hammer back on his buffalo gun and gripped it tight against his right shoulder. The recoil from the rifle brought tears to his eyes as his entire body was racked with pain. The ball hit Frank's horse, knocking it to the ground and causing him to run for cover. A hail of bullets sent splinters of wood flying as the men scrambled. Matthew painfully injected another cartridge into the chamber, cocked the hammer, and tried to aim. The second shot landed to the right of the small pile of wood Frank was crouched behind. The effort left him light-headed.

"He can't hit the broad side of a barn," said one of the men as he rose from behind a stump. Matthew had never seen him before. He was young and husky, with a shock of blond hair poking from under his hat. "You must have hit him good, Frank. I'll go finish him for you."

Matthew again cocked the rifle. His next shot sent the young man pitching backward.

"Gawd! That's another one I owe you for," Frank's voice rang out. "You're running up quite a bill, Manhunter. Five years in that hell-hole of a prison you put me in, my horse, and three good men."

"I thought one of your men was only wounded. What happened to him?" Matthew said as he loaded his gun.

"Latrobe? You shot his laig off. He wouldn't of been no good to me no more, so I put him out of his misery."

"I'm sure glad I'm not part of your gang." When he coughed, he could taste blood and figured his wound would soon be mortal.

"I wish you were. I'd like to put you out of your misery right now, Manhunter. How bad are you hurt, anyway?"

"Me? Nothing but a scratch. Why don't you come on in, and see?"

"Ha? You'd like that now, wouldn't you?"

"It would be nice. That way, I'd get this little girl home in time for dinner."

It grew quiet as one of Frank's men said something. They spoke too softly for Matthew to understand what was being said, so he turned his head and smiled at Caroline, who sat crumpled in the corner, covering her ears and whimpering. The men outside fired randomly at the doorway as Matthew fought hard to keep his senses. None of the bullets were coming close enough to do any harm, but he knew they were using it as a screen to move in closer. He also knew he was losing blood and it would soon be over for him and Caroline. He fired twice more to no avail, and the pain grew worse with each recoil of the gun. He lay the rifle aside and drew his pistol and waited. He was beginning to drift in and out of consciousness as his eyesight grew foggy. *Okay, God. If you're really there like Vicky says, take care of Caroline.* A sharp crack of a saddle gun sounded at the corner of the house as one of Frank's men yelled.

"Dammit, he's got help. That sonofabitch almost got me."

Frank and his men returned fire, only to be met with more coming from the same place. Several shots were exchanged before the men out front ran for cover.

"That damned Cotton must have followed me," Matthew said with a weak smile.

Quick steps on the porch and another rifle shot caused him to ready himself for whoever might enter. More splinters flew from the doorway and a shadow passed overhead as his benefactor dove for cover.

Matthew smothered a cry of pain as strong hands pulled him from the doorway. He stared as a tall, thin figure crouched behind the wall and reloaded the Winchester. He blinked several times as he thought his vision must be failing. The man quickly fired several more shots through the open door.

"Hank!" Caroline started for him.

"No, don't, honey." He held up a hand. "You stay right where you are. I'll see you in a minute." The child obeyed and he returned to his post to fire several more shots.

"Back off. We'll wait them out," Frank yelled. A moment later all became quiet.

Matthew watched his savior creep toward him. He was tall and skinny. Long, matted blond hair clung to the tattered collar on his coat. His smile revealed buck teeth protruding from a pock-marked face. Nimble fingers unbuttoned the buckskin jacket as he saw to the wound in Matthew's chest.

Caroline crept closer to stare.

"Mat-ew hurt?"

"Yes, he's got a bad hurt, honey," Otis said. Then, turning to Matthew he added, "You got a nasty hole in you, don't you now? Let's see if we can stop some of this bleeding. Funny thing, you know. Some folks don't think an Injun bleeds red like other folks. Look's the same to me." Matthew coughed hard.

"Got a little blood on yer' lips, too. Must have clipped a

lung." He rolled Matthew to his side. "Went clean though to the other side. Made a nice hole in yer' back too." He removed his jacket and tore a part of his dirty shirt, making two small patches and binding them tightly to his chest.

"Ain't much of a doctor, want you to know that. But it might stop the bleeding long enough for us to get some help. We'll probably have to wait 'til dark, then maybe we can slip out of here, if you can travel."

"I'll make it. If I don't, you can take the girl and leave."

"Na." He frowned. "You'll do. I ain't never known a Comanche who would give up in the middle of a fight, nohow. Know'd a puncher down in Texas once, who claimed he pumped five holes into one of your relatives a'fore he finally kilt him. You only got one in you." He shoved more shells into the Winchester and grinned.

"You're Slim, aren't you?" Matthew said weakly.

"Yep, shore one and the same." He scooted to his post at the doorway before pointing toward Carol. "You stay there and take care of your friend, okay?"

"You know I've been chasing you all over hell, don't you?"

"Yeah, I know thet."

"If I'd gotten the chance, I would have taken you back to Leon, or killed you."

"I know thet too."

Matthew grimaced in pain. "In reality, I might not make it. Why don't you take Caroline and leave. I can cause enough ruckus with my Colt to give you cover."

"And leave you here like this? Cain't do thet." He shook his head. "We'll all go."

"Why? Why are you doing this? I might have killed you."

"Vicky's God."

He was silent then. A sentinel at his post, protecting his enemy. And Matthew asked him no further questions.

Chapter 50

The rain whipped horizontally against the side of the cabin as night fell. Slim slid silently through the rear window and disappeared into the blackness. For what seemed an eternity, Matthew could only hear the silky sound of the rain and the whistling of the wind. He had begun to think Slim had abandoned them when the thin figure reappeared through the window.

"Got to be quiet, now," he said in a whisper. "Found your horse. He's sure bunged-up, but he'll have to do."

He helped Matthew through the window and onto the paint, then disappeared back inside the cabin, to reappear seconds later with Caroline bundled up inside his dirty jacket. Leading the horse and wounded rider, he mounted his own horse, placing the child in front of him. In a matter of seconds, they were headed through the trees away from the trail. Matthew had trouble staying in the saddle. One moment he felt chilled to the bone, while the next he wished he could remove his jacket. After Matthew fell from his horse, Slim decided it was best to ride beside him in order to hold him in the saddle. The travel was slow and Matthew could not keep his eyes open. Finally he gave over to a restless unconsciousness, leaning his head against Slim's shoulder.

As the horses stopped moving he opened his eyes to the

gray dawn. His mouth felt like cotton, and his throat burned like fire. The rain had stopped, but the wind was cold.

"We're here," Slim said, helping him to the ground.

"Where?" It took three tries for Matthew to get the word out.

"Mrs. Jamison's place. Come on, let's get you inside."

Matthew's eyes took in the small barn and the front porch where he had spent many an hour talking with Harold. Slim opened the door without knocking and helped Matthew inside. It was warm and cozy with the smell of fresh brewed coffee. Harold looked up from the table as his daughter ran to him. His coffee cup slipped through his fingers to shatter against the floor.

"Oh, Carol!" He wrapped her in his arms. Then, seeing Matthew he said, "Hank, what the hell happened?"

"This man's been shot." He kicked the door shut.

"I can see that. How?"

"I was follerin' him, 'cause he was follerin' them guys what took your baby. Well, he sure enough got her away from them, and killed a couple to boot, but they finally got 'em cornered inside a cabin and blowed a hole in him. Think they was trying to kill 'em both. Anyways, I snuck 'em out the back winder and we got away." He paused to shift Matthew's weight against his arm. "I didn't know where else to take him. Besides, I had your girl with me."

"You did right in bringing him here. Better get him into the bedroom." Harold whipped his chair around and through the curtain.

Slim laid Matthew on Harold and Vicky's bed, muddy boots and all. Harold began tugging at the blood-stained jacket. "Matthew? How bad are you, boy?" Matthew's answer was nothing but a croak.

"Hank, go get my wife. She's in the barn milking the cow." Otis vanished beyond the curtain without a sound.

"Mat-ew hurt, Daddy?" Harold glanced toward his wide-eyed daughter standing at the foot of the bed.

"Yes, honey. Matthew's got a bad hurt."

~ ~ ~

Vicky's mind was elsewhere, and she had not heard the horses as they came into the yard. She jerked up with a start as the barn door flung open and Otis rushed inside. "Oh, Hank, you startled me." She held her hand to her heaving breast. Then, seeing the dark look on his face and his blood stained hands, she added, "Hank, what's wrong? What happened?"

"Yer' husband needs you fast, in the house. I found Caroline, and...." He was cut off as Vicky bolted past him with a cry.

"Oh, God! Oh, no....Caroline. My baby!" She stopped beside Matthew's pinto to wipe her eyes on her sleeve before touching the red stains on the saddle with her fingers.

"He's hurt, ma'am," Otis said behind her. "Hurt real bad."

Vicky burst into the bedroom to find Harold doing his best to remove the muddy boots from the man lying in her bed. "Gunshot," he said, glancing up at her. "Same dirty bastards that shot Dave. Damn them all to hell."

"Mommy, Mommy!" Caroline jumped into her mother's waiting arms.

"Oh, my baby! How can I ever thank you, Hank? My little girl."

The saddle tramp smiled broadly as she covered her daughter's tiny face with kisses.

"Here, let me help you with that." Otis grabbed one of Matthew's boots. Vicky leaned over Harold for a better view, as she held Caroline in her arms.

"Oh, my God." Her voice trembled as she saw Matthew's ashen face. "Hank, heat some water as quickly as you can. This man's close to death."

"Yes, ma'am." He scampered to the kitchen.

"Then get my daughter some dry clothes, and see if you can't find something for her to eat." She sat Caroline on the floor with another kiss. "You go with Hank, honey, and show him where to find things."

Her fingers trembled as Vicky bathed the wound. "It's

already inflamed. Look." She glanced toward Harold. "Have Hank fetch my basket of medical supplies from the top shelf." She bathed the wound with a generous supply of brandy, then applied a mixture of milk and linseed oil in an effort to draw out the infection, then bound him tightly with clean bandages.

Harold opened the bottom drawer of his dresser to get some dry clothes for Matthew and stopped when he came to the revolver. He picked it up with a smile, rolling the weapon over in his hands before returning it to the drawer.

"Thank you," he said as he handed the clothing to his wife.

"You're welcome, but he needs a real doctor, very soon." She sniffed. "Forget the shirt. Let's just cover him with a blanket."

"Okay. But I meant, thank you about the gun." She stopped to stare at him.

"The other day when Hank came back, I saw you two coming from the barn and came in here to get my gun. I had every intention of killing him, but it wasn't loaded. If it had been loaded, he would not have been here to get Caroline and Matthew back today." He turned to the man standing at the foot of the bed.

"Sorry, Hank. I was scared you were going to hurt us. I'm real glad I didn't shoot you." Otis stared back, only letting his eyes drift to Matthew, then back again.

"You had better get the buckboard hitched, Hank," Vicky said after a minute. "We'll take him to town."

"I don't know if he'll make it that far," Harold said. "You'd be better off if one of us went. Hank, saddle one of our horses and go fetch the doc."

"He can't go, Harold. They might arrest him. What if they don't listen to him and the doctor doesn't come?"

"That's a chance we'll have to take. I can't take care of him like you can."

Matthew made a rasping sound as he tried to speak and Harold hurriedly wheeled himself to the kitchen. He returned with a different flask of brandy than the one Vicky had been using as disinfectant. "Got my own stash." He grinned and popped the cork. Matthew choked as he poured some of the liquid into his mouth.

"That's horrible." He choked again. "Are you trying to kill me? If Slim goes to town, have him go straight to the sheriff's office. Ask for Cotton. He's probably still there. Tell him what happened. He'll help you."

Otis was out the door before they realized he was leaving. Vicky watched through the window as he took the two spent horses to the barn and led her own horse outside. He had begun to put a saddle on the mare when Vicky turned back to see Harold watching her.

"He'll be alright. You know that don't you?" he said quietly. "I know you have feelings for him. I've known for quite a while now."

"Yes, I'm sure Hank will be fine."

"Yeah, he'll be okay, if he can find Cotton, but I'm talking about Matthew."

Vicky felt the blood drain from her face.

"Don't feel badly about it. I can understand how a person might love two people for different reasons. I know you are my wife, and you will always love me and be true. He loves you too. I've known him for quite awhile, and I've seen the way he watches you. You have an astounding effect on him. I just wanted you to know, that's all." She knelt beside his chair and held him tightly.

The door flew open and Otis dashed inside, holding a rifle. "No time to get to town." He shoved the board into its slot, bolting the door shut. "Riders coming. Same ones what shot Manhunter." Harold rolled his chair forward and pulled the curtains away to peer out the window. Three men on horseback were entering their yard.

"They must've follered us," Otis said as he wrapped Caroline in a blanket. "You'd better take yer baby, ma'am, and go out the back way. Hide and don't come back here 'til they're gone." Vicky stood frozen. "Move!" he yelled and pushed her through the back door.

Harold grabbed his shotgun from where it stood in the corner and readied himself for battle. "Do as he says and don't

232

argue," he said as Hank closed the door. "I'll take the first two, Hank. You can have the other."

Vicky saw her husband poised with his shotgun through the kitchen window as she grabbed her daughter. Holding Caroline in her arms, she ran from the back of the house toward the tall grass. Her heart raced and tears brimmed her eyes making it difficult to see. *The shotgun*, she thought. *My God, it's empty!*

She could hear Cuddles barking as she reached the edge of the clearing. Wrapping Caroline tightly in the blanket, she hid her in the grass. Cuddles let out a yelp and ceased his barking.

"Carol, listen to your Mother very carefully." She pointed a finger at the child's face. "You stay right here with your doll and don't move, okay?" The little girl sat wide-eyed and nodded her head.

"Now, be a good girl and don't leave this spot until Mommy comes to get you." She nodded again and Vicky raced back toward the house. *Where did I put those shells? Oh yes, on the top shelf behind the platter grandmother gave me.*

She burst through the rear door the same instant the front door gave way to the force of a heavy blow. The first of the three men loomed inside. Otis dropped his weapon and threw her into a corner out of the line of fire. Harold yelled for the intruder to stop and he raised his shotgun.

Frank Barnes' hand fell to the gun at his side as Harold pulled the trigger on the shotgun. Both hammers fell on empty chambers with loud clicks. An instant later Frank's bullet hit Harold in the chest, propelling him out of his chair and onto the floor.

Vicky jumped to her feet with a scream as the Mexican entered and leaped at her. Otis glanced at the rifle on the other side of the room before pulling the knife from his boot. He pounced on the swarthy figure, knocking Vicky out of the way. With a whipping action, the gleaming blade flashed across the Mexican's midriff. The man folded with a scream. Frank's gun boomed again and Otis hit the wall and slid to a sitting position.

Vicky grabbed the only weapon she could, and charged. She brought the cast iron skillet down, and Frank yelled as it connected with his left shoulder with a thud. She caught a glimpse of light from the corner of her eye as Frank swung his gun upward. Her entire head seemed to explode with a loud pop, followed by a rending pain over her left eye. Then, everything went black.

Chapter 51

"You bitch." Frank stood over Vicky rubbing his shoulder. "Damn, that hurt."

He turned in a slow circle, surveying the men scattered on the floor. He stared at Harold before bursting into laughter. "Look who we have here, Hawk. The big Army brass in person."

Harold rolled his eyes to look at his assassin.

"I told you this was the same son-of-a-bitch what wandered up onto us a few years back and messed up our deal with them Comanches. Look at his face. Well, ain't he?"

"Yeah, I think so." Hawk spat on the floor by Harold's head. "Hard to tell. It's been so long."

"Na, it's him alright. I knowed it when I seen him the other day. You know," Frank looked the dying man in the eyes, "I read somewhere that you told everyone it was one of them braves what shot you, and you got some sort of medal or something. I just want you to know, before you go to the devil, that I was the one what shot you. Yeah, I put that bullet in your back. Hell, them Injuns, they run like scared rabbits when they seen you comin'." Frank stopped as Harold's eyes went blank. He was gone.

"Frank." The Mexican writhed in pain. "That skinny bastard gutted me. I'm dying."

"He's right." Hawk knelt over him and shook his head. "Cut clean through. Hell of a way to go. Never make it."

Frank squatted beside Otis. "Like using this toad-sticker, don't ya boy?" He snatched Otis' boot knife from the floor and felt the blade. "Sure keep it sharp. This the same one you used on those two back in Leon? Ya know, I'll bet it is. Know that Hawk? I'll bet this is the same knife.

He turned to the Mexican and laughed. "Don't feel too bad, Mex. At least he's kilt you with a famous knife." Then he plunged the blade into Otis' heart. Vicky, who had just come to, saw it and screamed.

"Damn, don't you ever shut up?" Hawk said, and slapped her.

"Take her into the other room," Frank said as he knelt beside the dying Mexican.

Hawk grabbed Vicky's arm and dragged the hysterical woman toward the bedroom. He pulled the curtain back and stopped. "Hey, Frank. Come here, quick. Look what I found."

Frank stood beside Hawk, staring at Matthew. "Well, hell, ain't I stupid? In all the excitement, I plumb forgot what we came here for."

Chapter 52

Matthew had been listening to Harold's attempt at keeping Frank Barnes outside the house. He looked around for his gun and found it lying on the dresser. Bracing himself against the footboard, he rounded the bed in an attempt to reach the dresser, but collapsed on the floor as the front door gave away and the first gunshot rang out. Then Vicky screamed and a man yelled in pain, followed by another gunshot. Suddenly, Vicky stopped screaming. Everything grew quiet, and his heart sank as Frank laughed. *They're all dead.* He searched for some other kind of weapon, but found none. *She's got everything high and out of reach of her daughter.* Then he thought of Caroline. He had not heard a peep out of her. Where was she?

He glanced around the room once more. *Looks like you don't have any choice, do you? You don't have any weapon. And even if you did, how are you gonna fight? The great Manhunter's last battle!*

Okay, this might not be the correct way to do this.... He closed his eyes. *And this is no time to try and impress you. Please, keep that baby safe. I'm sorry for all this. I'm sorry I wasn't any better. So, please keep Caroline safe. Not for me, but....* The prayer was interrupted by a woman's scream. Vicky was alive.

The screaming stopped with the sound of a blow. *Bastards!* He could hear her crying along with the voices of men in the next room. The curtain was jerked aside as Hawk dragged Vicky into the bedroom. Her face was covered with blood from a wound above her left eye, and her mouth was cut and swollen. Hawk grinned at Matthew as he flung Vicky on the floor next to him and called for Frank. *God, please. A gun....anything.*

"Want I should bore him real good?" Hawk said, pulling his gun from its holster.

"Naw, I already bored him pretty good myself." Frank grinned. "Look's like that hole goes clean through you Manhunter. A forty-four-forty does a pretty good job, don't it? Does it hurt? Good, I want you to suffer a little, like I did in that hell-hole you put me in."

"He's dying," Hawk said. "Look at the blood 'round his mouth. You caught a lung."

"Yeah, I know. That's why I don't want you to plug him just yet. I want him to die real slow."

Frank hit Matthew on the bloody patch on his chest, and the pain from the blow brought a grunt of agony and made him light-headed. "Oh, did that hurt, Manhunter? I'm sorry." Frank laughed again.

He turned to a whimpering Vicky and back-handed her across the face. "I said, shut-up, bitch!"

"Don't beat her too bad," Hawk said. "I might want to use her later."

"Who are you kidding? Her face ain't the part what you're interested in."

Please leave the room, and I'll get Vicky to hand me my gun. With the Colt, he might at least stand a chance of keeping them out of this room. But then, what about Caroline? He still hadn't heard from her. The two men were leaving the room when Hawk stopped to stare at the dresser.

"Hey look at this." Hawk grabbed Matthew's gun. "Might make you a good souvenir."

"The Manhunter's gun." Frank grinned as he fingered the smooth walnut grips. "Do you mind if I keep it Manhunter?

I'll cherish it more than my own mother. In fact, I'll tell you what I'll do. When I get tired of seeing you sufferin' like that, I'll put you out of your misery with your own gun." He pointed the Colt at Matthew's head and winked.

Matthew allowed his eyes to drift from the gun to Vicky. That gun had been his only hope. The bleeding from the wound over her eye had almost stopped, and was becoming a dark purple knot. The blood had dripped from her face to mingle with tears, and soaked the front of her dress.

"Know something, Hawk?" Frank said. "I think them folks back in town were right. He kind of likes this woman. Do ya', Manhunter? I mean, like this woman?" He jerked Vicky's head back with her hair. Matthew lunged forward, but collapsed with a cry of pain.

"By God, I think yer right." Hawk laughed.

"Well, then, we just might have a little fun, right here in front of Manhunter. That way, he can see just how much we like her too." Frank wrapped his fingers in her hair, and pulled Vicky to her feet.

"Frank! My God, help me." The cry came from the next room. He let her go and walked toward the curtain.

"Get the whisky from my saddlebag and let's see about Mex," he said quietly.

~   ~   ~

Matthew knew it would only be a matter of time before they returned to carry out their threat. Vicky had stopped crying and sat in a chair opposite the bed, staring blankly. A dark cloud moved across his soul as he listened to the men in the next room. When they came back, what could he do? They had his gun, and he was too weak to fight. What they had planned for Vicky knotted his insides. He would be willing to die that second, if he could prevent them from abusing her. He held his hand up in front of him and let it fall back to the floor. *There has to be something I can do.*

"Matthew?" He allowed his head to roll her way. The blank stare was gone and she was looking right at him.

"Harold's dead. So is Hank."

"I know."

She crawled to his side and laid her head against his wounded chest. It could have been his imagination, but he thought the pain was not so great with her head there.

"What are we going to do?"

"I don't know," he whispered, caressing her head with his right hand.

"Mommy. Cold, Mommy," came the small voice from the next room. Vicky bolted upright.

"My baby! They have my baby!"

Chapter 53

"Would you look at what we found." Frank held Caroline in his arms as they entered the bedroom. Ya know, Manhunter, I gotta be getting old. In all the scrambling around, I forgot all about this young-un'."

"Carol," Vicky gasped.

"Cold, Mommy." The little girl started crying as she reached for her mother.

"What is it that you Comanches do to children you don't want?" Frank said. "Don't you hold them by their feet and swing them around like this?" He grabbed Carol by the ankles and swung her in a wide arch while she screamed. "And bash their heads against a wall?"

"No!" Vicky sprang toward her daughter, only to be shoved to the floor by Hawk as the men laughed.

Matthew struggled to raise himself. "You bastard," he said through clenched teeth.

"Wait." Hawk caught the girl in mid-flight, stopping Frank's movement. "That might be the Comanche's way, but we can get money for her. We might not be able to find Mex's man, but there's a lot of folks along the border who will pay dearly for a white girl."

"Yeah, you're probably right." Frank kicked Matthew as he tilted his head back and laughed. Hawk drug Caroline behind him as they left the room.

Matthew dropped his head back on the floor with a groan. They would continue torturing Vicky and her child simply to get at him. He regretted ever coming here. His past had nothing to do with this family. They were innocent. He was the one Frank should torture, not them.

He closed his eyes and listened to the men in the next room.

~   ~   ~

"Here, drink some of this; it might stop the pain."

Mex coughed. "It hurts like hell."

"Well, you won't be hurtin' much longer." Frank laughed coarsely. "You'll be stokin' coal for the devil pretty soon. Might as well spend the night here where it's warm, Hawk. Bet we can find plenty of coffee and grub in here too."

"With all this blood?" Hawk glanced around him with disgust.

"Hell, a little blood never bothered you before. Here, help me drag these bodies out to the barn. We might as well take their horses and anything else we can find. It ain't gonna do them no good now."

"What about Mex?"

"What about him? He'll be dead soon enough. Might as well drag his carcass out there too, so he'll quit bleeding all over the place."

"Damn you, Frank. Damn you to hell," the Mexican cried in a strained voice.

~   ~   ~

Matthew heared the squeak of the hinges as the front door opened, followed by the sound of scraping boots as the men dragged the bodies to the barn. He rolled his head to look at Vicky.

"I'm sorry. If they hadn't taken my gun, I'd at least have been able to try." Vicky looked up suddenly and whispered.

"Harold has a gun!" She glanced at the curtain before opening the bottom drawer. She handed Matthew her husband's Colt with both hands, then wiped her palms against her skirt.

Matthew felt a wave of relief as he studied the weapon, but his heart sank as he opened the chamber. "Dammit." He glanced at Vicky. "It's empty."

"I've got the bullets." She hurried to the top drawer and pulled the small box of ammunition from under her petticoats, then scampered back to Matthew. She had just handed the box to Matthew, when they heard Frank's voice at the doorway.

"What's going on in here?"

Vicky sat on the edge of the bed as he entered the room. Matthew carefully slid the weapon under the bed with his left hand and lifted Harold's brandy flask with his right.

"Let's see that." Frank grabbed the flask from Matthew. "Six-year-old brandy. Too good to waste on a dying half-breed like you, Manhunter." He snorted and left the room.

The Mexican cursed as they carried him toward the barn. Matthew painfully loaded the weapon and waited.

Chapter 54

Frank and Hawk sat by the pot-bellied stove drinking Harold's brandy. They soon tired of hearing Caroline cry and sent her to her mother. Vicky put her daughter in the bed and covered her with the heavy quilts, then sat stroking her head. Matthew was growing weaker and his breathing more labored. He caught her by the arm as she covered him with a quilt, and pulled her close.

"Take the gun and your daughter, then climb out the window," he said in a whisper. "Run as fast as you can. They're only interested in me. You just might make it."

"No." A tear dropped to land on his cheek. "I'll not leave you. Too much has happened already. They'll kill you."

"I'm already dead. Save your daughter."

"No, and I'm not going to argue with you, Matthew Blue. We will go through this together, no matter what happens."

Matthew nodded and cocked the revolver. Vicky locked her gaze on the curtain. Her husband and Hank were already dead, and Matthew would soon be if he didn't get some medical help. Ice swept through her veins as she realized what was about to happen to Caroline, and her too. They were going to sell her child, and the unspeakable things they had planned for her caused her stomach to knot. Her hand shook as she brushed the hair back on Matthew's forehead.

Oh, God! I don't know what to do. Please help me...tell me what to do...God, please.

~   ~   ~

The effects of the brandy and the whiskey on an empty stomach caused Frank's speech to slur. He revelled at his change of fortune. They could rightfully collect the fifteen hundred in reward money, and even more when they sold the little brat. Most of all, he relished the fact that the man he had hated for so long had been dumped into his hands. He wanted to cherish the victory to its fullest.

"Ya know, Hawk? Now that Manhunter and his deputy are out of the way, I got a feeling our luck's changed for good. Hell, we don't need to go to Mexico. We can have most anything we want, right here, and who's gonna stop us?"

It took most of an hour to finish the brandy and one bottle of whiskey. Frank's lips were numb, and his ears had started to ring as he rose to his feet.

"I think it's time to visit the lady of the house. Manhunter can sleep on the floor while we keep his bed warm, along with his woman."

They staggered to the bedroom and jerked the curtain back. A disheveled Vicky Jamison sat next to her daughter on the bed. The sight of the trembling woman sent a surge through Frank's veins as he entered the room. He gasped as Matthew pointed the cocked revolver at him.

Chapter 55

Frank reached for his own gun and Vicky dove across the bed, shielding Caroline with her own body. Mushroom smoke leaped from the gun as Matthew pulled the trigger and Frank was propelled against the dresser. He swung the gun toward the doorway and fired twice. Hawk howled in pain as he dove for cover and crawled toward the potbellied stove. Frank fired, and his bullet bit into the wall next to Matthew's head. Matthew swung back around and fired three more times, before the hammer fell with a dull click.

Vicky coughed and blinked at the smoke-filled room. There was only one man lying next to the dresser. She crawled to the edge of the bed and stared at Matthew. Her heart almost stopped as his head rolled to one side and the gun slipped from his limp hand. "No, God. No...."

She rolled off the bed and held a shaking hand against his forehead. There was a bullet hole in her wall, but Matthew himself had no new wounds that she could see. He felt cold and clammy. Her bottom lip trembled as she felt his chest. He was still alive. His breathing was shallow, and his heartbeat was weak, but he was still alive.

"Thank you," she whispered.

Caroline crawled out of bed and into Matthew's arms. He opened his eyes and pulled her closer, then nodded at Vicky, who had just noticed the moaning coming from the next room.

"Hawk is still alive and has a gun," he said in a hoarse whisper. He shoved Harold's Colt toward her. "It's empty. You'll have to do something, or he will kill us all."

She grabbed the box of ammunition, only to spill its contents on the floor. The bullets scattered like a child's marbles. She glanced at the doorway. He was still not there.

Scrambling on her knees, she raked at the bullets with trembling fingers, then tried to load the weapon, only to drop them again. "God, help me," she cried, clawing at the brass cartridges a second time.

With the gun fully loaded, she staggered to lean against the dresser. Frank's body lay partly in the doorway with a part of his temple missing and another hole in his neck.

"Dammit, Frank, he shot my face off! Frank?"

Vicky stepped over the body to see Hawk on the floor holding a blood-stained hand against his cheek. He cursed, and scrambled toward his gunbelt hanging on a chair.

"Don't!" Vicky rushed to point the gun at his head. Hawk froze as she pulled the hammer back with both thumbs.

"Oh God, lady, don't kill me." He held up both hands. Vicky saw where a bloody trough had been cut across his cheek.

"Don't kill you? You murdered my husband and friend. You were going to rape me and sell my daughter as a slave. You shot Matthew and he's dying! Why shouldn't I kill you?" She was a heartbeat from taking this man's life.

He made a quick dive for Otis' knife and she pulled the trigger. The roar was deafening and Vicky had to fight hard to keep from fainting.

"Oh, God, lady! You shot my ear off." He rolled on the floor with his hand covering the left side of his head. "Don't shoot me no more. I didn't kill your husband. Frank did. I swear he done it. I'll do what you want. Just don't shoot me again."

"Pick up the knife, carefully, and throw it out the door. Your gun too," she said.

"Frank?"

"He's dead, I think. Now, do as I say."

Vicky grabbed her coat from a peg by the front door and slipped it on.

"I don't want to kill you, but I will, if you don't do exactly as I say. You and I are going to go to the barn. I want you to hitch the team to the buckboard and wrap my daughter and Matthew in blankets. Then, you're going to put them in the back of the wagon. Do you understand?" Her voice trembled.

"Yes, ma'am. Then what?"

"We are going to take them to town, and you had better pray that nothing happens along the way. I'll kill you if it does."

"I'm bleeding, lady. I'll die before we get to town."

"You'll die right now, if you don't try."

She followed him, staying just out of reach as he carried out her orders.

"He'll never make it." Hawk eyed Matthew in the back of the buckboard. "He's too weak."

"Then, you won't make it either," she said. "Now, get in the driver's seat."

She sat in the back with her gun fixed on his back as Hawk urged the team through the cold night air toward Gueda Springs. Caroline sat wrapped in a warm blanket cuddled next to her. Matthew's head lay cradled in Vicky's lap while she rested the hand holding the gun against his wounded chest.

Chapter 56

Matthew sat by the window in the hotel room where he had been convalescing. His fingers dug into the arms of the chair as he watched the boarding house across the street. Jonathan Williams, along with the local reporter, was trying to crowd the small figure dressed in black as she exited the buggy. A photographer who had just arrived from St. Louis quickly set his tripod camera on the steps, trying to take a photograph. Matthew heard Sheriff Barry roar as he shoved them aside, knocking the camera over.

"Vultures! Leave her alone!" he yelled as Cotton and Barry rushed Vicky inside.

"Get back into bed," Dr. Truman ordered as he entered the room. "How do you think you're going to get well?"

"I was just...."

"I know what you were doing, and I don't blame you. But you still need to stay in bed."

Matthew obediently crawled back into the bed and pulled the blankets around him.

"I don't know how you had the strength to climb out of bed in the first place. You'll be fine, if you can learn to follow orders." Truman checked Matthew's pulse. "Actually, you know, by all rights, you should be dead. Except for that young lady's medical assistance, and the fact that you have the constitution of a horse, you would be in the cemetery with the others right now. Now, do what I say, or I'll have Sheriff Barry lock you in one of those cells at the jail. Maybe then I can get you to obey."

Matthew sighed as the doctor left the room and closed the door. *You'll be fine.* Matthew knew he would never be *fine.* He had died some time during the experience. It had taken place four days ago, but seemed like an eternity, and he had no desire for life anymore. He felt himself slipping away.

He had not seen Vicky since they arrived in town. There had been frequent visits by Sheriff Barry and Cotton, but they meant little to him. The only bright moments had been when Caroline who, with the aid of Alice Blankenship, came to visit. The child bounced into the room and jumped on his bed. She told him the latest news about her mother and the new toy Uncle Harvey had bought her. She also gave him a hug and kiss, which he cherished. Alice had given Carol a small book of child verses which she carried everywhere. She had crawled under the blankets beside him on her last visit, handed him the book, and said, "Read." The visit gave him relief from the emptiness inside.

He could not blame Vicky for not wanting to see him. The very thought of Manhunter would bring back all the horror of the past few days. The loss of her husband and the death of Otis were bad enough, but in saving her daughter's life and his, Vicky had desecrated one of the fundamentals of her faith. Matthew knew she would never be the same again.

The Reverend George Nelson and his wife had made daily visits. On one of these visits, they brought with them a small, balding gentleman with a pleasant manner.

"Matthew, this is William Ferguson. He is the head of the Missions Department, and in charge of placing missionaries with the Indians." Matthew shook his hand.

"Mr. Blue," Ferguson cleared his throat, "if what Pastor Nelson has been telling me is true, it's distressing news. Something needs to be done immediately. When does the doctor think you'll be able to travel?"

"I have no idea. You'll have to ask him. Why?"

"Because, I'll need some one to interpret for me. I don't want to go through the missionaries, since they might be at the root of the problem, and I don't want another white man who knows their language. I want to speak directly to the people themselves. If what you say is true, I'll personally guarantee, Mr. Blue, there will be immediate changes. Will you go with me?"

"That's all it takes? My going with you?"

"Yes, and a little Godly discipline. Very few ministers are corrupt, Mr. Blue. Most of us do love God, and are deeply concerned for the souls and welfare of those we minister to. The corrupt ones are the exception. Will you help me solve this problem?"

"Yeah, I'll go. Just as soon as the doctor lets me out of this prison." He laughed. "I don't know if anything's gonna happen, but if it does, I want to be there to see the expression on their faces."

~   ~   ~

"Matthew?" Alice Blankenship cracked open the door. "Someone to see you." Caroline ran to his bed.

"Mommy cry." She kept her large eyes locked on his as Alice hoisted her onto the bed.

"I know."

"Mat-ew cry too?" She caressed his cheek with her palm. He suddenly realized his cheeks were damp also.

"Yes, I guess I cry too."

"I love you." She threw her arms around his neck.

"I love you too, baby." He wiped his eyes with the back of his hand. "I love you a whole bunch."

"Read," came the familiar words as she handed him her book.

"You do realize, don't you, that she won't let anyone read to her but you?" Alice said with a laugh as she closed the door.

As Matthew read, the small head gradually dropped to his pillow. She was asleep. A few moments later, the door creaked opened and Matthew's heart skipped a beat as the black-clad figure entered. She looked much older than he had remembered. She was a woman. Same height and hair, but thinner, and her face had changed. There was a sadness that had not been there before. He felt a lump in his throat as she stared at him.

"You still look pretty, even in black," he said after a moment's silence.

"Thank you." Her voice was soft as she perched herself on the edge of the bed. "You look much better than I remember. You looked, so terrible that night. I...."

"I know," he said, touching her hand. "Thank you, too."

"Have you been reading the news lately?"

"No." He shook his head. "I haven't since we came to town."

"You might find this interesting, then." She handed him a folded newspaper. The headline read, *Bible Totin' Mom Tames Wild West*. There was a cartoon accompanying the article depicting an Annie Oakley type complete with hat, leather gloves, vest, boots and spurs. A small child with blond curls was shown peering from behind the flowing skirt. The character also had a gun belt with two holsters and cartridges. But instead of having drawn two revolvers, the woman held two Bibles, one in each hand. They were pointed like pistols at a desperado, who was clutching his chest as though mortally wounded.

Matthew coughed while trying to control his laughter and woke Caroline. "I'm sorry you're having to go through this," he said. "But this," he thumped the newspaper, "is rather amusing."

"That's not all," she said hugging her daughter as she climbed into her mother's lap. "There's a man who is trying hard to get me to sign some sort of a contract. He is the same author that has been writing the ten cent novels about Buffalo Bill. Anyway, he wants to do a series of novels about Caroline and myself. How we are supposedly claiming the west for Jesus, or something like that. He claims he can make us wealthy and famous. Besides the stories, we could travel the United States, giving shows and speaking engagements."

"And how do you feel about all this? What did you tell him?"

"That it was too soon to even consider such a thing. I'm still in mourning. I just lost my husband." She turned away as the lines between her eyes deepened.

"But I owe all this notoriety to you, Mr. Blue." She blinked her eyes several times and turned back toward him.

"Me?"

"Yes, you. It seems that you told Sheriff Blankenship that the reward money should be given to me. You told him I had captured Mr. Felts with my Bible. That's how the story got started. And then, Mr. Larkin came two days ago with a large amount of money and ten quarter horses. He thanked me and told the reporters what a wonderful and marvelous missionary I am, capturing killers and thieves with the Word of God. He took his prize race horse and left."

"You're kidding. I had no idea he would do something like that. I only wanted you to be financially secure."

"That's not all," she said as she absently played with her daughter's hair. "It seems that there was also a rather large amount of reward money offered by Wells Fargo for the capture of Frank Barnes and the men with him. They had robbed a stage line near Wichita and the news had just not gotten this far. In all, Mr. Blue, I owe you a lot. My daughter and I have approximately thirty-five hundred dollars in cash, ten horses, and we'll soon be known all over the United States as God's missionaries to the Wild West."

Matthew stared as the corner of her mouth crept into a grin.

"All this leaves me with a real problem. You see, I can't ever go back to that farm now." She took a hanky from her purse and dabbed her eyes. "So I decided that Caroline and I should visit my grandmother in Chicago. Mr. Blue, what in the world am I ever going to do with ten quarter horses in Chicago?"

They both laughed until Matthew's chest ached, then laughed some more.

"What are your plans now, Matthew Blue? Are you going

to continue chasing bad men?"

"No, I've decided to go home. I left for the same reason you can't return to your farm, but I think it's time," he said with a nod.

"I'm glad to hear that." She sniffed and blew her nose. "Perhaps you can take care of my horses."

"I'd be happy to. I'll take all your critters, if you want me to. I know that horse of mine's got his eye on that mare of yours. Hope you don't mind."

"No, not at all. Maybe Carol will have a pony of her own someday." She tilted her head to study her daughter's profile.

"Perhaps you and Carol would like to see my place before you leave for Chicago. It needs some fixing up, but I think its real pretty."

"I'd love to, but I can't. It's too soon."

"I know. Maybe some day?"

"Yes, some day."

They were quiet for a minute longer before Vicky rose. A single tear trickled down her cheek.

"Better tell Matthew goodbye, Caroline. We're leaving now." She waited as Matthew hugged her daughter and kissed her goodbye.

"I've got to go."

"I know you do, but I have to say something first. "What I said about you capturing Otis with your Bible? I meant no harm. I meant it as a compliment, because it was true. Otis told me that the day he saved our lives. I asked why he would help the man who was trying to take him back to Leon to be hanged. All he said was *Vicky's God.* With your goodness and love, you were able to change his heart. All Manhunter could have done was take his life. You can't blame yourself for what happened out there. You couldn't have stopped those things from happening. The loss of your husband, Otis, Frank, none of it. It's hard to understand, I know, and that hurt and empty feeling will take a long time to heal, but you can't blame yourself. It wasn't your fault."

"But I shot that man. I wanted to *kill* him, Matthew. I *wanted* him dead. You...you don't understand." She held her hands up to stare at them.

"Yes, I do. The empty guns were to protect your daughter. And that was right. Harold should have checked the loads before making his stand. He was a soldier. He used to tell all the new recruits to do that very thing.

"As far as fighting for your daughter and me? You can blame God, not yourself."

"God? How could you....?" She shook her head.

"Yes, God. When I thought you might die, or worse, I started praying. It was the first time in years. Me, the bounty hunter, Manhunter praying." He swiped a tear in the corner of his eye with his pajama sleeve.

"I asked God to save you and Caroline, and He did. Perhaps not in the way I would have thought. I was kind of hoping He would send a bolt of lightning through the roof and get them, but He didn't. I know it wasn't the way you would have wished, but, He still answered that prayer. So you are guiltless, Victoria Jamison. Believe that, above all else."

She mouthed the words, "thank you."

"There's another thing I need to tell you before you go." His voice became a hoarse whisper. "I love you Vicky, and I'll miss you."

She paused at the door and smiled weakly. "I'll miss you, too." She smothered a sob. "Goodbye Matthew Blue." The door closed, and they were gone.

~   ~   ~

Alice Blankenship sat on the edge of his bed, gently brushing his raven hair back with her palm. The sun had begun to set, causing the curtains to cast ghostly shadows against the wall.

"Harvey and Sheriff Barry kept those reporters away, and I saw them safely onto the stage, Matthew. They'll be alright."

He could only stare as tears welled in his steel-blue eyes.

"I know. But it's too soon. You know that. Much too soon. She will come back, but not right now. She has to heal first. You both have to heal."

Epilogue

The Indian slid from the saddle as his brown and white horse lapped thirstily from the pond. The two graves under the oak tree were surrounded by a freshly painted white picket fence. He smiled at the flowers and how carefully the weeds had been pulled away from the headstones. A squeal caused him to turn as his six-year-old daughter ran from the house to meet him, with her golden curls dancing in the summer sun.

"Oh, I love you." She threw her arms around his neck as he hoisted her off the ground.

"That's good." He repeatedly kissed her cheeks as he carried her toward the house.

"I missed you so much. Don't ever go away again."

"Really? I was only gone for one day."

"I still missed you."

"I missed you more."

"Na-uh."

"Yes I did." He paused to stare at his wife on the porch holding their three-week-old son in her arms. How he loved them!

He turned in a circle in an effort to absorb it all. God had blessed him much more than he deserved. The land was rich with grass and water. The horses were foaling and when weaned, the foals would bring a good price. Food and warmth.

His wife and children were beautiful and loved him. His life was full. Prairie Flower's spirit was happy now, and rested.

End

About The Author

MAJOR MITCHELL is the author of eight novels and two children's books. He lives with his wife, Judy, in Northern California. A member of The Western Writers of America and a frequent guest speaker at historical meetings and schools on the West Coast, he has also written several songs, and is currently recording a CD of traditional folk music. On rare occasions he will take the stage as a singer.

More about the author, his books and photo gallery may be found at www.majormitchell.net.

Correspondence should be addressed to:
Shalako Press
P.O. Box 371
Oakdale, CA 95361-0371

For your reading pleasure, we invite you to visit our Trading Post bookstore.

Other books by Major Mitchell:

Canyon Wind
The Doña
Mokelumne Gold
Poverty Flat
Dusty Boots
Joker's Play
A Reason To Believe
Charlie Shepherd (children's)
The Witch On Oak Street (children's)

Coming Soon by Major Mitchell

Where The Green Grass Grows

Shalako Press

http://www.shalakopress.com

CPSIA information can be obtained
at www.ICGtesting.com
Printed in the USA
BVHW041043140723
667244BV00001B/115